Blood

Blood On The Turf

by

GLENIS WILSON

DARF PUBLISHERS LIMITED
1989

First Published 1989

Blood on the Turf was awarded
the Nottingham Writers' Gwladys Bungay
Silver Rose Bowl Award for 1988.

ISBN 1 85077 213 4

Printed and bound in Great Britain
by BPCC Wheatons Ltd, Exeter

Dedication

"To my daughter Candis, who like me, has known the heaven and the hell of giving love to animals."

"White rails, green turf,
Flying divotts,
pounding hooves,
Galloping to the post."

CANDIS SMITH

Acknowledgement

"I would like to thank Mr Chuck Spares, Race Horse Trainer, Aslockton, Notts, for his kindness in checking technical details. Chuck was the Trainer at the time this book was written of the great 'Ibn Majed', the racehorse my daughter Candis rode whilst she was still at school."

"I would also like to extend my thanks to all the other people who have given me help and encouragement. In particular:– Derek Thompson, Television Racing Presenter and Racing Correspondent, Carole Carson, Racing, Neil Carson, Racing, Norma Macauley, Racehorse Trainer, Phillip Sharrock, Photographer, who took the back cover photograph, Gerard Rooney (Ireland) and all the staff of the bookshops in Jersey."

Chapter One

I STOOD by the winning post below the stands and hugged my sheepskin jacket tighter about me to ward off the insistent, penetrating, icy fog. If it thickened any more the rest of the races would be abandoned. Curling my toes up inside my heavy wellies and stamping alternately brought no welcome warmth and I gave up and instead pressed one side of my foot against the down post of the fence. Nothing. No vibration; they weren't close enough yet.

Just as a relaxed atmosphere is contagious, so is one of excitement. There was a charge of anticipation in the air, the whole crowd now on its feet ready to roar in the winner. I too felt the surge of adrenalin zip through me. But whereas the majority of people here were out for a day's jaunt, racing was my entire life.

The 4 to 1 ON favourite, Calypso Lad, would be approaching the last two or three fences now and would be visible at any moment. Riding him in racing colours of purple with blue stars would be Jack Hunter, my father.

My shiver of cold turned to a shiver of excitement. Now I could feel it: the slightest of vibrations and a few seconds later, I could hear it. The rhythmic pounding of galloping hooves on turf. It was a sound that had rung in my ears since babyhood. It had been the most natural thing in the world to learn to ride almost as soon as I learned to walk. Horses and racing had a pull like a magnet. I couldn't imagine a world without them. I looked eagerly down the course, frustratingly little of which was to be seen before the white curtain of fog obscured the last fence before the long run-in.

Suddenly a black horse burst the white barrier and barely a length or so behind came two more. Close on their heels thundered four others. There was a gasp of disappointment from the crowd of punters, broken only by a few encouraging yells from backers of the 5 to 2 Black Monarch. I felt I'd been punched in the stomach. Another horse trailed tiredly in. Eight I thought mechanically. Where was Calypso Lad? It had been a nine-horse race. More important, where was my father?

"A bloody fix," said an ample proportioned middle-aged blonde, her cigarette wobbling from her lips as she tore a betting slip in two, then into four and let the pieces flutter down to the grass.

I turned and ran as fast as wellingtons allowed towards the winners enclosure. The owner was a little tardy and I made it to Black Monarch before he did.

"What happened to father?" I yelled up as the snorting, much-lathered horse walked in from the course.

His lemon and white clad jockey flicked his whip in an involuntary backward gesture. "Fell at the third last, sorry love," Paul Reynolds had to shout above the crowd to make himself heard. There was no time to ask more. A beatifically smiling owner materialised and walked into the winners enclosure patting the strong black neck and making congratulatory noises.

The other horses and jockeys were all back now. Two followed Paul Reynolds to receive their lesser acclaim. I stood biting a lip in indecision. I had an odd feeling that there had been something in that interchange that I'd subconsciously noticed but couldn't recall.

It was pointless to think of running back to the third. By now the course ambulance would be there if needed. I looked through the thin crowd between here and the line of stables and saw Turton, our head lad, standing scratching his head in a perplexed way.

"A right devil ain't it?" he said as I reached him. "Never fell before, right cat-footed is Calypso Lad." His lack of comment about my father's condition was typical.

He'd been with us since before I was born and the

two of them were very close. Neither would admit it of course. But after a win, each would give the other the credit for it.

"If he's broken anything," I said, meaning my father, "he'll be as mad as hell. It will give Paul Reynolds a strong chance of taking the championship."

"Hmmmm . . ." Turton rubbed a stubby-fingered hand across his gingery moustache. He was frowning now and I followed the line of his gaze. I shivered again only this time it was with apprehension. The ambulance was crossing to the First-Aid room. Turton and I moved as one. Before we were half-way, the two ambulance men were out and had the big back doors open. They carried a stretcher carefully from the interior. I felt a wave of nausea hit me as the still, crumpled form of my father was carried through to the First-Aid room. Even from this distance, the blood stained racing colours were glaringly obvious. There was a loud hiss of indrawn breath at my side. I shot a glance at Turton. His face was grey and drawn.

A smallish man still clutching tightly to a white flag was now being helped from the ambulance.

"Fence Attendant," said Turton through clenched teeth as we covered the last few yards.

I could see for myself the Attendant was in a state of shock. Beads of sweat stood out and mingled with the misty wetness of the clinging fog on his pallid face. His hands shook so much it looked as though they were waving the flag.

The next few minutes were a kaleidoscope of horrific facts which didn't register in my numb brain.

"I'm Dr. Matthews. Are you the next of kin?" asked a gently spoken man.

"Yes, yes . . . that's right. How is he? I'm his daughter."

"Rather poorly I'm afraid. What about his wife?"

"Divorced . . . years ago."

"I see. Could I have your name then."

"Albertine Hunter."

He noted it down, cocking an eyebrow. "Unusual name."

3

"Doctor, don't try lightening the atmosphere, just tell me, how bad is father?" I stood there, hands clenched tightly into fists, determinedly trying not to breakdown.

"At this stage, Miss Hunter, I can't say. He's going to hospital. They'll be better able to say when they've examined him and run some tests."

"I'm going with him," I said.

"Tal, I'll come as well." Turton was making a pretence of blowing his nose on a large checked handkerchief.

Right now I desperately needed someone to lean on but somewhere deep inside a small voice said with conviction, you've got to take your father's place – it's up to you now.

I answered with difficulty, "No, you stay here. Box-up Calypso Lad, take him back to the Stables. Oh . . . and Turton," I said as I followed the ambulance man, "give him a thorough check . . . if father's like this . . ." I fought back the threatening tears.

Turton's hand bit into my shoulder. "You go where you're needed Tal. Leave the horse to me."

I nodded, not trusting myself to speak.

Outside the loudspeaker blared. The fog had thinned a little, racing and life was going on as before. An accident was a great crowd puller and a cluster of people, drawn perhaps against their better nature, watched with thrilled horror as my father was carried out. I looked for one particular familiar face: he was not there, but then, of course, he wouldn't be.

I climbed into the ambulance, after the stretcher with my father's inert body covered with a red blanket. It drove carefully out from the race meeting bound for the nearest hospital.

I sat in the hospital waiting-room and did just that. For how long I've no idea. It could have been two hours or two weeks. Time for once, wasn't governing my life. It was a limbo land I inhabited, the only other inhabitants being my thoughts. Some of them weren't comfortable companions. Just how bad father was I didn't know. I could hazard a guess from the little I'd seen of his face. That he was going to be disfigured was

4

certain. He looked like he'd been dragged through a jump. His neck and face were deeply raked and battered. One other thing was certain. He wouldn't be running Hunter's Stables for a considerable time – if at all. I threw the thought away from me. Jack Hunter was a fighter, he always had been. He wasn't one to give in. What he needed right now was someone to fight with him and run the business. That someone was going to have to be me. Looking back, all he'd had was me after mother left.

I couldn't even remember her. I'd only been two. It had been a case, he said, of opposites attracting. She was a willowy timid creature who had fallen for the handsome dare-devil man that hurled himself at life with a passionate zest. From her one photograph, which he had given me as my right to know what my mother looked like, she'd been a beautiful woman with violet eyes and ash blonde hair. At the time he gave it to me he'd said keep it if I wished but he never wanted to see it again. I still had it, tucked away under the bottom layer of padding in my jewel-case. It seemed strange to be thinking of her at this particular time when all my thoughts should have been for father. I hadn't bothered asking much about her in all the years of growing-up. We'd had a succession of housekeepers, none of whom seemed to stay long. The central character had always been my father. Whilst undoubtedly devoted to me, his pride and passion was horses and Hunter's Stables. It had been my paternal grandfather, himself a champion jockey, who had bought the land and built the big rambling house. He had married late in life and my father, being the only child, had inherited the lot at an early age.

I wondered now, as I sat in the hard, uncomfortable seat and stared at the blank ultra-clean walls, if it had been the money as much as the man that had decided mother she should marry. I'd never thought about it before.

The door swung open and a white-coated doctor entered.

"Miss Hunter?"

5

I stood up, the palms of my hands felt sticky. "That's right. How is my father?"

He motioned me to sit down again. "Mr Hunter has concussion, severe bruising to the left side and a broken left leg. Fortunately there are no internal injuries."

"Thank God," I said with heartfelt relief.

He held up a hand, "I'm afraid that's not all Miss Hunter. Whilst those injuries are serious, time of course will heal them. What I have to tell you will come as a shock."

I gripped the arm of the chair and waited.

The doctor looked at me searchingly. "Mr Hunter's eyesight is badly impaired."

I felt stunned. A picture of his bloody, mutilated face swam in front of me. I should have realised, been prepared for the possibility but it hadn't occurred to me. I jerked out the only words I could manage. "How bad?"

"At this stage, it's not possible to say exactly. One eye may retain some sight but, I'm sorry to have to tell you Miss Hunter, the other eye has had to be removed."

Blind! My father was practically blind. It should have devastated me but it didn't. Suddenly all I could think of was he's alive, he's going to live. Nothing the doctor had said could blot out that glorious fact. It was a terrible accident, the injuries were horrific but he was not going to die. We still had each other. Our roles would now be reversed. Where for twenty-five odd years he had sheltered and protected me, it was now my turn to provide the support he needed.

I felt very cold, very calm. I stood up. My voice came out strong and firm without a tremor and somehow I was not surprised. "Could I see him please?"

"Only for a minute or two, he's unconscious." The doctor looked faintly relieved as though he'd expected another patient on his hands.

He led me out along the echoing corridor from which rabbit warrened other identical corridors until we reached the small bare room where my father was. He lay unmoving, swathed in white bandages with tubes seemingly running from every orifice. I slid into the seat beside the bed. "Daddy . . . it's me Tal." Why I called him that I don't know. It was a name I hadn't used since childhood.

The doctor shook his head slowly. "I doubt he can hear you."

"How long will he be unconscious."

"It's difficult to say. Certainly for the next twelve hours. After that . . ."

"It's up to him?"

The doctor permitted himself a slight smile. "You could say that."

I stood up and held out my right hand. "Thank you all for what you're doing. It seems a bit ironic. People get sick through no fault of their own and here we are, as jockeys, tempting fate to hurl us to the ground."

"Our job is to heal Miss Hunter, just as yours is to ride." His eyes ran speculatively over me. Male interest ignited and was extinguished as rapidly. I was used to that. I resembled my mother facially although I had my father's thick black hair.

He shook hands firmly and correctly. "I should go home now. Ring first thing in the morning. We may have news by then. It will be pointless for you to wait around here all night."

"O.K." I fought down my natural impulse to stay with father. "I'll ring about six o'clock tomorrow morning."

"Good girl." He shepherded me out the door. "Try and get some sleep. He's our responsibility right now but when he's discharged then it will be up to you."

I retraced my steps down the labyrinth of corridors catching glimpses now and then of sleekly uniformed nurses moving quietly and efficiently about their duties. It was reassuring to know that whilst most of the world slept hospital care continued ceaselessly.

Reaching the main entrance hall I located the 'phone and dialled Turton's home number. His voice came through sounding strained. I depressed a coin and told him father was concussed with a broken leg but was in no danger. His relief was touching. He and father had been close pals for so long I simply couldn't tell him

7

over a 'phone of the extent of the injuries. To side-track him from the delicate subject I inquired about Calypso Lad. He was instantly animated and gave me a run-down from the moment he'd caught up with the horse on the far side of the race-course. It worked as therapy for me too as I forced my thoughts away from human injuries and concentrated on equine matters.

He paused for breath at the end of the saga and then almost immediately asked: "What are you doing now Tal? Will you stay the night?"

"No, I'm coming home now. He doesn't need me at the moment."

"How will you get back? Your Triumph's in the garage."

"Oh not to worry, I'll get a taxi. You go to bed. I'll be fine."

"O.K. then. See you at the stables in the morning." He rang off.

I scanned the various taxi ads that adorned the walls near the 'phone and chose one that traded under the name Canters, rather apt I thought in the circum-stances.

It seemed a long way back once we'd cleared city boundaries and were motoring down endless winding lanes. I paid the taxi off at the gates to Hunter's Stables and walked slowly up the curving gravel drive. I needed a breath of air and the fog, contrary as ever, had now been blown away in ragged wisps by a freshening west wind. There was a high, bright moon riding that spoke of frost before dawn.

I sucked the clean, crisp air deep into my lungs with the pleasure of a thirsty man downing a drink. Almost home now. Security and comfort awaiting. There'd be a fire burning away behind the fire screen in the big living room. Freda, the housekeeper, would have seen to it before she left. I'd make some fresh coffee before taking a last turn round the stables. And then I heard it. Rookey, the black spaniel, was barking spasmodically, half-hesitatingly followed by full throated barks. The sound seemed to bounce eerily off the trees that bordered the drive. I felt a thrill of alarm. He wasn't barking because he'd heard me returning. That bark would have been one of his glorious head back full-bore ones. This was a warning bark, a not too sure, yet something wrong bark.

I began to run.

Chapter Two

IF I'D EXPECTED a car parked on the wide semi-circular driveway in front of the house I was mistaken. It was as barren as a desert, not a soul in sight and saved only from pitch-blackness by the moonlight. There was never a light on by the massive main door, only by the back, which everyone used. Nobody stood on ceremony at Hunters.

I took the three steps up in one, tried the big door, locked. As it should be. There were two massive bolts as well on the inside which were always shot. No intruders then at the front.

The gravel slipped and scattered beneath my feet as I raced round to the back. Rookey set up a barrage of barks as I turned the house corner. "Great dog, good chap," I caught his sleek head in my hands and ruffled up his long ears. "Go seek!" I slipped the catch of his leash and he tore off. Despite the docility of his breed he was an excellent guard. Standing sideways and turning the handle of the door resulted in no opening inwards. The door was still locked. I abandoned the James Bond stance and fished for the key. It was always kept in the half coconut hanging high on the wall by the kitchen window. My fingers closed over the cold metal. If there had been a break-in it must have been by a window. Stepping back and scanning the run of windows on ground and first floor revealed no gaping hole, no jagged glass.

I opened up and went in switching on the kitchen light. Everything looked clean, tidy, normal. The butterflies in my stomach stopped dancing the highland fling and settled to a steady waltz. The hall was the same as the kitchen, nothing out of place.

I was about to enter the study when a noise from

behind froze me stiff. Here it comes, I thought, rear attack! A wet nose pushed at the back of my knee. "Rookey!" I said, half in exasperation half relief. He grinned up at me curling his dewlaps back to reveal white fangs. His stumpy wagging tail confirmed nothing untoward out in the grounds. He accompanied me into the study. It was father's actually. He kept all his racing trophies there. It was a fetish of his that only he cleaned them. Freda was not allowed to touch them. He lovingly dusted them most mornings. As far as I could see none of them had been moved by so much as a millimetre. His heavy silver cigarette box, quite a valuable item was still in its usual place above the blotting pad. Whilst father didn't smoke, a lot of his friends did. If we had had a break-in the box would surely have been taken.

Rookey deserted me and dashed off, nose hoovering the floor as he went. I waited for the barks but none came. Any prowler would have been flushed out immediately. If we had been burgled they certainly weren't around.

I started to relax. Still, there was also the cash in the top drawer of the desk. Better check it. Opening the drawer I unlocked the metal cash box, the bundle of notes was still intact. Casually now, completely reassured, I lifted up the folder of incoming letters . . . and froze. A sense of shock started the butterflies doing their mad dance again. So, after all, we had been visited by a person or persons unknown. Whoever it was had tried to be a little too clever and in doing so had given themselves away.

In the bottom of the drawer, father kept a few useful items that he used a lot but didn't want cluttering up the top of his desk. Stapler, elastic bands, letter knife and a box of paper clips. It was the paper clips that were the give away. Father always had a few shook out loose; I'd opened the mail with him that morning and used one or two myself. Now there were no loose ones just a neatly closed box. We had left the house at the same time this morning and since only I had returned, the desk should have been exactly as it was. Whoever had tampered with the drawer must have thought the clips had come loose when they removed the letter file and had most carefully put all of them back and closed the flap of the box. I stood stock still to consider the implications. This was no ordinary burglar. Someone who ransacked, stole and then defiled. That would have been bad enough. But this, this made my blood run cold. What burglar would have left behind a bundle of notes? I folded up into the padded swivel chair. When fate handed out a bashing it made a good job of it.

I trembled violently, the chair swinging slightly from side to side with the vibrations. Reaction, nothing great about that. After a racing fall I always got the shakes. Nothing physical this time though. Too much shock on the nervous system, too short a time. Waited for the worst to pass, tottered over to the drinks cupboard, poured a large measure of brandy into a whiskey tumbler and made it to the stoked up fire in the lounge. A black shadow appeared at my side. Rookey pressed his furry body close and leaned companionably against me as we both sat on the sheepskin rug before the blaze. I took the poker and clouted the top piece of coal which split suddenly down the middle allowing the flames to roar upwards and sending out comforting warmth fan wise. Rookey sighed in pleasure and sank down displaying his vulnerable under-belly to the heat. Obviously no intruder within miles.

Took a big gulp of brandy, pulled off my constricting boots. Better, much better. Spread my toes and wiggled them inside woolly socks. Had another long pull at the brandy. Fire-water, good name. It burned its way down inside, steadying, restoring, building confidence, lifting spirits. Two more sedate sips and the worst was over. Mind stopped feeling fuzzed and returned to its usual clarity. What the devil was the man looking for? Was it a man? Could just as easily have been a woman. Perhaps a search of the other rooms would give a clue.

I gulped the last of the brandy, reluctantly left the fire-side and started a room to room inspection. My stockinged feet made no sound but it didn't matter anyway, there was no-one else in the house. But there

12

was something left behind, the merest whisper of a smell – one I knew I'd smelt before somewhere but for the life of me I couldn't remember where. Nothing else appeared either to have been stolen or moved except in my own room. One can always tell if private items have been tampered with and the few papers I kept in an old cash-box in my bedside cabinet had definitely been moved. They were all still in identical order but put back exactly symmetrical. My drivers licence which I had carelessly tossed into the box had fallen with a page curled over and was now closed correctly. I shuddered. It gave me a sick feeling to know somebody else had been handling my personal papers. Thank goodness when I checked my underwear drawer that was still just as I'd left it. If it too had been rifled, the whole lot of undies would have gone on the fire.

There was only father's room left to check. I shyed away from the idea of prying but it had to be done. I didn't suppose for one moment that he had any dark secrets hidden but it gave me a queer sensation to know he was lying unconscious and helpless in hospital whilst I made free with his personal effects. As far as could be judged everything was neat and orderly, nothing scattered about. I was on the point of leaving the room when something caught my eye. Hanging on the wall opposite the window was an oil painting of myself astride my first pony, Gwillam, a sturdy little Welsh Mountain. Father had commissioned it and called it, "The start of my career". Suppose it was really. There was no future without horses as far as I was concerned. But what caught my eye was the angle it was hanging. Not a great deal out but certainly not square. Most people couldn't resist straightening an askew picture. Being no exception, I was about to adjust it when it occurred to me that since my room had definitely been singled out and this was a picture of myself, possibly the person unknown had been at it.

I lifted it carefully off the wall and sat on the end of father's bed and turned it over. A three corner straight cut had been made to separate the backing. A slow anger began to burn through me. Just what the hell was going on? There was nothing inside. But had there been? And if so, what? Something incriminating? My mind was full of speculation which led nowhere. The picture had hung there for years, well twenty-two to be exact. I'd been about three at the time it was painted. Not long after mother had left.

I put it back on the wall. A great wave of tiredness swept over me. What I needed was a good sleep. Would think straight in the morning. Certainly couldn't now. Ought to go and check the horses. Wonder if Turton had done. Went downstairs and dialled his number. Old Mrs Turton answered.

"It's Tal here. Sorry to ring so late but could I have a word with Turton if he's around?"

"Oh no, Miss Tal. You can't. He's not here d'y'see."

"Not there? But I spoke to him this evening earlier on."

"Yes. He was here earlier. Gone to look at t'horses he said."

"I see."

"But he's been gone a long time." Her voice quavered. "I don't like being on my own, not when it's dark."

"I'm sure he'll be back soon Alice," I said soothingly.

"What shall I tell him? When he comes back."

"Just that I rang, thank him for me for checking the stables."

I walked wearily into the kitchen, invited Rookey to pay a last call in the garden, locked the back door. Set some milk on to heat up and when it was ready laced it liberally with a spoonful of honey. Not that any rocking was needed tonight but it was a sure way of inviting sleep. Sat and sipped in comfort before the seductive fire. Bed was beckoning with a cajoling finger when the 'phone rang. Cursing under my breath, drained the last delicious dregs at the bottom of the mug and went to answer it.

"That you Tal?"

"Hmm. Hello David."

"Dear girl! I've been trying to get hold of you since the accident was on the news."

14

"The drag of being in the public eye. You can't even have an accident and keep it quiet."

"Are you all right Tally ho?" His voice sounded concerned.

"Sure, I'm fine."

"You don't sound your usual sunny self, more cynical."

"Bitter and twisted, you mean."

"No, not at all," he protested.

"Sorry David. Guess I'm dead beat."

"Then I won't keep you from the sheets any longer. But how is Jack?"

"Not in any danger." I stalled.

"Thank the Lord for that. He's not the age to go falling off."

"Look David, you know that, so do I, but retiring from racing never crosses his mind. He thinks he's Peter Pan and can go on forever."

"Tally, have lunch with me tomorrow, you can tell me how he is then."

"O.K. but not out David. Come over and I'll fix us an omelette or something. Come early, I'm not too sure where I'll be tomorrow."

"Will do. Twelve o'clock suit?"

"Lovely, bye David."

I crawled upstairs to bed and slutishly went to sleep with my make-up still on.

The alarm clock rang next morning at 6 o'clock. It didn't need to. I'd been awake since five wondering how soon I could decently ring the hospital.

Went to the bathroom, scrubbed off the ingrained make-up. A pale face with dark ringed eyes peered back from the mirror. Grief, I looked like a hung-over panda. Dragged on thermals, heavy jumper and tight slacks. Went down to the kitchen and was greeted rapturously by Rookey. Plugged in the electric kettle and made a quick, out of the jar, coffee, strong with a generous spoonful of honey. Turton would by now be down in the stables, better make the call before joining him. Reflected. Father usually started with Turton whilst I came on with Jimmy, our other stable lad, at nearly seven. Would have to re-organise the rota now. Not only the rota, everything would need to be re-scheduled. Walked through to the study and remembered with a bang the events of the last evening. Just for the first few minutes this morning I had forgotten the rotten welcome which had greeted me on returning. It surged back in force now as I sat down in the chair behind the desk. With great effort I pushed it from my mind and reached for the 'phone and dialled the hospital number. A cool, unemotional voice informed me that father's condition was stable. No change from the previous day. I sighed, leaned back in the chair and finished the coffee.

Rookey came dancing and begging to get out into the pre-dawn freedom where bladder relief and glorious sniffs combined. I caught up my old duffle coat, slipped on wellies and together we stepped outside into the chill dark morning.

As I had known he would be, Turton was already there. We had eight horses at the moment of which Calypso Lad was the star. He'd come on enormously this season winning four out of the five of his races. If it hadn't been for the accident it could have been five in a row. Rookey disappeared on his usual boundary patrol and I went into the Tack Room.

"Morning, Turton."

"Mornin' Tal. How's y'dad?" He straightened up from changing his boots for wellies.

"I've just rung the hospital. They say he's stable."

"Don't give much away do they."

"No."

"Aw, come on Tal. You know more than you're letting on."

"Honestly, that's all they would tell me."

"Now look here gel, don't forget, I was with you at the race course when it happened." He gave me a long steady stare.

My eyes dropped first and I screwed the toe of one wellie in a half-moon arc. However much I wrapped it up, this was going to hurt. It was as painful to me telling Turton as it so obviously was to him.

A staggered, incredulous look drained his face of colour. "By Gawd!" He said at last. "No wonder old Felton was took to First Aid in shock as well." He walked unsteadily over to a bale of hay and sat down heavily. "That's it then." He passed a hand in front of his eyes and in horror I saw the trickle of water on his cheeks. In all the many years and many sorrows at Hunter's Stables, I'd never known Turton to cry.

"Don't you understand," I grasped his shoulder urgently and shook it, "father's alive, he's going to live."

In an angry gesture he was up on his feet dashing the tears from his face. "No Tal, don't *you* understand. Your father died out there on that race course. Winning races was his life, Champion Jockey four times. Have you ever heard of a blind jockey?" He glared at me angrily. "No dammit, of course you haven't." His shoulders dropped suddenly and he picked up his boots and walked away. At the door he hesitated and said in a low voice with a gentle finality in it that was so much worse than a shout. "His life's over." He looked at me sadly and I realised that this man knew as much about father as I did, only more.

With a heavy heart I took a fork and went to the first stable to muck out.

It was Bright Boy scheduled for first exercise this morning and as I tacked up and swung into the saddle the relief of hard physical work countered the agony of mind. The exhilaration I always felt when astride a spirited horse with the gallops stretching out in front did much for my own spirits. A pale, winter sun crawled through the clouds touching the tops of the elms edging our land. Nothing killed off the sun or the seasons.

I squeezed my calves against the horse who responded with the joy of a true racehorse born to conquer the turf. Gasping at the raw air which tore at my throat, I leaned forward over the thick, coarse mane. The smell of hot horse filled my nostrils and I forgot everything in the thrill of drumming hooves, the feel of toned muscles and the flashing turf below me.

A family of rooks took flight with a cacophany of sound as we reached the far end. Jimmy, at the side of me, reigned in Court Jester. "Reckon this one's got a great future. Going really well," he panted, flushed and youthfully enthusiastic.

I nodded with sudden cold conviction. It had been grandfather's legacy to the Hunters all this, the house, land, our acceptance in racing circles, his vast store of knowledge about horses, all passed on to father. Hunters Stables was not going to be allowed to die. I'd see to that.

But had I known that the key to our future lay in the motive behind the burglary I wouldn't have been so sure.

Chapter Three

IT WAS NOT until breakfast break at 9 o'clock that I
had another chance to speak to Turton.

Jimmy was very subdued and hardly spoke save for,
"I'm real sorry about Mr Hunter . . ." He choked his
words off and busied himself eating. It was a sharp
contrast to his earlier exuberance whilst mounted on
Court Jester. He must have heard the details from
Turton. I hoped he wouldn't be put off his career
almost at the start of it. The lad showed real promise.
Racing was a dangerous game there was no doubt of it
but accidents like father's were rare.

One half of my brain started mulling over this
point whilst I debated how to broach the matter of
the burglary. It might be best to wait for the end
of morning session and speak to Turton on his own.
The less people who knew about it at the moment the
better. "When we finish tack cleaning, can I have a
quick word if you don't have to get home immediately?"

"That's fine by me." He finished his meal.

Turton only lived a few minutes away and usually
came in on a rackety old bike which he swore was more
reliable than any car.

We started the second lot of horses and I checked
over Calypso Lad. Turton had given me a thorough
report on the 'phone and the horse seemed quiet and
unperturbed enough now.

"I'd like to know what happened out there at that
fence." I said softly to him. He nuzzled my arm and
blew gently down his nostrils. Now the words were
spoken out loud. I realised that I very much needed to

know. There was something peculiar about the events of the last day. Something that didn't ring true.

"What happened to Felton yesterday?" I spoke up just loud enough for Turton to hear as he passed the door barrowing muck to the heap.

"Treated him for shock and sent him home."

"Did you get a chance to speak to him?"

"No. He didn't look so good. Fact, he looked bloomin' shockin'." We had finished the last horses and just starting to clean saddlery in the Tack Room, when we heard the swish and crunch of gravel beneath tyres and a discreet pip on a car horn.

"That'll be David I expect."

"Set him on if he comes down here," grunted Turton applying elbow grease vigorously to the saddle flap he was polishing.

I grinned "What in his best city suit?"

"Could always lend him my old mac."

"Have to leave you with it then," I said, dropping a pile of cloths. "Be down at 12 o'clock for a word before you go."

"O.K. I'm in no hurry."

I left them to it and walked up the path to the house. David met me half-way, a joyful Rookey circling round him.

"Bit late I'm afraid. Couldn't get away from one client. Seemed to think I would work magic with his declarable tax."

I laughed. "Couldn't you?"

He slipped my arm through his. "I'd rather work my wizardry on you, my raven-haired witch."

"Get away with you," I said but left my arm where it was. Companionably we walked back to the house. Freda had left at 11.30 and wouldn't be back until about 5 o'clock as she worked a split shift. I looked in the freezer. "Cheese and tomato pizza be all right?"

"Just right."

I knew better than offer him the ham ones. He was a strict vegetarian.

"Any further news about your father?"

"Not first thing. Stable, they said." I set the oven and left it to hot whilst I tried the hospital number again.

David looked inquiringly and I felt mean as I relayed their answer, "condition unchanged".

"Nothing we can do then?" he said.

"No, just wait." We'd have lunch first, the awful truth could wait until after. I recoiled from the thought of hurting him. First Turton, now David. And that was without the rest of the racing world plus the media who would doubtless turn the telephone hot once the news leaked out. I lifted the receiver off and left it to buzz gently to itself. The pizza in the oven I excused myself for a freshen-up and a quick change into gored camel skirt and chunky knitted scarlet sweater.

"You're good enough to eat yourself." David gazed frankly at me. The admiration showed plainly in his eyes. I knew his feelings were deep and genuine. It was a pity that I was dedicated to Hunter's Stables and a private dream all my own. That the chances of the dream attaining fruition were slim deterred me not a jot. Father thought eventually I would succumb and accept David's proposal of marriage. On average he asked me about once a month. I usually felt extremely guilty turning him down, knowing with woman's intuition that he would ask again. To hold power over another human's emotions whilst they kept on hoping seemed morally wrong. Besides, creeping up on me lately was another reason for feeling guilty. One that I would barely admit even to myself.

The scene of the crowd outside the First Aid room staring with thrilled horror as my father's stretcher was brought out came back vividly. Paul's face had been missing. The one person I had subconsciously wanted to see. Of course he had been changing silks for the next race. I would have known that and yet still I sought him in the crowd as I followed the stretcher. It was perhaps the most stressful moment of my life and it wasn't David I had looked for but my father's rival for the Jockey Championship this season, Paul Reynolds. A man who, until a few months ago, lived in the States and I didn't know existed.

"You're looking very pensive." David said as we started eating. "What are you thinking?"

"That you deserve an uncomplicated female, someone who would rather marry than try winning horse races."

He laughed. "Poor old Tally ho, full of remorse, the scalp on the belt theme again. You are a goose. Until you order me forever from the portals I shall likely remain your most dedicated marriage prospect."

"I'm a very fortunate woman, having all this," I ascribed an arc with my fork to encompass Hunter's, "and you too." Immediately the words were out I realised that the barricades of the last two decades had suddenly in the space of time it had taken for father to fall from Calypso Lad, begun to crumble. I put down my fork, no longer hungry.

"Finished already?"

"Yes, I guess so." I glanced at the wall clock. "Excuse me David, but I must catch Turton before he goes off. He won't be back until four."

"Carry on my sweet, I'll be in the lounge, if I may, unless you'd like me to come with you?"

"No," I said, knowing full well he didn't expect me to say yes. "Make yourself at home, you don't have to ask, shan't be long."

The news of father must come first before David learned anything about the burglary.

Turton was in the Tack Room sorting out saddle-cloths.

"Jimmy gone?"

He nodded. "Sent him off a few minutes ago. Thought you'd be coming."

"Good. I did want to speak to you alone."

"Gathered that. Something else wrong?" He put down the cloths and gave me his full attention.

"What time did you come to check over the horses last night?"

"Well, now, let me think." He chaffed a thumb nail across the ragged surface of one of his finger-nails. "Be about nine."

The surprise I felt showed in my voice. "That was early."

"Maybe it was a bit. But I was wanting to make sure Calypso was O.K."

"I'm not getting at you Turton," I said hastily, placatingly, "but I need to know. And what time did you leave to go home?"

"Bout ten."

"But you couldn't have, it was ten-thirty gone when I 'phoned your mother."

His jaw dropped a little. "What'd you 'phone her for?"

"To see if there was any need for me to do the rounds and check. I was nearly out on my feet but horses come first. Didn't your mother say I'd rung?"

"No. Anyway, I'd already done them. Didn't know you'd come back and, like you say, horses come first."

"Whilst you were here, did you hear anything, or possibly even see anything?"

He looked up sharply. "Like what?"

"I don't know," I shrugged. "A car with just side-lights on, footsteps perhaps, or a flash-light?"

"Why should I have?"

"Because last night someone broke into the house."

"Get away!"

"True."

"Take much did they?"

"Not a thing, as far as I can tell."

"That's funny, why break in then?"

"Just what I'd like to know."

"Maybe you're imagining it. Said yourself you were about kna . . . um . . . dead beat."

"So I was but it was not imagination, someone had been in looking for something."

He looked piercingly at me. "What?"

I spread my hands helplessly, "That's just it, I don't know."

He lost interest. "Ah, well . . ."

"But I intend to find out."

The interest came back. "Shouldn't do it."

"No? Why not?"

"Police go all over everywhere once they start check-ing. Don't want them down here upsetting the horses." There was an edge of concern to his voice.

"I didn't mean go to the Police."

"Oh?" He waited for me to continue.

I shrugged, "You slip off now for your lunch Turton. Forget I said anything."

"I think you're right," he said with relief, "don't want to get mixed up in anything unpleasant do you?"

David was relaxing in the lounge with a tray of coffee and Beethoven's 'Pastoral' gently flooding the room with beautiful sound. I sank down on the settee beside him.

"Coffee my sweet?"

"Hmm . . ." I closed my eyes and let the soothing music claim me. There was a healing quality about music. Even doctors, so sceptical of anything unproved by science, were beginning to acknowledge its beneficial effect on sick people. My thoughts swung automatically to father lying so still, enmeshed in unconsciousness. If the doctors agreed it might help him surface if he heard some familiar favourite pieces of music. "What do you think David?"

"To what?"

I'd spoken aloud whilst the thought had remained in my mind. "I was just thinking, father loves music, especially certain pieces. Would the doctors agree if I took some cassettes and a player for his room?"

"You know him better than anyone else. If you think it would help, I don't suppose they'll object."

David's words made me stop short. I had always thought I knew him best but Turton's outburst in the stable had shattered that. "I did think so but it isn't true. Turton knows more of the inner man."

David looked at me speculatively. "There's something else isn't there. You've not told me the full story."

"Yes," I said softly, "there's something else, well, two things really, but the second can wait."

"Go on, Tally, tell me the first."

I put the coffee cup down on a handy coaster with slow deliberate carefulness whilst I sought for a way of gentling what had to be said.

"With the look on your face, it's something momentous." David took my arm. "Get it out of your system, that way you'll put it into perspective."

"It's about father . . . his accident . . ."

"I rather thought so. He's more severely hurt than you've let on?"

"Yes."

"Tell me."

"He's blind." It was out. Said baldly, shockingly. No way of wrapping it up.

David stared incredulously at me. "Blind? You mean . . . totally blind?"

"More of less". I filled in the distasteful details whilst he grappled with the shock of it.

"Tally, darling," he reached for me and put possessively protective arms round. "I'm so very sorry."

I couldn't reply. I just nodded against the cool cotton of his shirt and thought quite irrationally my tears would make tramlines down the immaculate ironing.

"Cry it out my darling," David was smoothing my hair with a so-sweet tenderness. It was, of course, quite the wrong thing to do. It effectively demolished my high walls of defence. They shrank like a snowball in the hearth. And whilst Beethoven reached a thunderous crescendo, I howled. How I howled. On and on until I was shaking and spent and David's shirt looked like an over-used tea towel.

"Feeling better Tally?"

I sniffed and gulped then nodded. "Strangely, yes."

He lifted me onto his knee like a child and I snuggled close. It was a rare moment for both of us. Neither spoke, we just gloried in the warmth and closeness of each other and drew comfort from it. How easy right now to think of marriage to David. A secure cocoon of love and protection. The music leapt high and fell in silver cascade, faded and returned, trickling away exquisitely to a final triumphant flourish. There was a silence in the room. I opened my eyes and came back to an awareness of my surroundings. There was a roughness under my cheek where I was leaning against David's lapel. Our fugue in time had passed.

"I wish to God it could be like this always." David's voice was thick with emotion.

I put up my hand and stroked the back of my fingers

25

against his face. It so nearly could. So very nearly . . . and yet . . .

"I'm not asking you to marry me now Tally," he went on. "If I did you might agree. But it wouldn't be fair." He kissed me gently. "You're so vulnerable right now." We both knew how true his words were. "When you say yes, I want you flying high, winning races, business booming and . . ." his voice dropped a little, "your father recovered and back home."

"I needed that cry. It had sealed itself up since the accident. Thanks for pulling the plug."

"Any time." His smile was a little crooked.

I slipped from his knee and poured us both a brandy from the drinks cupboard. "Medicinal purposes, you've had an almighty shock too." We chinked glasses and sipped in silence.

"What's the second thing you were going to tell me Tally?"

"Something unpleasant."

"It can't be a fraction as bad."

"No, but it leaves a nasty feeling behind." I began from the point where the taxi dropped me at the gate and related the story to him. He stopped me when I reached the point about the paper clips.

"Was anything, anything at all, taken from the house?"

"Not that I know too."

"Don't you think on top of the accident it might just have been your over-active imagination?"

"Don't humour me, David. I wish to goodness that's all it was – but it's not." He listened in silence whilst I finished telling him about the old cash-box in my bedroom and finally the painting.

"Good heavens!" He jumped to his feet. "Have you reported it to the Police?"

"No."

He looked surprised. "Don't you think you should?"

"No."

"Why ever not?"

"Because there's nothing to go on . . . and besides . . . I intend to find out myself."

"Don't be silly Tally, how on earth can you?"

I was nettled by his attitude. "I'm not a child David. Stop treating me like one."

"But, Tally . . ."

"Look David, whoever broke in wanted something that belonged to me, or, something to do with me, right?"

"I'd say that was obvious, yes."

"O.K. so maybe they found it or again, perhaps they didn't. In either case, there are going to be further ripples."

He pursed his lips and looked thoughtfully at me. "You're right you know." He said at last. "How do you want me to help?"

I smiled at him. "Any suggestions welcome right now."

He jumped to his feet. "Let's have a look at the picture for a start . . ."

"I see what you mean by leaving a nasty feeling behind." David said as we came back downstairs. "It's practically worse than having the painting stolen. What was it anyway in the backing?"

"I haven't got a clue."

"Could be something Jack put there thinking it to be the last place anyone would look."

"You think father would know?"

"It's a strong possibility."

"And," I continued slowly, "If father knew what it was, it might point to whoever broke in."

"Exactly!" David was getting enthusiastic about it. "Grab yourself a coat sweety, let's go and look outside for some evidence of where they got in."

"None of the windows were broken, I checked them." I said, hastily pulling on my duffle coat and following him outside.

"Where was Rookey when you returned?"

"Normal kennel, close to the back door. But usually he's loose. Probably spent most of his time in the kitchen until Freda went home."

"Then she fastens him up outside?"

"Yes."

"Hmmm . . ." David inspected the leather leash. "It's long enough to reach the back door."

"So he can guard," I said absently searching round for footprints.

"But Tally, don't you see, if the windows weren't broken, someone must have come in by the door." David gripped my arm. "And if Rookey let someone through the door . . ."

We finished the sentence together. "It must be someone he knows."

"We're getting somewhere now," David said with a satisfaction I couldn't match. It made it worse thinking someone known, trusted, had taken advantage.

He walked to the corner of the kitchen wall and then called me. "There's just a confused muddle of footsteps around here and down the side-path, come and see if you can make anything of them."

I joined him slowly. The footsteps were indeed a jumble superimposed on each other, indecipherable.

"What about these thin tyre tracks." David pointed to some snaking double tracks by the cloakroom wall.

"Freda's bike." I said, scanning the ivy creeper. There were no snapped or trailing stems, nobody had tried to scale the walls. I looked up at the ivy covered walls, the windows reflecting the pale afternoon sun, so snug, so secure and felt betrayed. There was a niggle at the back of my mind something I hadn't remembered to tell David. Thrusting cold, blue hands deep into capacious pockets of the duffle coat I stood and thought it out. Went back over the whole of the burglary. And it clicked into place. The smell, familiar yet tantalizingly elusive. I opened my mouth to shout and tell him, then closed it again. Somehow I didn't want to tell him. It was absurd. Identifying the smell was a positive pointer to the burglar. The burglar who wanted something from me and who I must know. The whole business was beginning to take on a very personal note. I knew I needed to find out who it was first myself.

We continued looking around for a few minutes but discovered nothing. A horse whinnied eagerly from down at the stables, reminding me what the time was. My watch confirmed it was four o'clock. "Have to throw you out now David, unless you want to give a hand?"

"No thank you Tally. I must get back to the office, sign up and take myself home to my son. Housekeeper's child has measles so she's away and Tim will be coming back from school soon."

Despite myself, I smiled inwardly, yet at the same time, a little wryly. Nothing could induce David down to the stables.

"I'll give you a ring later to see if there's any further news of Jack."

"Righto. Thanks very much for . . . everything."

He caught my face between two hands and kissed me full on the lips. "Take care, Tally. Take great care. Promise?"

"I promise," I said shakily, suddenly, momentarily afraid.

His Rover scrunched on the gravel, accelerated and disappeared down the drive.

I changed and went to the stables, making a start on Pegasus. As the body brush hissed rhythmically in swoops over his already glossy coat, I let the facts swim gently to and fro in my mind. It had to be someone close, someone who knew of the accident and that I would be at the hospital and the house would be empty. The reason was an unknown quantity. What they were looking for completely out of my guessing reach. Stick to the facts. The facts I knew about. Pegasus soothed by the swishing, dreamed gently. A beautiful animal, temperamentally sound as a lamb. I lowered my head against his withers and willed myself to come up with the answer.

I pictured in great detail everything from that moment at the winning post. The fog, Black Monarch coming through first. The fat blonde. What was it she'd said? Oh yes . . . a bloody fix. Certainly bloody. But, a bloody fix . . .? Could the accident not have been an accident? Was it in fact deliberate? Had someone set out to cause father's fall? Answered myself – I didn't know.

Continued on with the cinematograph in my mind.
Every detail deliberately thought of and pictured.
Packed them all in right up to the moment I finally
crawled into bed that night. Was that it? Had I covered
every single scrap I knew? Yes. Satisfied, I handed over
to my subconscious. Handed over surely, confidently. I
even said the words out loud, "Over to you, get on with
it." It was a game I'd played many times before.
Usually when something had been misplaced. It never
failed to either give me the answer or point me in the
right direction. The answer could be given in a minute
or two or it could take a few nights' sleep for the brain
to release what it already knew. The trick, if you call it
that, was to have absolute supreme confidence in being
given the solution. Only this time, it wasn't a game. It
was deadly serious.

I continued grooming the horse, dandy brushing
down separate parts of his tail until it fell in a shining
stream to his hocks.

A face appeared over the half-door, it was Turton,
wearing a garish shirt.

"Did you call Tal?"

"Call? No . . . oh, I guess I must have been talking to
myself, sorry."

He withdrew.

I stayed immobile, frozen, the brush clutched in
outstretched hand. Of all the stupid, irrelevant things;
the loud-checked shirt Turton was wearing had trig-
gered the process of memory. He usually only wore it
when off-duty, not at the stables.

I knew now what the smell was and just where I'd
smelt it.

Chapter Four

FREDA HAD A meal waiting when I came in after evening stables. Despite being punch-drunk by my discovery, the delicious smell wafting to me as I opened the kitchen door brought realisation that I was ravenously hungry. "Smells fabulous." I kicked off boots, washed hands at the sink and sank gratefully into one of the wheel-backed chairs.

Freda grinned as she dished out a plateful of steak and kidney – no pie top – with a mass of vegetables. "How's Mr Hunter? It sounds a bad fall he's had." I nodded, mouth full. She prattled on. "We keep having calls but I can't tell them anything 'coz I don't know."

"You've put the receiver back?"

"Yes, shouldn't I have?"

"It's O.K. Freda. I didn't want disturbing this afternoon. Mr Blake came round."

"Haa . . ." she smiled knowingly.

It irritated me to follow her line of thinking but I let it go.

"If you get any more calls, Freda, just tell them father's suffering from concussion."

The morning paper was lying on the dresser and I reached over and glanced at it. There was a picture of father being stretchered from the first-aid room and a lurid headline. There was going to be no way of hushing it up once the full news story broke. There was the job of cancelling his rides too. I wasn't looking forward to it. It brought home the full impact of his disability knowing he would never ride in a race again.

A crunching of gravel under wheels had Rookey looking up and barking warningly at the door. The man who entered was very slim, wiry and looked every inch what he was, a tough jockey. His brown hair curled low in his neck and bright blue eyes smiled at me.

"You're sure a difficult lady to reach on the 'phone."

"Hello Paul. Have a chair."

He hooked a toe round a chair leg and drew it out from the table. "How's Mr Hunter?"

"Concussed at the moment." I held back the rest. "Have you eaten?"

"Nope, not yet. Just finished at Doncaster."

Freda anticipating my request, was already filling a plate for him. Her slightly arched eyebrows and lips drawn into a tiny smirk gave away what she was thinking. I could almost hear her unspoken thoughts, doing well today, that's the second one. I tried to quell a rise of excitement inside which her sensitive radar was bound to pick up. It was no good trying to disguise it to myself though. There was something about Paul. A compelling quality that seemed to draw me towards him. The chemistry between us certainly seemed to match.

He glanced at me from under curling lashes which strangely enough gave him a "little boy – love me" look. The expression in his eyes however, was anything but a little boy and I felt my cheeks warming. To cover, I dug a fork into a heap of golden sweet corn and concentrated on getting it to my mouth without spilling any.

"How did the horse do?"

Inward relief flooded through at finding myself on comfortable, familiar ground. "Just a few superficial scratches, that's about all. Turton said he was pretty worked up and had a job catching him at the race course. He's as quiet as an old donkey now."

"Glad to hear it." He shovelled in a forkful of vegetables with gusto; chewed, grinned, "No lunch. Who'd be a jockey?"

I grinned back. "Everyone who wants to be and can't."

He stopped with fork in mid-air and stared at me. "Right! You know, you're dead right." The fork continued its upward journey. "When are you riding again?"

"Two fixed, end of the week."

"Will you do them, with your dad in hospital?"

"Depends on whether or not he's still unconscious or if he needs me."

"Sure, see your point." He finished off the remains on his plate.

"Are you dashing off, or will you stay for coffee?"

"Don't mind if I do thanks." He stretched his legs under the table and battled to disguise a big yawn. I knew the feeling. He'd probably had 5 rides that afternoon and given his all to each one. Coming over from America as a top class jockey one could see why he looked like an odds-on to take the championship over here. There was a steely determination to win, very visible in his riding. A total concentration with sights set for the top. Not for the first time I fought a battle with envy. When it came to choosing jockeys for their horses, owners nearly always preferred a male. Stronger than a girl, was their argument. Costs as much to put on a girl as it does a man. It was a sore point with me and had been for years. What the owners didn't see was the intuition and rapport that girls had with horses, the ability to get that little extra spark from them.

Paul had been round to dinner quite a few times before the accident. Despite their professional opposition, they had seemed to get on extremely well. It was not surprising. Paul was a very likeable chap, humorous and witty and enjoyed playing poker every bit as much as father did. With Turton a willing third player they had often carried the game on until well into the night on a Saturday.

"Coffee in comfort, I think Freda if you wouldn't mind."

"Of course, Miss Tal. I'll bring some through to the lounge."

"Guess I could use a soft chair right now," Paul followed me through from the kitchen, lowered his voice and added, "or a soft settee."

A thrill of excitement prickled its way down between

my shoulder-blades. I knew father disapproved of Paul making passes at me. I'd previously been firmly packed off after dinner leaving them to settle to an all male card game. This was the first time he'd been here when father was absent. It was David who had father's blessing to pursue his wooing. Perhaps that was why Paul had this fizzing effect upon me. Forbidden fruit and all that. I reproved myself, acting like a silly sixteen year old, I should know better. But it didn't put out the fizzing. "Sit wherever you like," I waved a hand round the lounge. "I must just make another call to the hospital."

"Take all the time you need. I've got all night." His eyes added volumes to the words.

I took a deep breath and went to make the call. There was a more sympathetic soul at the other end this time, but the message was still the same – "no change, ring again." Replaced the receiver and returned to the lounge. At the door I hesitated a moment. Ought Paul to be told about the injuries? He had been a friend of father's. Another unpleasant confrontation coming up.

Paul was stretched out flat on the sheepskin before the roasting, big fire, his eyes closed, limbs loose. I stirred him gently with a stockinged toe. "Freda's bringing the coffee. It's difficult to drink lying flat."

He smiled, eyes shut. "Blame your seductive fire, it's nearly as potent as you."

I hastily withdrew my toe.

The sound of Freda's footsteps reached the door and I went to take the coffee from her.

"Your ring's on the tray, Miss Tal. I found it this morning when I cleaned your room. Forgot to tell you before."

"My ring?"

"Yes, it was under the radiator near the window, think it must have rolled there. I didn't know whether to put it back in your jewellery case or not."

"No you did right to give it to me Freda, thanks." I hoped my voice sounded steady. The ring had been with my driving licence in my old cash box. The burglar had lifted out the contents and the ring must

34

have rolled out. Had he searched for it to replace it and if so, had he got into a sweat when he couldn't find it? I was sweating now. "I'll see to the coffee cups Freda, you can go off when you've finished in the kitchen."

"Thanks very much. There's a good film on the telly soon. Wouldn't mind seeing it." She trotted off and Paul heaved himself up from the sheepskin rug and took up the ring.

"Very unusual, attractive too."

"Father gave it to me – for luck."

"Oh?"

"Racing luck."

"Aah! And do you wear it at all your races?"

"Never without it. Father gave it to me just before my first ever race. A talisman he calls it."

"Does it work?"

"Who can say. Sometimes I win." I stroked the top of the ring with my fore finger. "A black cat is supposed to be lucky." The ring had a cat carved from onyx set in gold.

"I thought a rabbit's paw was the thing." Paul took a gulp of hot coffee.

I shuddered. "Poor rabbit. Surely you don't have one do you?"

"Me? No, I stick to things closer to me."

"Oh?" I was intrigued. "Such as?"

"Well, my whip. It's got a lock of my mother's golden hair wrapped around. Woven in with the leather and varnished."

"How original! And do you find it lucky?"

"Of course, very lucky." He smiled a private sort of smile.

"You're very set on the championship aren't you?"

"Dead set girl, as concrete." There was a ruthless hard quality to his words that I didn't care for.

"If father hadn't had the accident he'd have taken it again this year." I said needled, reminding him that father still officially held the title.

"And doesn't father carry a talisman for himself?" Paul said in a mocking tone.

"As a matter of fact he does. On a chain round his

35

neck." I frowned. "That reminds me it must be with his racing gear that I left for Turton to bring back from the first-aid room."

Paul gave me a sideways look. "Cut them off did they?"

I gave a slight nod, not wanting to picture the scene again in detail.

"Wouldn't bother if it was just concussion."

I didn't answer him.

"So," he persisted, "what's he got?"

"It's not pleasant. Do you really want to know?"

The front door bell jangled before he had chance to reply. Rookey barked furiously in the kitchen.

"Freda," I yelled, "you still here?" She didn't call back and the bell jangled again. "Didn't hear Freda's bicycle bell ring did you?" I asked Paul.

"No, should I?"

"She usually pedals away ringing her bell to let us know she's knocked off for the evening and the kitchen door's unlocked."

"That's sure the only bell I've heard." Paul tipped his head towards the front door as the old Church hand bell in the hall jangled loudly for the third time.

"I'd better see who it is. They're persistent." I scrambled to my feet and padded to answer it.

"Miss Hunter?" asked a tall man with a too wide smile.

"That's right."

"About Jack Hunter's accident . . ."

"Sorry, but just now, no comment, O.K.?" I said as the man waved a press card at me. I made to close the door but it was too late, he'd quietly slipped round the architrave and actually inside the hall. "Do you mind! This is a private residence."

"Just a few questions, Miss Hunter. When do you expect your father to be back? He is in hospital I take it?"

"Please go, I'm not answering anything."

"Come now. What about all the fans? They want to know when he'll be racing again."

"Put 'no comment' because that's what I'm giving

you, no comment. And now please leave." I held the front door wide.

"I'm sure you could just tell me how long he'll be in hospital . . ."

There was a movement behind me and Paul's voice said, "Out." It was pitched low but the menace behind it was unmistakeable. The reporter opened his mouth to argue, thought better of it and stepped back outside. "No questions then, but what about a 'photo Miss Hunter?"

Paul seized hold of the heavy door and crashed it shut. "So bloody persistent. Never take no for an answer."

"Thanks, next time I'll use the peep-hole and check before I open it."

He took my arm and led me back to the cooling coffee. "You were about to tell me something," he prompted.

I sighed. "Obviously the facts can't be contained any longer. Better you hear it from me direct." I told him the facts as the hospital had given them. He took it badly.

He swayed, raised a hand to his forehead. "A whiskey, Tal, if you wouldn't mind?"

"You look ghastly Paul, sit down."

"Bit of a shock, I didn't expect it to be that bad."

I pushed a tumbler into his hand and he downed the spirit in one gulp. "What's going to happen now?"

I was puzzled. "About what?"

"The stables, the whole set-up."

"It's going on just as before, only I'll be running it."

"You? Run it?" The disbelief in his voice put my hackles up.

"And why not? I do hold an Assistant Trainer's Licence."

His eye-brows shot up. "The hell you do!"

"Didn't father tell you?"

"No we never talked shop. Strictly cards when we met off the race course."

"Very single minded of you."

"It's the only way to succeed – in anything."

"Maybe I should take a few lessons."

"I shouldn't think you need any." He was recovering fast, his eyes appraising. For me the fizz had fizzled out and a sudden depression had dropped down. The reporter's visit had left behind a nasty taste. A foretaste of the next day when I would have to play fair and inform the media of the end of Jack Hunter's racing career. "Paul, I'm not very good company at the moment. If you don't mind I should like a quiet evening, probably watch that film Freda mentioned."

"And you'd like me to go?"

"Up to you."

"I'd just as soon stay. No sense in wearing out two television sets, one at my place and one here just to watch the same film."

"Is that really all you'd be doing tonight?"

"Sure is. As a matter of fact, I was looking forwards to seeing it."

"Go on."

"It's about the Canadian rockies, used to live there when I was a kid."

"The rockies?"

"No, Canada you idiot." He pulled a face at me. "Come and sit on the settee, I'll protect you from the grizzlies."

"Now who's being the idiot?" I flicked on the set and shoved two logs on the crackling fire. "Mind if I let Rookey in? He's fire-mad."

"Go ahead. He's a cute dog."

Rookey overjoyed at being allowed through washed Paul's hands vigorously in sloppy licks before throwing himself down before the blaze.

"I wouldn't describe him as cute," I said watching the dog stretching his legs out luxuriously, "he's no lap-dog. Quite the reverse. He's a good guard. I was very glad of him last night."

"Why was that?"

I'd said it quite without thought and realised I hadn't meant to let Paul know of the burglary since the flash of insight in the stables I wasn't going to mention it to anyone. "You know, being on my own." It sounded lame even to me. He raised a quizzical eyebrow at me but said nothing. We relaxed on the settee watching the cool grandeur of the mountains and forests and Paul, sensing my need for peace, contented himself by slipping an arm round my shoulders and lost himself in the picture. My depression lifted as quickly as it had dropped. I leaned against him and closed my eyes. It was all very restful. Just the balm I needed which my battered emotions took advantage of and re-generated themselves. I must have dozed off for the next thing I was aware of the music signifying the end of the film was playing.

Paul smiled down at me. "You're great company, even when you're asleep."

"Sorry," I smothered a yawn.

"Don't be. At the end of a gruelling day what could be nicer than a cosy fire and an unresisting girl in your arms?"

"We'll have a hot drink than I must go out and check the stables."

"Turton not doing it?"

"Yes, he'll be doing the rounds but there's something I want to check with him."

"Privately or could I give a hand?"

"Thanks for the offer, I might take you up on it sometime Paul but not this evening, O.K.?"

"O.K. M'am. I'm at your disposal." He smiled disarmingly and I left him watching the television and went to fix some coffee. He took it scalding, black and sugarless.

"That will put hairs on your chest." I curled my legs up and sat on the rug sipping my paler, honeyed version.

"Some people," he said with mock severity, "are fortunate to be naturally below the weight limit. Us others, we have to suffer." He slid down from the settee to sit beside me. "I'm going to ease my suffering right now."

Before I could object Paul had pulled me against him and kissed me hard and passionately. "Pure caveman," I said struggling to get my breath and pushing hard against his chest.

"It gets results," he replied breathing hard, but releasing me. "I've been wanting to do that all evening."

"Do you always get what you want?" I straightened my disarranged jersey trying to calm my racing emotions.

"Pretty near. If I want it badly enough."

"Be careful you want the right things then." My voice was a little unsteady.

"Oh I do," he said softly putting his face close to mine. "And what do you want Tal?"

"Right now," I said firmly levering myself up off the floor and inwardly cursing for putting myself in so potentially explosive a situation which I should have foreseen, "right now, the horses want me."

"I want you too Tal." He'd uncurled from the floor and caught me against him in one swift move. His kisses cut short my protest and I felt my senses reel. His body was like pliable steel and the superior strength it could exert to get his own way was frighteningly obvious.

"No, Paul," my voice rose. I stumbled backward as I struggled to free myself.

There was an anguished yelp and Rookey leapt up cannoning into Paul's legs. He let go of me fast, clutching the mantlepiece to avoid falling. I was furiously angry for allowing a dangerous situation to develop but I was angry not only with Paul but with myself moreso. For a few seconds I had felt my self-control go as completely as Paul's had. And it scared me. My emotions were something I prided myself were on a tight reign and the last thing I wanted was to find out the opposite. To get heavily involved with Paul at this juncture was out of the question.

"I'd be pleased if you'd go Paul." The coldness in my voice was deliberate. Knowing little of Paul as a private person it had been foolhardy to encourage his company with father away.

"I'm going. I'm sorry, real sorry." He looked dispirited. "I sure didn't mean to rile you." A lopsided smile appeared on his face. "What you could call mis-timing. Guess I'm guilty of rushing my fences. My own stupid fault if I come a cropper."

40

I had to smile back, he was so like a little boy caught at the jam-pot. "I'll see you out."

"Can I call you up tomorrow to see how Jack is?"

"Yes of course. You certainly can't leap on me from the end of a 'phone."

"I promise you Tal, never again, unless you want me too."

I looked into his so-blue eyes and felt disturbed by the swell of emotion within me. There was something I couldn't describe which drew me to him, a magnet like quality that I'd never before experienced. He gazed back at me. We both knew without saying that we felt the same attraction.

The cold, sharp air met us as we stepped from the house and crunched over the gravel. The moonlight showed up Paul's car clearly. He gave an exclamation of annoyance and kicked a rear tyre. "Slow puncture, noticed it was a bit soft earlier."

"Wait, I'll switch the garage lights on. There's a foot pump you can borrow."

Brightness flooded out from the twin fluorescent tubes and we entered the big garage.

"Taken up cycling?" Paul enquired patting the seat of a bicycle leaning against the far wall. I lugged the footpump down from a shelf and turned to see what he'd found. "That accounts for it. I'd forgotten in the midst of the accident and everything."

"Hmmm . . .?" Paul squatted down examining it. "It's crook."

"It's Freda's, which is why we didn't hear a bell. The chain came off a few days ago. I said I'd ask Turton to fix it for her. I'd forgotten." A coldness came over me which had nothing to do with the weather. It was a confirming factor that pointed unmistakably to the identity of last night's intruder. I had hoped desperately to be wrong. Now I knew I wasn't.

Paul connected the pump, filled the tyre and drove away with a discreet pip of the hooter.

I returned to the house for a coat and, Rookey at my heels, headed for the stables. Turton was already there checking haynets and talking softly to the horses. For a

41

moment I stood uncertain. It was all so familiar – and I was about to shatter it. I looked up at the star studded night sky and drew in a long, deep breath. Turton walked down the yard and went into Bright Boy's stable. Psyching myself up deliberately, I followed.

"'Lo Tal."

"Evening Turton." I pulled the door closed and stood silently watching him. As the tension in the air intensified he turned slowly to face me.

"What's up?"

I held his gaze with what I hoped was an impassive face. My lips felt wooden as I framed the one word, "Why?" It came out as a harsh accusation.

"Why what?" he licked his lips nervously.

"Why did you break into the house last night?"

Chapter Five

THE WORDS stood between us like a fence. For half a life-time Turton had been ally and friend to father. It was so against his character that the spoken words were like knife cuts. What had happened in the last two days? Life so ordered and comfortable had been turned on its head. For Turton to let us down was unthinkable but on top of the accident it was doubly staggering.

Turton dropped his eyes and muttered, "I didn't."

Hope, bright as a flame, lit up inside me. Could I be wrong after all? Pray God I was. At least part of my life would re-assemble.

"Didn't have to break in. I just used the key."

The starkness of the words hit me in the stomach like a blow. The hurt I felt wasn't caused by anything physical: it was a compound of bitterness, betrayal, loss.

He met my eyes and I shook my head slowly, "Why, for God's sake, why?" It came out not as an accusation this time but a hoarse whisper.

"I can't tell you."

"You knew father was at the hospital, me too. You chose your moment well. The house was as vulnerable as father. What did you want from it?"

There were unshed tears in his eyes. "I wouldn't hurt you Tal, nor Jack neither, not for the world."

"It wasn't money you were after was it?"

He pulled himself erect, pain striking across his face. "I'm no thief."

"Tell me why then." I urged.

"It was something important," he said slowly, choosing his words, "but right now it wouldn't do you any good to know what it was."

"Something of value?" I spread my hands in bewildered frustration.

"No, well not in the sense of money."

I changed tack. He was obviously not going to tell me outright. "Did you find . . . it?"

"No."

We stared at each other.

"If you tell me what it is, I'll give it to you," I said at last.

"Tal, it may not be what I think. Probably imagining things, what with your dad an' all."

"What's father got to do with it? He's miles away."

"Yeah, miles away, smashed up." He clenched a fist. "If only I *knew*. If I'd found the danged thing I could've checked."

"You're not telling me a thing Turton. I'm not a mind reader."

"Damn good job you're not."

I could have shaken him. "You're not going to tell me are you?"

He shook his head. "I'm not causing you any more heartache than you've got. Anyway, that's only the tip of the iceberg the rest of it's all dark, hidden."

"Something to do with father's accident isn't it?"

"Accident, pah!"

"You don't believe it was an accident?" Purposely I kept my voice flat without emotion but a thrill of apprehension fluttered in my stomach.

He studied his hands, rasping at a finger-nail before answering. "Where do horses fall Tal? I've lain awake last night pondering it."

"They fall anywhere, on bends, slip on wet grass, after jumping the fence."

He seized me roughly by the shoulders. "That's it gel, that's it! You've just said it. *After* jumping."

"So," I shrugged my shoulders, "what're you getting at?"

"Your dad's face, it was a right mess wasn't it?"

I nodded, trying to put a thumb-screw on the feelings that swelled up at his words. "Lacerated, raked."

"That's right. Calypso Lad couldn't have caused that if he fell after the fence."

44

I narrowed my eyes and mentally pictured how it would have been. The horses approaching the fence. Calypso most probably in front, sweating by now, his neck lathered where the leathers brushed, sounds of deep gusts of breath as he exhaled, the power coming from the muscles of the hind quarters propelling him forward. Father collecting him ready for the take-off shortening reins, eyes on the height of jump, mind already over and landing, moving as one. Fully confident in the forged ability of horse and man. Already visualizing streaking past the post and the crowds, leading the rest of the horses home, taking no chances yet already assured of his place in the winner's enclosure – collecting his 10%. It would have been his thirtieth win, a psychological boost in itself. Only he didn't win it. Would never ride that thirtieth winner, would never ride again, ever.

But if Turton was right, Calypso hadn't jumped the fence, father had been out the saddle before take-off, I simply couldn't picture it, it didn't add up. Calypso Lad was a superb jumper knowing to an inch what demands to make of himself in order to clear fences. Conserving his energy in a canny way. This was why however long the run-in, he'd still plenty of steam left to go clear and why we'd picked Cheltenham race course.

"I don't buy it Turton. He must have cleared the jump. He's not a horse that runs into the bottom, you know that."

" 'Course I do, like I've said many times, Calypso's right cat-footed. But I'd stake all I've got that he never cleared that jump with Jack still in the saddle."

Cat-footed. I'd heard that before quite recently. Then it dropped into place. Turton had said it straight after the accident at the race course. To him it seemed incomprehensible. And to myself knowing the quality of his judgement after forty years with horses, I felt he was right. Impossible to have happened that way, yet it must have done. It would explain how father had got his face in such a mess but left a huge question mark over Calypso's future ability.

Father was to have ridden him in March in the Grand National for Lord Vardy, the owner. There would be murmurs from that direction when the news reached him. The excellent form Calypso had shown the last two seasons coupled with father's capabilities and experience would have been sure to have made him hot favourite.

Turton spoke again. "Did any of the nearest riders see what happened?"

"Paul Reynolds simply said he fell at the third. He meant the third from home."

Turton's face darkened. "Closest was he?"

"Yes, I'm pretty sure he was."

There was something about Turton's manner that made me feel guilty to have been in Paul's company to-night, especially when I realised I'd had the ideal opportunity for asking questions and let it slip by. There was Leicester races the day after tomorrow and I was down for riding Badinage. An opportunity could be contrived to ask Paul about those last few moments before the third. I forebore to mention to Turton that he'd been to dinner tonight, albeit, without invitation.

"The news will have to be given to the press tomorrow but I've decided to drive down and see father to begin with. Can you manage here if I just do first lot?"

" 'Course. Seeing t'horses ain't the worry. It's what the owners will say to you Tal that's going to be the headache."

"What do you mean?"

"Like, can you train as good as your dad?"

"I see, a lack of confidence."

"Could well be. Might even withdraw the horses from Hunters."

"Very doubtful." I said decisively. "You have confidence in me don't you?"

"Oh aye. Born in a stable you were, weaned on racing."

"Leave the owners to me Turton. They're more temperamental than the horses but they'll eat out of my hand too, you'll see."

He chuckled. "Always a determined little beggar you was even when you were in rompers."

I smiled fondly at him; sometimes I forgot he'd known me from birth.

"What you just said, about me being born in a stable, it's not true is it?" Turton's words had aroused my curiosity. I'd never asked many questions about my early life from father, had never felt the need to.

"You very nearly were. Your ma came down to look at a new horse, your dad insisted, he was that thrilled with it. Last box before the Tack Room it was. Anyway, her pains started." His eyes were far away, seeing it all happening again.

"Would you tell me about her, when we've more time? Father never mentions her and there's nothing of her in the house. I think it might still be painful for him to remember."

"Nothing of her at all?"

"No, not a thing."

"Aah." He sighed gustily.

"Will you, there's so much you obviously know that I don't?"

He was silent for a moment or two then said, "After all she did, Jack still loves her y'know."

"Not after all these years surely."

"You've a lot to learn yet gel." He said it with affection. "Do you still remember Quillam?"

I stared at him, taken aback. "Quillam, you mean my first pony, dear old Quillam?"

"That's exactly who I mean."

"I couldn't forget him, I adored him."

Turton smiled and cocked his head sideways which said quite clearly, "you see what I mean?"

"You'll tell me then, when we've time?" I persisted.

"I'll tell you all you need to know anyway." His smile had disappeared now and a guarded look took it's place. "One thing, gel?"

"Yes?" I said briskly to cover the flutter of apprehension which had started up again in my stomach.

"Why were you so sure it was me who broke in?"

"Remember, on your mother's birthday, you were off

47

duty at the time? I came round with some chocolates for her. You were wearing that loud-checked shirt and smoking a menthol cigarette. It's a distinctive smell. No-one else I know smokes those. I could smell it faintly inside Hunters after the burglary."

"A little thing like that eh?"

"As you say, just a little thing. I'll see you first lot in the morning."

He nodded abstractedly as he twitched at Bright Boy's haynet and I walked out the stable with a mêlée of confused thoughts batting around in my brain.

I awoke next morning to rain drumming hard against the pane. It was coming down stair-rods. My spirits weren't exactly high and the weather did nothing to raise them. Gulped down black coffee in the kitchen and considered. There was no point ringing the hospital. I was going anyway. And after that? It was time to admit to the world that father was out of the saddle for good and Hunters was now being run by yours truly. Although I'd answered Turton in a confident manner much of it had been for his benefit. It was one thing to be Assistant Trainer quite another to be in complete control answerable for any slip. I dragged on a waterproof, made a hasty plait of my hair and stuffed it down underneath.

Outside the savage wind snatched the branches of the trees and slapped me wetly in the face. It was an unpromising start to the day. The rain had a subduing effect on the horses and we splashed through the stable yard in a steady, collected walk. Within minutes the horses flanks, below the rugs, were slicked dark, tails bedraggled and torn by the wind. The going at Leicester tomorrow would be heavy unless the deluge abaited. There was no winter sun touching the elm tree tops at the edge of the gallops today. Even the rooks seemed to have lost their caws. But as I asked for speed from Badinage, the big horse took off like a train. His joy in running was as complete as mine in being astride him. The feeling of power flowing through him lifted my spirits as nothing else in life could. In a world full of misfits, people in dull, soul-destroying jobs, I thanked God that I was lucky enough to be a jockey, totally content with my work with all the unmatched pleasure it brought me. For all it had brought about father's disability, I knew he would not have altered his life-style for anything in the world. But that particular race? If he could have foreseen the outcome? He was as human as the next man and he'd have ducked the ride. Turton's attitude showed clearly he didn't think it an accident And if it wasn't, it must have been deliberate. What did I think? I slowed Badinage to a trot. Events hadn't rung true from the beginning. I had felt that strongly but instead of analysing the facts and clarifying them the deeper examination of them had led into a maze of confusion. The one person who could tell me what actually happened was lying in a hospital bed.

We finished the first lot exercise and clattered back down the stable yard. Stripping off the saturated rug from Badinage, I made a twist of hay and worked away at his coat drying and cleaning. It was strenuous, heat inducing toil and both the horse and I steamed companionably but I was impatient to be off. Guilt was creeping in every time I thought of the motionless form between ultra clean, stiff sheets, knowing I ought to be there when he came round. But training from the cradle had also instilled in me that whatever, even the moon exploding, horses came first. They were the hub of our world and their care was paramount. After all, as father had said before on occasions, when I'd jibbed at putting self last, whoever heard of a jockey without a horse; get your priorities right girl. If he were in any shape at all it would be the horses he'd be enquiring after.

This last fall however was different from any of the others. Always after those falls there was the carrot dangling of getting back in the saddle. It was the spur needed to a swift recovery. But this time there would be no carrot and I didn't know how he'd react.

An unfamiliar, nervousness began churning my stomach as I closed the stable door behind me and walked back to the house. It persisted all the time I was turning pink in a hot soapy bath and when attired in a snappy, emerald green suit eating Freda's scrambled eggs in the warm, comfortable kitchen. Rookey turned his back on me in my 'going out' clothes and stumped off into his basket where he flopped down heavily with a big sigh. I almost wished I could climb in with him. His strength lay in his faith at relying on my return but where was my strength? My foundations right now were feeling decidedly shaky as I realised how much I'd relied on father to deal with life's more unpleasant aspects.

Slipping through the rain between house and garage, I turned the key in my sports car ignition. It fired first time and I backed out and swung round onto the drive. Freda came out and waved from the kitchen door-way – I couldn't hear her words but I lip-read them. Good luck. I certainly needed that. Raising a hand back, I snaked the car away down the drive towards Gloucester.

It was an uneventful drive with less traffic than I'd anticipated and plenty of scope for thought. I wasn't nearer an answer when the car engine cut in the hospital parking area but one thing was clear. Decisive action was needed, there'd been enough time spent treading water, adjusting to the changed circumstances, now positive action was required. Exchanging driving shoes for some gravity-defying black patent ones, I collected up the cassette recorder and a few selected tapes from the passenger seat, slammed the car door, locked it and made my way to reception.

Simply getting away from the home environment helped put life into perspective and had a therapeutic effect. Coupled with the almost subconscious awareness that the emerald green rig-out was doing great things for my figure built up confidence rapidly. I was working on the theory that if you look right, you'll soon begin to feel right. I took a couple of deep breaths which I really didn't need and tapped my way as quietly as the nonsense shoes allowed down the endless hospital corridors and was shown into father's room.

A nurse straightened up by the bed. "Mr Hunter's starting to come round. He's rambling a little naturally but apart from that he seems disturbed by something."

"I'll sit with him for a while nurse, see if I can make out what it is."

She nodded as she went to the door. "Just ring if you need me."

Turning my attention back to father it was a relief to see the grey pallor of his skin had gone, replaced by a pale but more normal colour.

"Hello father . . . can you hear me?" I took up one of his limp hands from the bedspread and squeezed it gently. He did not respond. For a few minutes the only movement was a nerve twitching in his cheek then his lips fumbled to form a word. It was whispered in so low a tone I had to place my ear almost to his mouth to catch it.

"Cheated." It was repeated harshly a second time and he became increasingly agitated. I was on the point of ringing for the nurse when the whisper died away and he lay as still as before.

What did it mean? Was he just rambling . . . or did the word have any significance?

"Father, I'm here, it's Tal." I squeezed his hand again. "I'll stay with you until you come round." It could have been imagination but for a fleeting moment I thought the pressure seemed returned. I gazed down at what still remained visible of his dear, familiar face. It wasn't a great deal. Eye pads and bandages obscured the greater part. I felt isolated from him yet still able to touch – an odd sensation. Automatic reaction is to look someone in the eyes and the thick, gauze covered pads alienated the feeling of communicating. I glanced round the small room. A power point was sited near floor level on the far wall. Plugging in the cassette recorder I selected a Schubert tape and turned it on keeping the volume low. Father seemed very peaceful now and I sat by the bed holding his hand and just waited.

Once a nurse popped her head round the door, cupped a hand to her ear, smiled, nodded and withdrew.

The music seeped into me relaxing tension and inducing a dreamy state in which I recalled times past when father and I had been together. Happy times. No

51

tears times. The tape finished and I slipped across to slot in another – Beethoven's 5th. A little premature in the circumstances, but perhaps the symbolic victory music would assist father's fighting spirit. It was a tape I usually played after a race win when I felt high and victorious: the world shrinking to football size and I standing with one foot, controlling my destiny, on top. Quite ridiculous of course, but marvellously exhilarating whilst it lasted.

I was holding father's hand as the first few bars thundered out. It reminded me irresistibly of tons of water hurtling and crashing down over a weir. Majestic, frightening music, sweeping man along with it, raising deep surging feelings of power within him. The hand within my own jumped and gripped seemingly shot through with an invisible electric charge.

His head rolled sideways. "Cheated." The word was clearly audible, his voice stronger, "Cheated." He repeated it again several times, his hands clutching the bedclothes in a tormented fashion.

I rang the bell. Within seconds the nurse appeared, summoned a doctor and I was banished to the now familiar waiting room. This time however it was a comparatively short acquaintance compared to the last.

A doctor entered and said "Mr Hunter has regained consciousness if you would like to see him now." Would I? It was what I had wanted to hear since the accident. Just as we were about to open father's door the doctor put a hand on my arm. "Miss Hunter, obviously you brought in the cassette recorder and tapes. Why did you choose to play that particular one?"

I countered the question with one of my own. "Was it that tape that brought him round?"

He gave me a keen glance. "We think so. He was coming round before you understand, but the sudden acceleration into full consciousness was due to some outside stimulus."

"The first tape was Schubert's Trout Quintet. One of our favourites. We've often played it together at home. It seemed to have a soothing effect on him today so when the tape ended as a contrast, I put Beethoven on.

Since it symbolized Churchill's victory, I thought it might help father to fight back. Apart from that I really don't know why I chose it. It's one of my personal favourites; I bought it myself."

"Does your father play it? At home, I mean."

I hesitated, then said, "Now you come to ask, no, no he doesn't. In fact . . ."

"Yes, Miss Hunter?"

"In fact . . . thinking back, we've never listened to it together. Whenever it's playing, he . . . he leaves the room." The doctor and I stared at each other.

He spoke first. "It obviously has unpleasant associations connected with it. I would say very strong ones."

"Strong enough to bring him back to consciousness?"

"Exactly. And you have no idea what it signifies to Mr Hunter?"

"None at all. It's a jolt to realise I must have played something obnoxious to him."

"Don't worry about it Miss Hunter. It's a case of good coming from bad. The main thing to remember is he's conscious now."

"Can I see him please?"

"Of course." The doctor opened the door and we both went into the room.

I approached the bed. "Hello father."

He moved his head in the direction of my voice. "Tal? That you?"

"Yes it's me." I bent, kissed his face and then wished I hadn't.

He winced sharply and said, "Made a right mess of myself this time haven't I?"

"Afraid so."

"How long before I can get home?" Despite the weariness in his voice it was so typical of him that I could have broken down and wept.

"Several weeks yet I should think, what do you say doctor?"

"Let's be optimistic and say three at least Mr Hunter."

"Hmmm! That's no damn good to me man, season's underway."

53

I opened my eyes wide with horror and looked across at the doctor. Father didn't know! Didn't know he was blind! But how could he? Unconscious since the accident until today, of course, he hadn't been told. The doctor shook his head warningly at me not to say anything.

"You've had a really nasty fall this time Mr Hunter, it's going to be a while before you're on your feet again. We can't rush nature I'm afraid. All we can do is assist her and that includes you getting plenty of rest."

Father tightened his lips in a grimace and moved his head slightly. "O.K., O.K. I suppose so." He sighed gustily.

"I think you should sleep now Mr Hunter. It's the best medicine I can prescribe."

"Bye father. I'll be back to see you soon." I squeezed his hand but it was slack and I could tell he was already asleep. A normal sleep, as the doctor had said, nature was swinging into action to repair the race course ravages.

"Can I call back this afternoon to see him, doctor?"

"You can certainly visit, whether he will be awake or not is something you'll have to take a chance on Miss Hunter."

"I'm used to taking chances. I'll call back about two o'clock."

I left the car where it was and walked into the town. At the first telephone box I saw I dialled Turton and gave him the good news that father had regained consciousness. After that I 'phoned the newspaper and gave them an abridged version of father's accident. Despite the condolences of the reporter on the other end, I could practically feel the vibrations of his concealed excitement. I'd just placed an exclusive scoop in his lap. I brushed aside his effusive thanks and replaced the receiver. It would be splashed across the next issue and the whole country would know Jack Hunter was finished as a jockey.

With a heavy heart I left the kiosk and went in search of a light lunch. I found a clean, cheerful, vegetarian cafe not far away and slipped onto a chair and ordered egg salad. When the delicious, crisp salad topped with bean sprouts was set before me I realised just how hungry I was after the long drive down. After eating, much fortified, I left a generous tip and sauntered back to the hospital.

Father had awakened before two and was plucking restlessly at the sheet as I went in.

"Tal?"

"Yes father."

"Thought it was you, nurses don't wear high heels."

"How are you feeling?"

"Rough." His voice was clipped and brusque. "What's wrong with my eyes Tal?"

I gritted my teeth. I hadn't expected him to ask so soon. "Your face took a beating that's all."

"It's bloody not all! I've asked the nurse point blank but she wouldn't give me a straight answer. Now I'm asking you. I want the truth Tal. Am I going to see again or . . . am I blind?"

He was my father and I told him.

Chapter Six

LEICESTER was only a flea bite away from where we were in Nottinghamshire. If the horse box left at 11 o'clock there was still all the time in the world to settle Badinage down in the race course stable before his race at 2.30 p.m. Turton had packed the hamper last night but I checked through it again. No-one was infallible and arriving at a race course to find something like the passport or even the cooler missing was not a prospect to relish. The normal morning routine held a delicate tinge of excitement.

Over the years I had grown used to race morning atmosphere, that it was different from other mornings couldn't be denied and yet it was pegged down firmly. Horses were sensitive creatures that responded to mood and I wanted Badinage sweatless and calm as possible when we cantered down to the start. The nervous energy they could burn up before a race was phenomenal. I wanted all that energy still in reserve as we jumped the last and approached the run-in. Today's race was in no way a push-over. We had been preparing him for weeks for this but the opposition was stiff. Last night's paper had given him odds of 9-2 with three more at shorter odds. The danger looked like coming from Cherrytop, one of Brice's stable. Paul was riding him. I felt a harder than usual edge of determination rise inside me. So what if Paul was on Cherrytop? I was riding Badinage.

Feeling someone's eyes on me I swung round. Turton was studying me with a calculating, assessing, shrewdness. And I knew just what he was thinking. That look hadn't been for me to see but now he knew of my awareness, he didn't bother to try to hide it.

"Do I measure up?"

He didn't reply immediately but rubbed a stubby finger across his moustache, his face still serious, still assessing. I waited edgily. His reply was important to me.

"I reckon so gel, I reckon so."

I know my breath came out in a gust although I didn't realise I'd been holding it.

Turton carried on. "You've changed Tal, since yon accident. Grown-up suddenly p'raps. There's a new hardness about you that wasn't there before. I won't say it's something I like to see but it's necessary, if we're all to survive."

Impulsively I hugged him. "Don't worry. I've not changed Turton, not the real me inside. Circumstances have hardened the crust but the filling's still soft."

He grinned. "Now, and there's me thinking you're steel hard right through."

I aimed a mock punch at him which he ducked.

We called a halt for coffee at a quarter to eleven and a few minutes after were leading Badinage up the ribbed ramp into the horse box. Down the stable line heads were put over half-doors as the other horses watched. They all knew what horse boxes meant. One or two whickered and blew down their flared nostrils while inside the horse box, Badinage pranced a little and whinnied back.

"All set then?" Turton clipped the ramp shut.

"All set." I climbed up into the driver's seat of the cab and switched on. Turton clambered in beside and I nosed the massive vehicle out of the stable yard and shortly we were bowling down the A52 at a steady forty-five.

The morning was clear and fine, no rain today. Whilst the going wouldn't worsen, it wasn't drying enough to improve and I expected it to be heavy. Badinage was used to heavy going and I wasn't too concerned. What did concern me was the pair of us should make a good showing.

The morning paper had, as expected, splashed across a headline proclaiming Jack Hunter's demise from racing. At the moment, I blessed those thick, gauze covered pads across his eyes. At least he would never have to read the terrible words, if of course, he were ever to be able to read again. I pushed the ghastly headline out of my thoughts and thought about the race meeting. People were going to be watching. Watching from curiosity and from a critical view point. Their thoughts were bound to be can she carry on without him? I wanted to boost confidence in all quarters that it was most definitely business as usual. Which meant winners. Thinking of winners made me reach in my jacket pocket for the little box containing my talisman. Pushing up the lid with my thumb I juggled the box between both hands on the steering wheel before managing to slip the black cat ring on my left hand.

Turton glanced sideways to see what I was doing. He stiffened perceptively at the sight of it and I remembered what Freda had said.

"Freda found it, under the window by the skirting board."

"Good. Wouldn't want it to have got lost." He replied matter of factly but I knew he was much relieved at its re-appearance.

Swinging right off the Oadby road, we bumped gently across the grass at Leicester. Brice's distinctive blue and red horse box was already parked and Paul was leaning against the side talking to the trainer. It crossed my mind it seemed rather an odd thing he should have chosen to rent a cottage so close to where we had our stables at Dalting. With the world's racing headquarters acknowledged to be Newmarket it was strange that he wasn't living there. Still, he did ride for Brices and they were the nearest stables to us so perhaps it wasn't so unusual.

I dismissed Paul from my mind and went to help Turton unbox the horse. He clattered down the ramp with head high and ears pricked. He was a horse that knew what was expected of him and was only too eager to oblige. His staying power like Calypso Lad's was pretty well bottomless. It would need to be. There were puddles everywhere. The going would be a test of stamina for all the horses today. We walked Badinage

58

over to the line of boxes. It took us far longer than normal. From every angle friends in the racing world stopped us and expressed their concern, regret and genuine sorrow that my father would no longer ride. It was touching and comforting to know just how many people cared about him. I left Turton murmuring gentlings to the big horse and walked across to the weighing room. Before I reached it a shadow unhitched itself from the corner of the wall and came up to me.

"Hello Miss Hunter."

I eyed him with distaste. He was a big man, built like a mountain with a broad nose and an even broader smile. His skin had blemishes and bumps all over it. He reminded me of a complacent toad beaming at a fly before swallowing it.

"Sorry to hear about Jack."

"Are you?"

The smile didn't slip a millimetre. "But of course. He's going to be a great loss." Theatrically, he removed his trilby and held it in front of his heart. "Yes, a great loss."

"You can put your hat back on Mr Snodgrass, you don't have to stand on ceremony with me."

"But my dear young lady, my heart bleeds for you. All the worry of keeping the stables running until you can find a buyer."

"No, Mr Snodgrass." I said shortly.

He feigned not to hear. "But that's where I can take some of the trouble from your elegant shoulders. A client of mine is desperate to obtain a racing stable Miss Hunter." He put a smiling face very close to my own. "Simply desperate."

I held his eyes with my own, deliberately kept my voice low and let all the dislike for him come through. "And I said no, Mr Snodgrass."

"Oh, come how," his jovial manner didn't falter.

"For the last time the answer's no and will remain no. Goodbye."

"He'll make you a very good offer."

The tenacious gall of the man slipped the catch on my temper. "Shall I tell you something to your advantage?" I bent forward towards him.

"Yes?" He was all eagerness.

I stuck the barb in where it would hurt most. "Go on a diet and while you're at it, have a facial."

The smile left his face like a horse leaving the stalls. Pure undiluted hatred lasered at me from his grey eyes. "You'll live to regret that. Or . . ." he laughed unpleasantly, "you may not . . ." With incredible swiftness for a man of his bulk, he strode away.

It was the first time I'd ever had my life threatened and it shook me. There was something going on that didn't meet the eye. Why the sudden urgency to buy Hunters Stables? Had father's so-called accident been a pivot to try and force a sale?

Turton's voice cut through my thoughts. "What's up?"

"Snodgrass just made me an offer *he* thought I couldn't refuse."

"And you did?"

"What do you think?"

"For Hunters was it?"

"Yes."

"Haa . . ." he tugged at the side of his moustache in agitation. "Reckon we're facing something bigger than we know."

"I get the same impression Turton. He just gave me a life threat."

"No!"

"True."

He turned very pale. "Better inform Police."

"No!" Now it was my turn to say it. "There's absolutely nothing to go on. An accident that might not have been. A burglary with nothing stolen – which you reckon you did. An offer to buy the stables . . ."

"With a threat thrown in."

"Maybe, but he didn't actually say, sell it to me or wake up tomorrow with your throat cut."

"No, he wouldn't. He's far too cunning a bastard to say something incriminating. Look how he took poor old Fosdyke's stables over when his wife died. Poor bugger never stood a chance. Picked the time when the man was at his lowest and put the pressure on."

I nodded. "And made it appear he'd done Fosdyke a big favour."

"He'll not get Hunters." Turton's fists clenched in tight knots.

"We'll make sure he won't, but we can't bring the police into it."

"Who is he acting for, did he say?"

"No, just 'a client'. A client who is desperate according to him."

"I don't like the sound of it Tal gel. Watch yourself every step of the way now."

"Believe me, I will."

"And for gawd's sake be careful in the 2.30. We don't want another accident."

"An accident that we can now be pretty sure wasn't."

The weighing room bell had clanged and several of the jockeys walked to the parade ring together. I made a quick exit and caught up with them. There was safety in numbers.

Kevin Grundy, Badinage's owner was standing waiting in the parade ring. He clapped a hand on my shoulder. "Every confidence in you Miss Hunter. He looks in superb form."

I was grateful to him for saying it. Confidence was half-way to winning. "He's certainly at his peak. We've been working on him for the race."

"You've done a good job." He patted the horse's glossy neck.

I took the golden opportunity and jumped in. "You'll be keeping him with us then, despite father's accident?"

"Can't think of anybody I'd rather have training him. Don't lose sleep on my account."

"Very good of you Mr Grundy. We appreciate it."

He pumped my hand up and down. "Get both of you round in one piece and give the others a damn good run for their money. If you can pull off a win, I'd be highly delighted."

"Do my best."

Turton hoisted me into the saddle. He caught hold of my left hand and rubbed the onyx ring furiously. "Good luck Tal. And don't forget gel. Watch yourself."

He took hold of the rein and I squeezed my calves gently against Badinage's sides. The horse obediently walked a couple of times round the ring before going out onto the course. Turton released his hold as Badinage pranced with eagerness, half-rearing in his excitement to get going.

I could feel all the pent up energy tuning through him. It took judgement to know when to ask for full power but Badinage and I knew each other well. At the critical moment when the maximum drive was wanted, I knew he wouldn't fail me. We cantered down to the start with the rest. The bright colours of the jockeys a cheerful note atop the dark green of the saturated turf. As we walked round before the tape I thought for a fleeting moment of father's accident. There was no way he'd been aware of his danger and the element of surprise had been in the attacker's favour. From now on that advantage was gone.

I decided to let the others go in front. Badinage had enough steam to open up at the last. Even his owner wanted him in one piece in preference to being first past the post and for that I was grateful. As desperate as I was for a winner today, it would do no good to get myself fouled up and be out of the saddle with injuries. I was acutely aware that with father not riding it was now my feet in the irons that Hunters rested on.

The starter's voice cut through, calling for us to get in line and I pulled down the goggles. The tape flew up, we were away and I was back marker. From between Badinage's ears I watched the thrusting rumps of the other horses and rose and landed over the fences in their wake. For the first circuit I maintained the same steady pace but it was taking all my technique and strength to hold the horse back and I knew he was resenting it. Easing the reins, I gently let him make up ground on the two in front. The familiar sound of heavy drumming battered against my ear-drums as forty-eight metal shod pounding pistons hit the unresisting earth. Divotts flew high with globs of white sweat and spittle mingling. I eased up Badinage, passed three more chasers to take the lead over the back half of the field. So far it had been a normal race. If only it could all have been imagination.

The exhilaration and joy of riding was overcoming my cautious start. There was no way I was going to let anybody take away my delight and sheer blissful pleasure in winning races. I took Badinage to the outside and eased the brake still more. There was about five furlongs to go now and I held the big horse steady with just two in front. At the second last the horse in front pecked badly on landing and shot the jockey into the air. That left Paul Reynolds out in the lead on Cherrytop. I shortened the gap between us. Paul looked round once, very quickly, and then gave his horse a slap with the whip. Cherrytop increased speed and headed for the last fence. I booted Badinage and he responded magnificently. We both took the fence with half a length between us. Slowly, inexorably Badinage gained on Cherrytop. We flashed past the one furlong marker neck and neck. Paul was using his whip freely now and not only on the horse but in his familiar style of swinging it past the horse's eye. The horse responded. We raced nip and tuck. I gave Badinage one flick and for a few seconds we were leading. But Cherrytop wasn't odds-on favourite for nothing. The horse gamely found another burst of speed and right on the line was a short head in front.

We dropped back into a canter and Paul shouted across. "A bit too close for comfort this time!"

"You think so? Wait until next time."

He laughed and turned Cherrytop for the winners enclosure.

Turton was waiting by the gate for me. We walked behind Cherrytop into second place in the enclosure.

"By, Tal, you rode a damn good race." He fussed over the horse, holding the bit wide.

"Didn't win though. I played it too cagey at the start. Should have moved up sooner." As I spoke I undid the girths and slid the saddle from Badinage's steaming back.

"You're still in one piece gel, don't knock it."

I went to weigh-in leaving him tenderly spreading the

cooler over the sweating animal. Being cautious and letting others make the running didn't win races. I knew Badinage could have had that race and I'd allowed myself to be intimidated by Snodgrass' threat into playing safe. And that was not what racing was all about.

Paul had just finished weighing-in as I entered through the glass doors. He had a happy smile on his face. Why shouldn't he have. That was number twenty-six so far for the season. I sat down on the weighing chair and stared glumly in front.

Paul waved his whip at me. "A bit more of this Tal and who knows, you could have pipped me."

It was no good being a sour grape. After all it was my fault I'd lost the race. Receiving the O.K. I left the chair and went over to him. "Let's see the lock of hair you were on about the other night."

Immediately he looked shamed-faced. "About the other night . . . I'm real sorry losing control."

"Forget it. I have."

"Have you Tal?" He was standing very close to me and the look in his eyes made my knees feel like water. Allowing myself emotions was not in the form book right now.

"Can I see the whip Paul?" I made a show of reaching for it to cover what I felt.

He obligingly handed it to me. "There, see, around the bottom of the hand grip?"

"Oh yes!"

It was a skilful job. A plaited lock of hair, palest honey colour, was woven into the whip leather and had a hard, clear varnish on the top.

"I take her everywhere with me," he said, stroking it lovingly. Before I realised he let his hand slide up over mine. "Can I see you tonight Tal?" He said it in a low voice so the others couldn't hear.

The strange magnetism of the man seemed to draw me to him and I had to force myself to shake my head. "I'm sorry."

His eyes looked deep into mine. "So am I." His fingers still stayed over mine.

64

I released my hold on the whip. "Father and I would be glad for you to come round when he returns. He'll need his friends."

"But I'm more interested in you."

"I must go and change Paul. I'll probably see you at other races."

"You'll certainly do that. I'll be out in front, winning."

His complete confidence had the effect of shrinking mine. He was so sure of himself, didn't he have any self-doubts?

Driving home in the horse box I had to admit to myself I had plenty. Snodgrass' threat had undermined the psyching up process I employed before racing. Without the right mental attitude there wasn't going to be any winners.

"You're getting depressed gel, ain't you?" Turton had picked up my negative vibrations.

"I guess I am but it's enough to make you."

"There might be some better news from the hospital when we get back, that'd cheer you up."

I stiffened my elbows and stretched against the steering wheel. "It was a funny thing, father repeating that one word yesterday."

"Oh, what was that?"

"Just one word he said, kept on repeating it, 'cheated'."

There was silence in the cab.

"Any ideas what he meant?"

"Could mean anything."

Turton's reply was a little tardy and I flashed a quick glance at him. He was gazing down at his hands, his face impassive.

"Hazard a guess." I urged.

"What did he do? Just came round and said it?"

"More or less. The music seemed to get through to him."

"What music?"

"Beethoven's 5th."

My eyes were on the darkening road and I sensed rather than saw Turton stiffen.

65

"Why'd you play that one?"

"Thought it might stimulate him."

"It'd do that all right."

The way Turton blew down his nose deprecatingly as he said it made me realise that he knew something.

"O.K." I changed down, pulled to the side of the lane, just passed a bend and stopped the big vehicle.

"What you doing Tal?"

"Now, tell me. What do you know that I don't."

He began to bluster. "Come on! Move it off. It's bloody dangerous stuck here."

"I know."

"Well shift it then."

I wound down the window. "Not 'till you tell me why Beethoven's 5th should have had a strong enough impact to bring father round and why he said that word."

"If Jack wants you to know, then he'll tell you."

"We'll stay here then."

"Look Tal," he licked his lips. "If you don't hurry up and move, somebody's going to come round this blasted bend and ram right right up our backsides."

"Yes."

"Think of the horse Tal. He's the one that will cop it."

"I haven't forgotten him."

There was a faint sound of an engine some way behind. We both heard it.

"Are you going to move?"

"Not 'till you tell me."

"I'm getting out! I'm not staying to get smashed." He put his hand on the door handle.

"Fine, save your own skin. I'm still going to be here, so's the horse."

The sound of the other vehicle grew louder.

In desperation, Turton drew his hand away from the door and slammed it down hard on his knee. "Right. I'll talk about it, when we get home. Now get the hell out of it."

"My pleasure."

I hastily let in the clutch and the horse box glided away smoothly.

"By, you had me worried there."

"Some folk scare easily." I said staring straight in front and hoping Turton wouldn't hear just how hard my heart was pounding against my ribs or notice the tell tale sweat marks on the steering wheel despite the cold of the afternoon.

"Huh!" He grunted and was silent for the rest of the journey.

We pulled in on the gravel drive avoiding a highly polished white car already parked near the house.

"David's here." I remarked and received a grunt in reply. My conscience was beginning to prick over the way I'd blackmailed Turton into agreeing to tell me. "Be an angel would you, take the box down to the yard and see to Badinage."

"Sure."

"I'll see you in a while, just want to have a quick word with David first."

"Sure," he said again in a more relieved tone which I detected smacked of the condemned man being reprieved.

I gave him a quick grin, slipped from the driving seat and ran across the scrunching stones to the kitchen door.

David was in the study, his broad shoulders bent forward over the desk. The table lamp, already switched on, shone on his sleek, dark hair. The sight of him gave me a reassuring, comfortable feeling. As David's wife I should enjoy a life free from worry or death threats.

"Hi David."

He looked up, his initial smile at seeing me changing quickly to a grave expression. "Hello Tally."

I frowned. "What's the matter? Is something wrong?"

"You didn't mention anything about selling up. Don't you think you're being hasty making that decision?"

"Selling up?"

"I thought you'd have consulted me." His manner was stiff.

"Look here, David. I don't know what put that idea

67

into your head but there's no possibility whatever of Hunters being sold."

Relief spread across his features. "You're not thinking of selling?"

"Not while I draw breath." A picture of Snodgrass' face floated momentarily before me and I mentally kicked it away.

David's relief changed to puzzlement. "Then how come you received this?" He handed me a letter. "It wasn't in the mail I opened. It arrived about half-an-hour ago, delivered by hand."

I felt a tremor run through me as I took the letter and read the name at the top. Snodgrass and Associates. The swine hadn't wasted any time. It was an official offer to buy Hunters.

Chapter Seven

IT WOULD HAVE made me feel better to have told David of the brush with Snodgrass this afternoon but I didn't. "The man's heard of father's accident that's all. He's just banging in an offer hoping I'll take the easy way out."

"You could be right."

"'Course I am." I tore the offensive letter into small pieces and threw them in the waste basket. "Stop worrying David."

He relaxed, the crease line between his eyes smoothing out. "It had me worried I must admit."

I steered the conversation away to business matters and was delighted to find I'd been booked on two rides the following week. David carried out the paper work and day to day assistance excellently.

"Any news from the hospital whilst I was at Leicester?"

"I rang up a bit earlier. Quote: 'comfortable'."

"As forthcoming as usual. Could you stay for a meal or do you have to rush back?"

"No rush at all Tally. I've solved the problem of dividing myself up."

I cocked an eyebrow. "How come?"

"I've just employed a new live-in housekeeper. One Mary Frankish. Nice girl, no ties now her mother has passed on. She stayed home to nurse mother and now finds herself unqualified for a job."

"Has Tim taken to her?" I said referring to his eight year old son from his previous marriage.

"Like a duck to water."

"Oh good."

"Yes thank heavens. You never know with children.

If they take a dislike to someone, you've had it. Mary's on a month's trial but I can tell she's just what Tim needs."

"It will be a weight off your mind."

"Well, with Jack out of action, I knew you'd need me here more to give you a back-up in the paperwork department."

"And how right you are David."

He stayed for a meal and I totally forgot about meeting Turton at the stables. It wasn't until we were talking of father's recovery later that I remembered.

"And he's recovered enough to talk?" David asked.

I nodded. "He's his old battling self. Except . . . ."

"Yes?"

"After I levelled with him, about his eyes . . . after that he was very quiet. Hardly spoke at all. Asked if I'd come the next day to see him. Told him no because I was riding at Leicester."

"You could have scratched."

"Scratched! Don't talk sacrilege David. Give up a race? Never!"

"But if Jack wanted . . . ."

"Knowing I was riding was the best thing for him. He actually did a little smile and said 'Keep going girl, keep going'."

David looked at me a little wryly. "Like father, like daughter."

"Anything wrong with that?"

"No, no, I just wonder how long it will take that's all."

"How long what will take?"

"You, Tal. How long it will be before you give a tiny bit of yourself to me. I'm not stupid enough to think you'll ever give up racing but even a fragment of your heart, if you could spare it, would be nice."

I laughed. "Don't be so melodramatic David."

"Marry me, Tally," He said gently taking hold of my hand. "While there's still time."

"You make it sound as though I'm about to pass over."

"Be sensible, Tal, marry me, say you'll marry me."

His grip tightened and I knew he was speaking from his innermost feelings.

"David let's get passed this period of our lives first. It's impossible to make such a decision with father still so ill and Hunters relying on me." I stroked his cheek, "You do understand, don't you?"

He sighed deeply. "Oh yes, yes I understand only too well." He released his hold on me. "Think I'll be going now Tal. You've the stables to check in a while and my Tim will just about be getting ready for bed. He likes to say good-night before he settles down."

"Of course." I followed him out the kitchen door. As he walked away to his car, shoulders hunched dejectedly under the thin cloth of his suit, he looked suddenly ten years older. I watched him drive away and felt every bit a louse.

The 'phone rang about nine o'clock. It was Turton.

"Would you mind Tal, I'd be obliged if you could do the stables without me tonight. Mother's had one of her dizzy spells this evening and doesn't look too good."

"Not to worry. You stay and look after her Turton. Don't give the horses another thought. I'm sorry I didn't get to speak to you earlier but I'll see you in the morning. O.K.?"

"Sure," he sounded relieved, "thanks Tal."

Turton wasn't a man to shirk his duties in any respect and I had no doubts that old Mrs Turton needed him. It was equally certain when I saw him in the morning he would talk as agreed about the piece of music and its strange effect on father.

Whistling gently I collected up Rookey and we walked across to the stables. It had turned bitterly cold and the stars twinkled down sharply like cut diamonds from the winter sky. Over by the side of the building the horse box stood with ramp still down. I went over. There were whisps of hay and clods of part-dried clay as well as horse droppings littering the rubber ridged floor. Have to get Jimmy onto it in the morning and have it hosed out. It seemed a little surprising that Turton hadn't brushed out at the very least before going off duty. I chuckled. Bet he'd worked like mad to finish

71

attending Badinage and assisting Jimmy with the feeds in order to be away before I finished chatting to David.

I worked my way steadily down the line of horses. Everything was in order and the animals complacently swung an acknowledging head in my direction or nuzzled and whickered as Badinage did whilst I ran a hand down each leg, relieved as always to find them firm and cool with no hint of tenderness. Closing his door I went on to the last one. Calypso Lad blew down his nose at me and I blew back. I encircled the glossy neck with my arm and pulled gently on his ear, telling him what a smasher he was and didn't he know he was top horse. He was too. With the pulling and staying power of a train he was to have carried all our hopes in the Grand National. It was warm by the side of him with the sweet smell of fresh hay coming from the rack and I dreamed contentedly and leaned against his shoulder. He snorted and side stepped suddenly and I nearly went sprawling.

"Steady there boy, steady." I regained my balance and ran a soothing hand down his neck. "What is it? Something caught you didn't it?" I slipped off his rug and ran an exploratory hand down the side of his neck, over his withers and down the shoulder. He seemed calm enough. I checked his near side fore-leg, still nothing. He swung his head and butted me gently as I bent over. I responded with a pat on his side. As my hand connected with the bright chestnut coat he snorted loudly and kick stamped the near hind leg.

"O.K. boy, take it easy." My slap of affection had pin-pointed the trouble. But it was no easy matter to explore the tenderness. Whenever my hand reached the right place he countered by swinging his hind quarters away. In the end I gave it up. It wasn't doing him any good at all getting excited and sweating. "You win my big boy," I gently stroked the plush velvet nose, dotted here and there with its contrastingly sharp prickly whiskers. "We'll look at you in daylight, out in the yard."

Calypso hrumphed at me, curled the soft lips back to show large, white teeth and shook his head: plainly saying 'scored there didn't I'.

72

I chuckled at him. "We'll see who wins tomorrow. Can't be much wrong with you, you big hunk, you're too lively." I rugged him up, closed his door securely, switched off the stable lights and went off to an early bed.

At two o'clock in the morning, the telephone rang. I groaned, rolled over, squinted with one eye at the clock and reached for the receiver. Smothering a yast yawn I mumbled, "Dalting 5238, Tal Hunter."

A man's voice, full of life and vigour which defied the hour said, "This is Portishead radio ships telephone service. We have a call from the Q.E.2 for you."

In an instant I was wide awake and sitting up. Meeting trouble lying down only magnified its proportions. That the call would be trouble was something to be relied on.

"Hunters?" A tough, cultured voice rocked the memory cells of my brain as I swiftly tried to put a name to it. Recollection coincided with his next words, spoken now with an edge of impatience. "Hello, hello, Hunters?"

"That's correct. Hello Lord Vardy."

"Ha, Miss Hunter. About my horse."

"Which one are you referring to Lord Vardy?"

"Calypso Lad of course." His voice had an acid cut to it. "I've just learned that it lost the George Stevens Handicap Steeplechase."

"I'm afraid so."

"And your father came off?"

"Yes."

"Fill me in."

I did.

"And he's out of the saddle for good?"

I winced. "Yes." The pain of those words was still so sharp.

"So, there's only you in charge?"

"Until he returns from hospital."

"And did you ride Badinage for Grundy at Leicester?"

"Yes."

"And the result was what?"

"We came second."

73

"In other words, you lost?"

"I'm afraid so, yes, this time."

"Well the next time I want a lad put up. You understand? Girls simply aren't strong enough. Takes a man to lift horses over fences."

I writhed and fought to keep my temper. "It's not just a matter of strength Lord Vardy. The rapport between horse and rider is everything. Keeping the horses in our stables as I do gives us an advantage from the start."

"And yet despite this 'advantage' you still lost." The sarcasm was barely veiled.

I could hardly say I'd been afraid. Afraid to go in amongst the horses and risk possible injury. Couldn't say a death threat had penetrated the bubble of self-assurance, bursting it, leaving me a negative nothing. So I said nothing.

"It's not a very satisfactory state of affairs. I'll be quite honest Miss Hunter, I shall think seriously whether to keep my horses there with just a woman in charge."

Before I could answer he rang off. I sat in bed, staring at the inert piece of plastic in my hand which had just delivered a body blow. I knew then that the fear of Snodgrass' threat was nothing. This threat was the one that could kill. It only needed to get round that Lord Vardy had lost confidence in Hunters and taken away his horses for the other owners to do the same. That would be the end. I didn't blame him, there was little room for sentiment in racing. Either you won or you didn't. The next day whatever the race course result, the horse kept right on eating exactly the same. And that cost. There'd be more cost tomorrow if I had to call in the vet to Calypso. It might be nothing but with the value of the animal I was not going to take chances. All the same it might be that one extra little nudge that would push Lord Vardy.

Bright Boy, his other horse, was down to run next week at Warwick. It would have to be a win that was for sure and I'd have to ring round and fix up another jockey. My thoughts immediately jumped to Paul. His assurance was fully intact, his will to win almost a killer instinct. It could be he was already fixed up. I tossed and turned in bed sleepless churning it over and over.

When five-thirty on a winter's morning arrived it had never been more welcome. I slipped from the rumpled sheets and stood in the shower for ten minutes with the temperature on hot. When honeyed coffee followed, I began to feel a little more human.

For once I beat Turton to the Stable yard and started work. Moving among the big animals had its usual absorbing effect and until Turton touched my shoulder I wasn't aware of his arrival.

"Stole a march on me this morning gel."

"If you will lay in bed all hours . . ."

He raised a mock threatening fist at me first before peering intently at me sideways. "Bad night huh?"

"Does it show?"

"You look more like a panda than the real thing."

"I've never claimed to be a beauty like mother."

He frowned. "Your beauty's inside as well as out, her's never was."

"That smacks of disloyalty." I carried on forking straw up the sides of the box feeling a lurch in my stomach. It was the first time any comment had been passed about her.

"She didn't command loyalty. Led Jack a right dance . . . talking of which, I made you a promise about him yesterday Tal. Haven't forgotten y'know."

"I knew you wouldn't. Leave it 'til breakfast, there's something else I want to have your opinion on."

"Oh yeah?"

"Hmm, Calypso Lad."

"Gone lame?"

"No, something wrong round the girth area. Can you get him out after first lot, it'll be a bit lighter then. Couldn't see much last night."

"Will do." He ambled off.

"Oh and Turton," I called after him, "I'll be going to the hospital later, leave you in charge."

He jerked his head in reply and disappeared into the Tack Room.

I rode Flyght Path first lot and found Turton had

Calypso head-collared and tied up in the yard when I returned. After untacking, wiping off sweat and settling the big grey I went to look at Calypso. He trembled nervously as my hand reached the danger spot on his chestnut coat. In the morning light I could see exactly where the trouble was and feel it. There was a burning swelling just at the back of where his girth would be placed and below jockey length stirrups. I placed two thumbs either side the swelling and parted them with slight pressure. There was a showing of yellow pus in the centre and the horse kick stamped and swung his quarters in a half circle. "Have you seen this Turton?"

His head came round one of the doors. "Nasty." He came over. "Don't like the look of it. Vet job I reckon."

"Hmm . . ." I agreed. "Need a jab. Can't take any chances."

Turton pushed back his old cap and scratched his head. "What d'you reckon caused it?"

"It's been coming a day or two. Could it have been something from the accident?"

"Suppose it could. Vet'll be able to tell us likely."

"I'll ring him when we have breakfast, see if he can come in this morning before I treck off to Gloucester."

"Are they going to transfer Jack to Nottingham Hospital d'you know?"

"I don't. Be a lot easier if they would."

"Any ideas when he'll be back, at home I mean?"

"No, they haven't said anything. I'll ask one of the doctors when I'm down there. See if we can get to know."

During breakfast, I 'phoned Peter Upland, our Vet. I caught him before he started his rounds. "Don't think it's serious Pete, but I'd like the horse to have an injection to be on the safe side. You'll be here sometime this morning? Great. See you then."

As good as his word, Peter's big estate car pulled into the drive later and he strode into the yard carrying a bag. With him was a former race course acquaintance of mine, James Crack. Everybody in racing called him Jim. It was inevitable of course with a surname like that and he'd taken a lot of stick when first starting out in racing. However his ability to bring home winners had rapidly brought respect and one and all we'd been shocked when a crashing fall at Uttoxeter brought his superb racing career to a premature halt. He worked now as a private investigator and had an office in the nearby little market town of Bingham.

"Didn't think you'd mind Jim coming," Peter said, "had to treat his cat Matty, for a cut paw just before I left so . . ."

"I took advantage." Jim grinned down at me.

"Nice to see you again. Still sleuthing for living?"

"Yep, it's a great game."

Neither of us referred to his racing past. However much he enjoyed his new life-style we both knew it couldn't compete and any excuse that offered itself to visit a stableyard was seized upon avidly.

"How is Maternity, still living up to her name?"

"Afraid so, expecting again soon."

"Have you tried bromide in her milk?" said Turton and we all laughed. But we weren't laughing long.

Peter took a cursory look at Calypso's wound, filled a syringe and insured the horse against infection.

"What caused it?" I held Calypso's head-collar and smoothed my palm down his soft spread of cheek.

Peter straightened up. "Difficult to say exactly but something penetrated quite deeply. Probably why it's taken two or three days to become apparent."

"Could it have been anything to do with the accident?"

"Bad business," he looked soberly at me, "convey my sympathy to your father will you?"

I nodded. "I'll tell him. Today as a matter of fact. I'm going over later."

"And any help I can give, don't forget, you've only to call."

"Thanks very much Peter."

"Make mine the same Tally," Jim added. "Anytime Jack'd like a chat . . . I've been there as well . . . it might help."

I reached for his hand and squeezed it. "I won't forget."

Peter turned back to the horse, palpating the swelling gently with sensitive fingers. "I should say it probably did happen the day of the accident but . . ." he stopped and frowned, ". . . it couldn't have been caused by the jump itself. The brushwood twigs are of much thicker diameter than whatever caused this."

Turton and I exchanged quick glances. "What d'you reckon caused it?" Turton queried.

"Difficult to say with any certainty."

"Just give us some idea Peter."

"Don't hold me to it Tal, but I'd say something fairly slim in diameter and smooth, yes, definitely very smooth and certainly extremely sharp." He pursed his lips and added, "Something rather like a lady's hat pin almost."

There was silence as we all four looked at each other in shocked bewilderment.

"But that would have to have been deliberate." Peter stroked Calypso's nose. "From the depth of the wound it went in with considerable force."

He issued instructions to foment the swelling several times a day with warm water and antiseptic and he and Jim took their leave.

After they'd gone, Turton and I sat on a hay bale and took stock of the situation.

"Sods!" Turton spat the word out. "Injurying a horse deliberately."

"For an end result."

"Somebody wants Hunters pretty bad, that's all I can say."

"Was it done to try and kill father or did it go hellishly wrong? Do they just want the owners taking horses away?"

Turton narrowed his eyes. "Is someone pulling out of the stables?"

"Wasn't going to worry you with it but I had Lord Vardy breathing ominously down the 'phone early this morning."

"Oh my crikey, that's all we need."

"It seems to hinge on Bright Boy winning the race at Warwick next week."

"He should."

I nodded in agreement. "Yes, if father had been riding him but he's not and now I'm not either."

"Now she tells me!"

"Orders from Vardy himself Turton. He wants a man in the saddle."

Turton pulled furiously at his moustache. "Who do you reckon on?"

"First choice has to be Reynolds."

He spat deliberately out of the corner of his mouth.

"Look, I know you're not keen, see him as father's rival and all that, but he's a brilliant jockey."

Turton grudgingly admitted it. "Likely he'll be booked already though."

"Yes I know, but the first thing to do is to ask."

We sat there each busy with our own thoughts. It momentarily crossed my mind I could present the problem to Jim in his official capacity as investigator but a dark corner of my mind perversely, stubbornly, didn't want to. Somehow it was too personal a mystery.

"It's beginning to snowball Turton." I said at last. "Unless I can get to the bottom of it, we're headed straight for the slips. We can't rely on the horses winning, you know as well as I do, horses aren't machines. You get everything set, horse working beautifully, sound as a bell, the going just right for him, the weight O.K., right distance, good jockey, should be a walkover – still he loses."

He nodded absently, "Nothing's a certainty in this game."

"And it's because of that I'm asking father what exactly happened during that race. I don't want to. It's going to be rubbing in the salt for him but I've got to. If we could just get a lead on someone . . ."

"There's Snodgrass."

"Yes, but he's only front man for someone else."

"We haven't seen the last of him. He'll be back pestering."

"When he doesn't get a reply to his letter he will."

"Aye?"

"When we returned from Leicester, there was a letter waiting. David was screwed up about it. Thought it was for real and I was considering selling-up."

"What'd he say?"

"A very large offer to buy Hunters . . . for 'a client'."

"Phew," he blew through his front teeth, "he didn't waste any time."

"You're telling me."

"One thing is sure gel, whilst he thinks there's a chance of you considering an offer, he's not going to get violent."

I laughed shortly, "That's some comfort I guess."

"Look Tal, when we were coming back from Leicester . . . about that promise . . ."

"I'm not holding you to it Turton, it was blackmail whichever way you see it. I'll be damned if I'll sink to Snodgrass's level especially with you. I was just pretty desperate to see if it had a bearing on what's happening."

"I reckon it has," he said slowly, "don't know how but things you do today have a bearing on what happens tomorrow."

I stared at him. "Cause and effect?"

"Something like that."

There was silence and I didn't rush him. If he was going to tell me anything I wanted it to be because he was free to without any pressure.

"Your dad and me, we've been together a long time, a hell of a long time," he began.

A quiver of excitement started low in my stomach and crawled up my spine. Turton was about to reveal things that I wasn't even aware of and I was scared and excited at the same time. There were cupboards to unlock and skeletons to be taken out. If I wanted to draw back, now was the time before the safe, protective cocoon I'd grown-up in was finally ripped apart.

He looked questioningly at me, almost as though he knew how I was feeling. "Sure you want me to tell you?"

"Go on Turton," I said shakily, "I'm listening."

Chapter Eight

"YOUR DAD and me, we've been together a long time," he repeated, "been through a lot together. Seen a lot. Some things, like in most folks lives, are far better forgotten." He plucked a long length of hay from the bale and chewed the end. His eyes were fixed on the far wall of the tack-room. I knew he wasn't seeing the white painted bricks but instead was visualizing again the world he had lived in forty years ago. "I was thirteen when your grandad set me on as a stable lad. Proper green, never ridden a horse in my life before, barring a seaside donkey on a day-trip."

"What was he like? My grandfather?" I couldn't help interrupting.

"He was a hard man, you had to work fast, pick things up quick. He wasn't above giving you a twitch with a riding whip if you put a toe out of line."

I listened fascinated, having no idea that Turton had been with the family through three generations of Hunters.

"He had an old hack he used himself to ride out on gallops and I was taught how to ride on that." Turton chuckled a little, "First time he put me up on a race-horse it bolted. We were cantering down the long field when a covey of partridges rose from the grass tussocks flapping like mad. Well, the horse swerved and reared and when his hooves came back to the ground again he took off. Terrified the life out of me. Lost the irons, lost the reins, ended up half-way up its neck with my hands tangled in its mane. But I didn't come off . . . Your grandad was watching from the bottom end, nothing he could do of course, or anybody else. There was no way of stopping that two-year old."

"I was expecting a bawling out and more than likely a few goes with his whip. I got myself back into the stirrups and collected the reins when the horse had finally blown to a stop and walked him back gently like to where your grandad was waiting."

"What happened?"

"D'y'know, the old man was as nice as could be. He put his head on one side and looked careful at me and said 'You'll do'. And that was it, no come back at all. I went to bed that night as happy as ever in my life. I'd ridden a race-horse – and stayed on!"

He stopped for a minute, eyes bright with the memory, enjoying the experience all over again.

I knew how he felt. The first time astride a race-horse was definitely a memory to take on with you through the years. I'd had to wait until I was fourteen before father allowed me up. I'd ridden ponies since babyhood of course, but how I'd longed to be in one of those tiny saddles, knee flaps reaching far forwards, the almost ridiculously short leathers that you didn't appreciate until you were actually riding the horse. I could still remember that first horse's name: Miss Felham. I hadn't come off either, but then she'd been a super ride and father knew exactly what he was doing. He'd graduated his choice of rides for me, bringing me on gently, almost as though I were a race-horse myself. He'd built up my confidence both in myself and in my riding. There was everything to thank father for. I'd been lucky and I knew it.

I slapped Turton on the shoulder and smiled at him. "Carry on."

"Life was pretty tough and you had to be the same. Your grandad worked us to dropping point, but, give him his due, he worked like a horse himself. All the lads respected him for it and it made it doubly hard when he had to sell Hunters.

I couldn't believe what I was hearing but Turton was in full spate.

"We'd had five bad seasons one after the other, you'd hardly credit it. Falls, virus, infected feed, whatever could go wrong did. The last season, we'd been reduced to the dregs. The horses were poor quality and so were the owners. By that time your grandad was grateful to get any owners and he believed them when they said payment was difficult that month and they'd pay the next. 'Course they never did. There was only me left in the yard by then, he'd had to let the other lads go. Couldn't pay the wages. It was a good job your dad was working in the yard too else I couldn't have managed. Me and him, we got on like smoke going up a chimney. He was a few years younger than me. Suppose he'd be about eighteen, yeah, guess so, I was twenty-three that year. By gawd! I remember that year!" Turton took the soggy length of hay from his mouth and spat viciously. "I'll never forget it."

"When the boss had to sell the stables, it broke your grandma's heart. Reckon that's what really finished her off. She died y'know, a few weeks after. She'd been ailing but she lost the will to live, gave up fighting it. It turned your dad sour. He really hated the man who bought the stables. It was misplaced o'course but he saw him as the cause of your grandma's death. She used to indulge him something rotten, they were as close as could be you know."

"And who was he, the man who bought up the yard?"

Turton turned and gave me a peculiar look. "Your other grandfather."

I gaped at him. "My other . . . what on earth . . ."

He forestalled my question. "Your dad married this bloke's daughter."

I sat there feeling sandbagged and dizzy.

"Are you saying that father married my mother in order to get the stables back?"

"Good gawd no!" Turton exploded.

"So, it was from my other grandfather that I inherited the stables?"

Turton shook his head. "I didn't say that."

I passed a hand across my forehead, my brain seemed to have gone into neutral and lost the power to think straight.

"Your dad fought against his feelings for the girl.

He'd always been a dare devil but now he was down-right reckless. We'd both been set on at other stables and Jack took any opportunity of a ride that was going. Even the bad 'uns. Didn't care what he rode. Day after day just about working himself to a standstill. He practically lifted horses over fences, took so many chances it's a wonder he didn't kill himself. But it paid off: he started winning. The more races he won the more your mother became interested in him. Up 'till then it had been all on your dad's side. From the first time he'd seen her, it had been like a disease had struck him. He was wild about her. Didn't seem able to help himself. Still, love's like that, no logic, no reason behind it, common-sense out the window. Well, y'know don't you." Turton didn't expect a reply and I didn't give one.

It was then I knew David wasn't the man for me. If it was how Turton had just described it, I certainly wasn't in love.

"Your dad tried to smother his feelings in sheer hard graft," Turton went on. "But it didn't work. When he realised how strong a force he was up against, he changed course completely." Turton reached for a fresh stalk of hay and chewed it thoughtfully. "He's a proud man, your dad, and decisive. Once his mind is fully made up, nowt'll shift him."

I nodded, that at any rate I understood: as to the rest, my head was in a whirl.

"He made his mind up over the girl," Turton continued. "I can't say I blamed him, she was a good looker all right. Anyway he decided she was for him but as circumstances stood he'd nothing to offer. Don't forget, we were both staying in lodgings."

"And what about my grandfather," I interrupted, "where was he living?"

"He was very fortunate. The bloke that had bought the stables rented him the small cottage on the estate."

"But there is only one, where . . ."

"I live now." Turton finished. "Yes it's odd ain't it how life swings in a full circle."

"It's incredible, I can hardly take it in. All these

years I've thought Hunters was handed down from my grandfather . . . and now . . ."

"Wait gel, whilst I finish telling you, there's not much more. There was no possibility of your dad buying Hunters back and that's what he'd decided he was going to do – get the stables back. He reckoned as a property owner, he could court the girl and ask her to wed. But there was only one property he was interested in: Hunters. And he was determined to get it. Like I say, once his mind's made up"

"But if he couldn't buy it back how on earth did he manage it? I take it he did manage it?"

"Oh, yes," Turton drawled the words, "he managed it all right. Just think Tal, what's racing people got in common? Apart from a love of racing that is."

Before I could think of a reply Turton answered his own question. "Gambling. A love of gambling. You know as well as I do Tal what jockeys do in the weighing room at race courses. They gamble. And trainers are the same. Usually for higher stakes."

I was forced to agree with him. I'd seen gambling sessions going on in every weighing room I'd ever been in. The jockeys often made more from the card games at the races than they made from winning them.

"Your dad and me, we weren't any different from the rest, we gambled. Jack was hot stuff at it. Weren't many times he'd drop. Always knew when the luck was running out, never over stretched himself. Made a tiny pile he did before he started on the big stuff."

"The big stuff being the wealthier trainers?"

"That's right. It was all to try and win Hunters back."

I nodded. It sounded too high flying to work but I recalled a few years back a titled trainer who had got in too deep and ended by losing his yard in a card game.

"He thought of nothing else," went on Turton meditatively, his eyes fixed on the far wall of the tack room, "suppose you could say he was obsessed with the thought of getting Hunters back. 'Course he didn't let on to anyone, only me, what was in his mind. The stakes would never have gone that high if it had been common knowledge what he was after. No, he kept that close to his chest."

"He was seeing your mother regularly by now, he'd money y'see to do it with. It was through seeing her that he ended up being invited to the stables for a meal and o'course it wasn't long after that he sat in on the card games. He didn't rush it. Didn't need to, just bided his time until there was a big game fixed."

"But he'd need a huge stake to put in."

"Yes, he knew and he went to his dad and used the proceeds of the sale of the stables."

"What a gamble! Risking total destitution for them both. Did my grandfather agree?"

"He did in the end. Your dad talked him round. Said it wouldn't be long before he was back at Hunters again and the thought of it was too tempting to resist.

"The night of the big one, I went with Jack, it was strictly men only. By the end of the night it was just the three of us, me, your dad and your mother's father."

I leaned forward on the hay bale, "Go on," I urged, "what happened?"

"That's it. Jack got Hunters back." Turton said in even tones, eyes still fixed on the far wall. "End of story."

I was perplexed at his sudden stop. "There's got to be more. The old man, my paternal grandfather, what happened to him?"

"Jack handed Hunters back to him."

"So we did inherit from him after all?"

"Yes."

"But what about the girl, my mother?"

"She and Jack married a short time later. After both occasions, your dad put that record on."

"Beethoven's 5th?"

He nodded gravely, "Said it was only played to symbolize victories. I never knew him to play it again after that, not even when you were born."

"Maybe he didn't think I was worth playing it for."

"As far as Jack was concerned you were the most momentous thing that happened to him. Right from the cradle he had it all mapped out. He was going to prepare you for a great career in racing."

My heart suddenly lurched and my throat seemed to have difficulty in breathing, a large lump was in the way. "Pity I wasn't a boy." I said lightly, belying how I felt.

"Far sighted, that's what Jack is," Turton went on. "He told me the tide's turning, women are making their mark now. One day Albertine will be a great jockey, maybe even champion, flat or steeplechase. It's never been done yet but who knows. Perhaps she might even win the Grand Natonal or the Derby."

We were both silent, seeing a man's dreams down the years. I knew my commitment to racing was absolute, that most of it was inherited was certain and the bit that wasn't had been fostered by my upbringing. I could understand better now why I was in no hurry to try marriage. Marriage meant a dividing of that special commitment so vital to success.

Thoughts of marriage made me think of David. In fairness to him he must be told but it needed the right moment. For such a long time, it seemed like years, he'd gone along with hope sitting on his shoulder that I'd become his wife one day. Patience had been his middle name. Now, when I knew that marriage was not on my priority list it must be broken to him gently. It was going to be delicate and very difficult.

"How long did father's marriage last?"

"Around three, four years maybe, not much more. She went off you know, with another bloke, went abroad where her father had gone."

I'd suspected it must have been a triangle situation but it was still a revelation. "But she left *me* Turton."

"Ha," said Turton giving his cap a tweak further over his eyes. "Well you see, your dad, he's very possessive like. First of all when he married her, he was like it with her, then when you came along, it transferred to you d'you see."

"And she was left out in the cold?"

"Something like that. When she left she . . . well she was expecting this other bloke's child . . ." Turton scuffed the toe of one boot in embarrassment. "She was a woman with strong feelings . . ."

I looked directly at him. "Did she make a pass at you Turton?"

"Not just me . . ." he said unhappily.

"It's all right Turton, I get the picture. All that was a long time ago . . . it doesn't matter any more." How wrong I was, but I didn't realise it until a long time after.

Jimmy's head popped round the door. "Sorry Mr Turton, but could you have a listen to Flyght, think he's got a bit of a cough."

"Right lad," Turton was on his feet. He was grateful for the diversion. "Better have a look," he said. I nodded and he hurried off.

I went to fetch warm water and antiseptic and talked honeyed words to Calypso as I bathed his injury. The rattling of old skeletons had given me a lot to mull over and I wanted to digest it before setting off to visit father. The warm water softened the swelling and a trickle of yellow poison came away. "That should ease it sunshine," I said patting him. "Mustn't let it stay in and fester." Even as I said it I thought of the letting out of old poison in my own case. It had helped me to understand a little but I knew underneath there was more to spill out.

There was no racing for us today and I left the stables in Turton's charge and returned to the house. David hadn't arrived yet, he worked from home as well as a freelance financial consultant and I was grateful for the chance to adjust before seeing him. I went upstairs, plugged the bath and ran the water at full pressure. Extravagantly, I tipped a generous amount of exquisitely perfumed foam bath in, peeled off my stable clothing and climbed in. As I stretched my legs luxuriously in the soothing warmth, my conscience pricked; David had given me the expensive foam bath as an impromptu present. I wasn't playing fair with him and it was one more problem to add to all those others. Regretfully leaving the warmth and comfort of the hot bath I towelled vigorously and dressed in calf-length grey flannel skirt with high grey boots and topped them with a bright turquoise fluffy jumper. Some discreet make-up and a spray of 'Arianne' perfume all but finished the good work. I brushed loose the thick dark hair from its working plait and an attractive woman looked back at me from the mirror. Even if father couldn't see what I was wearing, I could and knowing I looked smart and cheerful would make me act that way. Snodgrass and his threats receded and confidence came back.

I padded across to father's room and looked around for something to take with me to remind him of home. I nearly settled for his watch which had been returned with the rest of his things after the accident but realised he wouldn't be able to see the time anyway and it would only emphasize his loss of sight. In the end, getting desperate, I picked up the tiny horse statue of Marchioness, father's all time favourite horse which he had commissioned specially before she died. If he couldn't see it, he could at least run his fingers over the beautifully moulded body and intricately featured head. It would give him pleasure in an alien environment and hopefully bring home a little closer. I had a last quick look round, pocketed another treasured article and ran downstairs. The drive to Gloucestershire was problem free and I kept the speedometer needle high most of the way. Jockeys have one way of driving – fast! With so much time sent behind the wheel it has to be.

I parked the sports car in the only available space, alongside a coal lorry that was hogging up the car park. It looked incongruously small and shiny beside the coal dust begrimed double wheeler. The driver jumped down from the cab and swung the door to with a flourish. He was as begrimed as his vehicle but a broad grin split his blackened face showing a flash of white teeth. "You'll not let on to the old man will you?" He said grinning more broadly than ever as he saw me look in his direction.

"The old man?"

"Me boss."

"Oh no, of course not."

"Couldn't resist, y'see. The round goes past here today so I thought I'd pop in and surprise her."

"You did?"

"Yes, well, I know it's not our first but each one's just as precious. The fourth this time." His pride was bursting out of him. "Boy again, Don't know how I do it."

I couldn't help grinning back.

"Life's precious lass, very precious." He swaggered off, head high sublimely oblivious of his black state.

I watched him go. How ironic it was I had taken pains with my dress and apparel for a man that couldn't see and the coal man hadn't had time to even wash his hands for a wife that could. But there was one thing we had each brought with us that was the same. And it was the one thing that mattered. Love. I followed the man up the stairs and through the hospital doors. It was claustrophobically hot inside. I slipped off my shoulder bag and shed my woollen coat. It made it marginally better, but not much. Used as I was to working outdoors in any weather, the heat made me feel like a goldfish who had been placed in a tropical fish tank by mistake. Father must hate being incarcerated like this.

Following endless corridors, I eventually arrived at his room and went in. At the sound of the door he turned his face in my direction.

"Tal, is that you?"

"You bet it is." I hurried over to give him a hug.

"I'd know your perfume anywhere."

His bandaging had been reduced a little round his face and I found a spot to plant a kiss.

"You look better, a great deal better considering the short time you've been here."

"The sooner I get better the sooner I'll be out."

"Talking of out, any ideas when you might be?"

"I'm just going to tell you. Had a good go at the doctor yesterday . . ."

"Oh father!"

"I want out Tal, as fast as possible. I told him, so O.K. one eye's gone, can't do anything about it . . ."

"Daddy . . . I'm so, so sorry," I interrupted him, cradling the side of his cheek in my palm.

He motioned impatiently with his hand, "I've had one maudlin' day, full of self-pity. It gets you nowhere Tal, you understand, nowhere. That's not the way to get better. Pulls you down further. When I'd done feeling sorry for myself, I was in worse shape than after the fall."

I didn't say anything but stroked his cheek gently marvelling at his tremendous will power. A normal person would have wallowed for a long time before they realised what father had done after just one day. But then father wasn't a normal person, in that sense. He was a jump jockey which meant a built in acceptance of risk, an acceptance of inevitable injuries and the positive mental attitude to get well quicker afterwards.

"I wanted to know the score about my other eye, what the chances were on seeing again."

I all but held my breath. "And what did the doctor say?"

"Took off the wrapping and had a rummage round. Hummed and hawed a bit wouldn't commit himself. Said what I needed was a specialist eye surgeon."

"An eye operation?"

"Yes. The man I need is based at a different hospital."

"Will he come here to do the operation then?"

Father shook his head, winced, obviously realising it was not the thing to do and went on, "No, this is the best part. I'm to be transferred Tal. To the Queen's Medical Centre at Nottingham."

"Oh great! You jammy old bugger." I hugged him tight.

The Queens was a newly built hospital, one of the most up-to-date and well equipped in Europe. And the best part was Nottingham was the nearest city to us being only a handful of miles away from Hunters.

"When are they transferring you?"

"Soon. The doctor was pleased how I'm going on, said I healed quick. Apparently if I want to chance this operation it's a case of the sooner, the better."

"Just a minute father. What's this about chance it?"

"There's a little sight in my eye at present. Not a lot.

91

Enough to see largish objects across a room. Not good enough to read a book though."

"But that's better than I'd anticipated." I said eagerly.

"Don't get carried away Tal. It's not sufficient for me. If I can see I want to be able to read form books, do the paper-work at Hunters, not see just light from dark or big objects. That's why I've already agreed to this operation."

I felt cold despite the heat of the room. "And if the operation isn't a sucess, what then?"

"Then I could lose what little sight I've still got. So you see, Tal, my love, as far as I'm concerned there's no choice."

I knew as I looked down at him that he was living by the code he had always done. Take the chance, however slim and go all out for it. It was why he'd made champion jockey, why he was who he was and also, since Turton had told me, why I would inherit Hunters. I bent down and kissed him. "I wouldn't have you any other way father. I'm right behind you."

He gripped my hand hard. "I knew you would be Tal. You're my lass, part of me, we're built the same."

"Hey, hey, now who's getting maudling?" I said ruffling the top of his dark hair and biting the side of my lower lip to keep control. Tears were something father hated, regarded as a weakness. "I've brought you something." I released his hand and fished down in my shoulder-bag.

"What's this then?"

"Hold your hand out and guess," I placed the bronze statue on the outstretched palm and his fingers closed around it. He explored it with light fingertips tracing its every mould and angle.

His lips curved and he said with pleasure, "It's Marchioness, from home."

"Dead right. She'll keep you company when I'm not here."

He carried on lovingly fingering the horse. "How'd you do at Leicester yesterday?"

The question caught me off-guard and I just stopped

myself in time from blurting out 'I was warned off'. "Came second," I said and added, "I'll be first next time."

He nodded apparently satisfied.

"Oh yes, and there's another thing." I had another dip in my bag and handed over the next item. "That's for luck."

Again his hand closed over and examined it. "My buddy," he said his fingers stroking the thin chain, the ugly little Buddha's face and passing on over the rotund belly. There was a tiny click and I watched with amazement as the front portion of the belly slid away to reveal a flat compartment behind it.

"I didn't know about that." The surprise in my voice was obvious.

Father tutted with annoyance at himself. "Didn't mean to do that. Blasted eye, must have caught the mechanism with my finger nail."

"What's inside?" I queried curiosity eating at me.

"Suppose you'll have to know now you've seen this much." His voice had a jarring hardness to it, most unlike normal. He turned the Buddha round towards me and I could see there was a stiffish piece of thick paper folded inside. "Go on, take it out," father instructed.

I did so and unfolded it. The paper was in fact a very old sepia photograph. I smoothed it out and felt a shock of distant recognition.

Chapter Nine

"YOU WON'T KNOW the man of course," father was saying, "he's dead anyway by now so I suppose it doesn't matter anymore."

I was struggling to put a name to the face but it eluded me.

"You never met him you see," father continued, "so you can't possibly know him."

"But I feel I do."

"It was way back before you were born so there's no way you could know him."

"All the same . . ." I persisted screwing up my eyes and looking at the photograph from different angles, "it's familiar to me."

"No, no Tal, my love. Although . . ." he hesitated a little, "perhaps what you see is a similarity."

"To whom?"

As he spoke his head bent forward but he didn't need to try and hide his face from me, the bandages did a fine job of that. "To your mother."

Of all the people he could have said, she was the last one I would have chosen. I felt distanced from him and wished with all my heart we could have looked each other in the face as he said it. Did he still love her despite the years and her infidelity? Without seeing his face it was impossible to say.

"I never knew my mother," I said carefully watching his reaction.

"No you never did," he agreed. "Well, only when you were a tiny scrap in diapers bumbling around. Your memory at that age couldn't have persisted."

"Then how come this photograph seems so familiar?"

"I don't know what you did with the one I gave you Tal, whether you threw it away or kept it but there was a photograph of your mother . . ." his voice dwindled away.

"I've still got it," I said gently, "but you said you never wanted to see it again."

"Don't suppose I shall now," his hand went up instinctively to rub against the bandage.

"Father," I caught hold of his hand, "after the operation if . . . when you can see again, do you want to look at it?"

Inside my grasp I felt his fingers stiffen.

"No! No, I bloody don't," he almost shouted the words. "Never, ever again do I want to see her." His vehemence startled me.

"Steady on, you'll have the nurse running in."

"You don't understand," he said tiredly, "it's not just her, but all she represents, all she reminds me of."

"And doesn't this?" I indicated the Buddha still held in his hand. "Doesn't this remind you of her?"

He didn't reply immediately and I continued. "Turton told me about grandfather having to sell Hunters and about you winning the stables back so you could marry her."

"I'd have done anything in the world to get her." His voice was low in contrast this time and I had a job to catch what he was saying. "What else did Turton tell you?"

"Just that she went off with another man, no more."

He nodded slowly, "Turton's a good chap. The best friend you could find. He's stuck by me right along the line."

"Father who is this man in the photograph?"

"Him? Oh," he drew his thoughts back, "that's your mother's father, your other grandfather."

I stared at the photograph, "Since I didn't know anything of him, why do I feel he's so familiar, as if I could have met him yesterday? It doesn't make sense."

"No it doesn't," he agreed. "The only explanation is that 'photo of your mother. Guess it must have stuck in your mind."

"Why should you keep his 'photo inside the Buddha?"

"When I have a win . . . had a win . . . on the race

course, I used to open up the slide and take the picture out. I'd look him straight in the eye and say 'won that time didn't I'. I suppose it became a sort of ritual. A thing I did after a win to encourage the next."

"I still don't see why him. Why not mother?"

He snorted contemptuously, "Her! I don't owe her a thing. The only good thing she ever did was leaving you. She levelled any score when she left."

"And what score do you owe her father?"

A tense, heavy silence which lasted a full half-minute greeted my words.

At length he said, "He allowed my dad to stay on, on the estate. It meant everything; the estate was all he thought about after mother died. Just to be near kept him sane. I shall always owe the man for that."

"He stayed in Turton's cottage didn't he?"

"Yes." Father lifted his head towards me. "How did you know? From Turton?"

"Hmm."

"Did he tell you anything else?" Father said it lightly enough but behind his words I sensed an urgent anxiety.

"The music, Beethoven's 5th. He told me about that."

Father's breath came out in a gust, almost a hiss. I looked at him in surprise. His jaw muscles were clenched hard drawing his lips into thin strips over his teeth. "What'd he tell you?"

I had the sensation of walking over thin ice and it wasn't pleasant.

"That you played it when you won the stables back and again, when you married mother. To you it represented victory."

"Why should he have mentioned it?" Father shot the question at me.

"Because the music brought you out of unconsciousness after the accident and it had to be something important associated with it in your mind."

"I see." Father rubbed the back of his hand across his mouth as if to rub away the tension. "You sat with me then, when I was out cold?"

96

"Yes, for a short time anyway."

"Did I . . . was I rambling at all?"

"Not really. You just kept repeating one word."

Again I could sense that heavy, tense silence in the room.

"Which was?"

"You said 'cheated'." My words hung in the air, suspended between us. He made no response and I continued. "What did you mean father? Was it about the race? Did you feel you'd been cheated of it?"

"Yes, yes, it was the race." His words came out quickly, hoarsely, as though his throat muscles were constricted. I thought for a moment that I could detect relief in them but I brushed the thought aside as he continued. "I know I was cheated Tal. Something happened at the third fence." His voice was now normal and deadly serious. "I would have won that race if something hadn't happened."

"Can you remember what it was? I waited eagerly.

"That's the damn fool thing about it, Tal. Since I came to, all I've done is to think about that race. Bits of my memory are there but a good deal is still muddled, or blank."

"Does the doctor think it will come back?"

"Oh yes, he talks that way but doctors have to be optimistic in front of patients. At least my memory is perfect of the time leading up to the race and I'm thankful enough for that."

"Take it easy father, don't push yourself. It'll come back when it's ready."

"I've a recollection of the fence attendant doing something odd." Father rubbed a hand through what little hair was still visible on the top of his head in an effort to think straight. "I know there was something odd about him. I remember thinking at the time, what's he doing? But in a race Tal most of your attention is directed straight in front. Anything happening past the edge of the track you don't notice."

"Could he have been waving his arms, warning you of a hazard?"

"No, I'm sure it wasn't that."

"They brought the attendant in you know, from the course, in the ambulance. Suffering from shock as far as I can gather," I said.

"Most unusual," father pounced on the information. "Why should he suffer shock?"

"Because," I tried to slide over the difficult words, "you were a bit of a mess when they brought you into the First Aid."

Father waved a dismissive hand in the air. "Attendants are used to seeing falls, they're prepared for it. It has to be something more. If only I could remember." His mouth screwed up in perplexed frustration.

"Give yourself a few more days and you will," I said trying to soothe him. "If you don't try so hard to remember maybe it will just click back when you relax."

"Could be." He yawned a cavernous tired yawn.

"I'll be off now father. See you get some rest." I collected the 'photo and replaced it inside the hidden compartment of the Buddha. "Lean forwards," father did so and I slipped the thin chain over his head. He lay back against the hard, white pillow and I kissed him, promised to ring before I came again in case he'd been allocated a bed at Nottingham Hospital, and left.

On the long drive home, I puzzled over father's words. Just what could a fence attendant do that would strike a jockey as odd during a race? Once the goggles were down and the tape up, concentration was riveted on the track. It would have had to be something completely out of character to be noticed.

One jockey only was close enough at the time to possibly notice anything and that was Paul Reynolds. After our meeting in the weighing room, I was reluctant to seek him out deliberately. A chance meeting would be far better but that would not be possible until next week's rides.

I pulled out to overtake a lorry and a sharp blast from a hooter ticked me off. Easing off the accelerator on to the brake, I nosed the Triumph back to safety as another vehicle came tearing past, its driver's face a mask of annoyance. As he flew past I realised that with my mind grappling with problems I had sloppily neglected to check in my rear mirror. At the next junction I thankfully changed down and left the polluted air of the main stream traffic and ambled gently back home through the scenic route. Stopping altogether in one lane to allow a file of ducks to cross in safety I looked for a decent spot to have a precious few minutes out of time. Half a mile further on a stream ran under the road and down in the field was a fallen dead elm tree lying parallel by the side of the bridge. It was as good a spot as any.

With a gentle sun brightening the running water and an absence of breeze from the shelter of the bridge, it could have been mistaken for April. I leaned back against the solid stonework and uncorked the flask of coffee I'd slipped into the dash-board before leaving home. It was piping hot still. I closed my eyes, sipping luxuriously at the honey- sweetened beverage. Deliberately letting my mind go blank I escaped the twentieth century. With peace all around and just the gurgling of the stream for music it could have been any time in any century. I finished the coffee, found a comfortable hollow amongst the stones for resting my head and dozed agreeably. How many countrymen down how many years must have done the self-same thing I wondered idly and it brought home the enduring permanence of the land and as it did so my problems shrank into perspective taking with them much of my anxiety.

In my euphoria with eyes closed against the reflected brightness of the water, I failed to see a man approaching from the other side of the field. The sudden flapping take-off of a pair of partridges followed by the excited yapping of a dog snapped me back to the here and now. Making heavy weather of it, the partridges laboriously evaded the black and white collie. The dog tore after them with all the vim of a horse from the stalls but in his case it was probably due to insufficient exercise. The man accompanying it was waving his arms and calling but with the quarry in sight the dog paid no attention.

The course of the birds took the collie in a swing to

the right and for a second as they disappeared over the boundary hedge the dog hesitated and looked back to its master. That was its undoing. The man had obviously been waiting for the moment. Whistling one last time, he turned and ran. I smiled, the good old dog psychology bit. And it worked. The collie forgot the vanished quarry and saw instead he was being left behind. Tongue lolling widely to one side, he loped across the tussocks after his owner. Man and dog, their figures etched like a charcoal drawing against the bright blue sky, disappeared from my view.

As I sat for a moment eyes still focussed on the point where they had last been visible, the 'click back' I'd spoken of to father happened to me. I knew with certainty what had happened to the fence attendant the day of the accident.

I didn't spare any time on the rest of the way back and as I drew up in front of Hunters the speedometer needle thankfully returned from rarefied heights. Turton by now would be on afternoon break but I didn't intend to wait until the time he came on duty. A 'phone call would suffice: I just hoped he knew the answer to my question. Heading through the kitchen to the hall I bumped into David.

"Hello Tally Ho, been to see Jack?"

"Yes, he's coming along fine. Battling away as usual."

"He's like a rubber ball," David chuckled. "Can't stop him bouncing back when he hits the floor."

"To be honest, I'd forgotten you'd be here today. Have there been any problems?"

"No owners playing up if that's what you mean."

"Good. Look, David I've just one call to make and then the 'phone is all yours again. Do you think you could find out if Paul Reynolds is booked for next week at Warwick when Bright Boy is down to run? If he's not, snap him up would you?"

"You're the boss Tally but you were going to ride weren't you?"

Lord Vardy says it has to be a man so there's no arguing with that."

David pursed his lips, "Being difficult is he?"

"Just a little. He'll be eating out of my hand again if . . . when Bright Boy wins."

"Let's hope he does. Just going to fix myself a coffee, would you like one?"

"Love one, thanks."

We parted, David to the kitchen, I to the study. I dialled Turton's number and waited. After a couple of rings he came on the line.

"Tal here Turton. Do you happen to know where Felton lives? You know, the fence attendant when father had his accident? Somewhere near Cheltenham. I see. Somewhere what? That sounds religious? You can't pinpoint any closer? No, well, never mind it will do. No, there's nothing the matter and I'm not doing anything silly." I stifled the annoyance both from the lack of detailed information and from the over protection. He really was worse than father at times.

David appeared at the door with a tray of coffee. I was touched to note he'd placed a jar of honey on it too. My conscience pricked hard. He was really a most considerate man and I was far from considerate with him. But today was not for levelling. It would have to come later. There were far too many other thoughts buzzing around in my head demanding attention.

I finished the coffee and the business chat as quickly as was decently possible and, taking the road atlas with me, went to my own room. Closing the door, I sat on the bed and opened the atlas. It should be child's play to locate the village Turton had mentioned and from there I could find the nearest Post Office. I knew they could supply me with Felton's full address from their records but I didn't intend telephoning from the house. I would set-off in the right direction and use a call box along the route. David would undoubtedly be even stuffier than Turton if he knew. I didn't intend to tell him.

Next I went to the dressing table and took out my jewellery box. Tipping out the top layer of assorted frippery in a cascade over the bedspread, I removed the red velvet tray and from the bottom of the box took out a photograph wrapped in flimsy tissue paper. Walking over to the window I looked at it with the daylight full on the beautiful woman's face. She was beautiful, it could not be denied. I stared at it with mixed feelings. The woman was my mother. It was the photograph father had given me long ago, the only one I had ever seen. For several minutes I stood and looked at it. Many years ago I'd put it away, carefully hidden in the base of the box, and I had forgotten what she looked like. Finally lying it down on the window ledge, I drew from the pocket of my skirt another folded up photograph. Smoothing it open on the ledge besides my mother's, I compared the two. Father, bless him, was innocently unaware that his Buddha was minus my grandfather's 'photo. I was gambling he wouldn't try opening the sliding compartment at least until I'd managed to smuggle it back. As he had bent forward to have the chain put over his head, I'd slipped the 'photo out and into my pocket. Now I had the two side by side to examine. There was not a great deal of likeness, no instant, yes of course they were father and daughter, recognition. And yet as I poured over them one thing became apparent. The expression in the eyes was the same. I left them lying by the window and went over and sat at my dressing table. Cupping my chin in both hands I stared at my own reflection. If I had secretly wished to see that expression looking back at me, I was out of luck. My eyes were the same as father's, dark and deep holding something of a brooding quality.

I folded mother's 'photo back inside its tissue paper and hid it again in the jewellery box, replacing the velvet tray and scooping up the assorted pieces of jewellery on top. The other 'photo I lingered over. The familiar quality which had struck me in the hospital was still there. Comparing the two together hadn't convinced me that having seen mother's 'photo years ago was the reason for it. The time however was trickling by and I needed to be away. Even leaving now it meant my return would be extremely late tonight. I quailed at the thought of the hours of driving still in front. Gathering up the perplexing likeness and my bag, I ran downstairs. David was bent over some receipts and a ledger in the study.

"What do you think to this?" I handed him the 'photo.

Staring at it for a moment or two brow creased, he finally said, "I don't know him but I've a feeling he's known to me. If you follow that . . ."

I nodded. "Exactly. It plagues me in the same way."

"Who's the man? Obviously it's an old photograph, is he still living?"

"Actually he's my grandfather. Not grandfather Hunter, my other one. Father doesn't think he's still alive but I couldn't say."

"Your maternal grandfather! Really!" David concentrated on it again with increased interest. "Of course I never saw your mother but he doesn't resemble you at all Tally."

"I take after father."

He glanced up at me. "Yes . . . yes you're very like him. Strange though this chap in the 'photo does strike a chord with me somehow."

"What about the eyes? Could it be those?"

"He resumed his scrutiny. "I believe it could well be. Not sure of course but this feeling of being known to me, it's uncanny. Annoying too because I can't put my finger on it."

"It's been bugging me ever since I saw it."

"Where did you get it from?"

"You wouldn't believe me if I told you."

"With you Tally, I'd believe anything."

"I'm not sure which way to take that but, O.K. then, it belongs to father."

"Did he give it you when you visited this morning?"

"To be strictly honest, no. I stole it."

"I believe you." David kept a dead straight face which was marred only when a corner of his mouth twitched.

"It's true," I started to laugh, "well, perhaps borrowed. It goes back next time I see him, hopefully before he notices it's gone."

"I don't see why Jack should be carrying a photograph of this chap with him."

"It was concealed inside the Buddha, you know, the good luck mascot he wears racing? I thought it would make him feel closer to home if he had it so this morning I took it to the hospital with me."

David stared at me, "Darned peculiar."

"It is rather. I think there's more behind it than the reason he gave."

"Which was what?"

"That he owes the man, for giving grandfather Hunter a room over his head when he needed one. After a win he takes out the 'photo and acknowledges the victory?"

David shook his head slowly, "Sounds a bit lame to me, still if he doesn't want us to know the real reason that's up to him."

I took the photograph and slipped it in my bag. "I'm going out for a while David. Could you leave Freda a note to feed Rookey for me? I'm not sure what time I'll be back."

"Will do. Take care Tally Ho."

"Bye David."

And I was away. Heading down the drive back to Gloucestershire. The sports car sang sweetly and I tried to curb my rising excitement. Felton knew what happened at that third fence; all I had to do was persuade him to tell me. However difficult it proved, I was determined to get the information from him.

Chapter Ten

TURTON'S directions had been rather vague but he was sure the fence attendant lived close to Cheltenham. A place with a religious sounding name. Not a lot to go on but enough. I'd motor for a good way and then consult the map.

The Triumph made nonsense of the intervening distance and just before Stratford, with pangs of hunger increasing every mile, I swung off into the forecourt of a wayside garage-cum-cafe which sported a call box. Taking the Shell road atlas, I entered the cafe. It was basic but clean. Since it was now late afternoon, between set meal times, no-one else was eating. Ordering a Tuna fish salad I opened the relevant page of the atlas. Ignoring the social niceties, I poured over the spread pages. To be awkward, of course, the specific bit I needed to follow was continued on different pages. Flipping back and forth I tracked the route. I would finally be motoring down the 435 which would pass very close to the actual race course itself. The salad arrived and I propped the atlas up on the condiment set so I could eat and read at the same time. A place with a religious sounding name Turton had said – and there it was. Bang in the middle of the 435 about four miles from Cheltenham. Bishop's Cleeve. I was about to close the atlas in triumph when, following the distance down into Cheltenham, my eye caught the one word, Church-down. A small village from the look of it just off the A40 below Cheltenham. I swore under my breath. How many more religious sounding villages counld there be? It took the rest of the salad and the following coffee to establish the fact there were three. The third was some little way up from Cheltenham but still close enough to be considered. Follow a 'B' road to Aston Cross, add on the odd mile and I was left looking at Ashchurch. They were all so close, twenty miles if that between them, a local directory would doubtless list them all. I paid for the meal and went out to the car.

I slid back behind the wheel and headed south. Giving the sports car it's head and applying right foot pressure as the hands of my wrist-watch urged it on, soon saw me ten miles north of Cheltenham. The signpost up ahead said Aston Cross and I eased up, swung right and motored on. There should be a call box somewhere close at hand. As it happened, I drove right past before noticing and had to reverse back. Thankfully vandals had disregarded this kiosk and the 'phone was not only humming efficiently when I lifted the hand set but there was also an up-to-date Gloucester directory sitting on the side shelf. It was a long shot that the attendant would actually be on the 'phone but it was quicker than going through to the British Telecom in Cheltenham. Thumbing through the 'F's and running a finger down the small block of Feltons showed no-one lived at Ashchurch but with a thrill of anticipation I found a C. Felton listed at Bishop's Cleeve.

My hand hovered over the dial but didn't make the call. Surprise was always on ally in a sticky situation and this one had all the makings of tacky treacle.

A quick about turn left Aston Cross behind and landed me back on the 435 with a handful of miles between me and C. Felton. If he were at home or not had to be chanced. What I would say to him wasn't rehearsed either, still I reckoned a woman's devious thought patterns set against the straight forward thinking of a man would give me verbal advantage. The question of superior physical power was something I didn't allow myself to consider.

On the outskirts of the village I stopped and asked a girl pushing a pram the way to Millicent Street. Following her directions brought me to a long street faced by old teraced type houses all looking pretty much the same and identified as individuals only by the

different coloured front doors. I pulled up outside No.
32. An orange painted one this and obviously many
years since the application of the paint, for it was
peeling away and the shine had been covered by the
dust of many summers. I knocked. And knocked again.
No-one answered. There was a passageway down the
side and I walked through to the rear. The path ended
at a grimy back door which faced a long thin strip of
sad garden. A peep through the kitchen window confirmed the owner's absence. It confirmed as well the
state of the interior matched the exterior. Except for
one thing. Standing beside a grease laden cooker that
must have come out of the ark was a gleaming, new,
white refrigerator. I found that very odd and very
interesting. The rest of the furniture and floor coverings
that could be seen in the room next to the kitchen
followed the pattern of having been there so long they'd
taken root. So Felton had recently acquired a new
fridge-freezer in the last few days. Since the day of
father's accident possibly? Another thought struck me
too. Strange that Felton should be on the telephone. It
was the state of the whole place that made it seem
incongruous. Unless someone needed him available and
on tap.

"D'ya want Mr Felton?"

A voice from somewhere above made me jump and
spin round. A curler-encrusted head was thrust from a
bedroom window next door. From the way the woman
was leaning an elbow on the windowsill and smoking
a cigarette suggested she'd been watching me all the
time.

"Yes, as a matter of fact I do."

She smirked with satisfaction. "He's out."

I smiled back at her. "That's right."

The smile disappeared. "Well he'll be back soon," she
snapped and slammed the window shut.

I returned to the car and idled along the street and
parked just before the next junction. From here I could
see both ways. If Felton were due back I couldn't miss
him. And I didn't doubt the truth of the woman's
statement. If I'd asked her straight out she'd probably

have said she didn't know. I settled down in the driver's seat, prepared for a good wait. I nearly missed him. Felton arrived almost straight away not on foot as I'd anticipated but in a disreputable old, blue van. The registration number wasn't very distinct but as the vehicle pulled away from Felton's house it came straight towards me. I took an address book from my bag and copied down the number plate HTV 144C. The driver was a huge man wearing an old checked cap pulled so low over his forehead it met his eyebrows. He didn't give me a second look. At the intersection he turned right and disappeared.

I left the car and walked briskly back to No. 32. Felton had gone down the side passageway. Obviously the kitchen door was the usual point of access. It was still ajar. Felton had his back to me shovelling a pan of coal in the adjoining coalhouse. He was a weedy little man with dirty tow coloured hair that need a cut and stuck out sideways above his ears. The hand that held the coal shovel was thin and bony bereft of watch or ring. I couldn't help comparing his build with the driver of the blue van and feeling relieved.

"You're getting your hands dirty."

The words had an electrifying effect. Felton straightened up fast dropping cobbles of coal over the yard. "What the . . . who the bloody hell are you?"

"Come now Cuthbert, you know me!"

"My name's Claude. You've got the wrong man."

"Claude is it? Hmm . . . you see, Claude, the telephone directory only gives initials."

"What'd you want? I don't know you."

"Oh I think you do."

His eyes darted all over me.

"Try imagining me dressed in silks – and I don't mean dresses."

Recognition flickered over his face. "You're his daughter ain't you?"

"Whose daughter would that be Claude?"

"He's not dead is he?" Felton tried to keep the fear out of his voice but didn't succeed. "Papers didn't say he was dying."

"Keeping up-to-date with his condition are you? That's nice. Shows concern."

"I'm not concerned in it. Nothing to do with me."

"You don't say?"

"I don't know anything about it."

"And that's why you were suffering from shock when you were brought back in his ambulance?"

Felton ran a quick hand across his face. "I didn't want to get in the ambulance. Told them so."

"Made you feel worse did it, guilty?"

"You can't tie me in with it. It was a mistake it happened like that anyway." The words hung in the cold air.

"I think you just tied yourself in."

"You can't prove anything, you can't pin it on me." Felton began to bluster. "Besides, you said he's getting better."

I decided to lie. "He's not."

"Well it's not my fault." His voice rose sharply. "I only . . ."

". . . carried out orders?"

"I didn't do it." His grip on the coal shovel tightened making the bones stand out even more. He took one aggressive step towards me. I deliberately stepped forward one pace.

"You see, I know who gave you the order."

"I didn't do nothin'."

"Except turn and run."

His mouth dropped open. My inspired guess had hit target.

"How d'you know? You weren't there, nobody was there."

I was saved from replying by the curlered woman from next door. She came puffing down the passageway carrying a very fat old Jack Russell.

"Thought I heard you shouting Claude, I've brought Millie back safe and . . ." her voice tailed off as she arrived at the end of the passage and saw me. Felton snatched the dog from her.

"Ta, Lil."

"S'all right."

She looked me up and down. Nobody spoke.

She sniffed. "Right then, I'll get back."

Felton nodded. "See you Lil."

She marched off down the passage, sniffing every two or three paces.

The little bitch squirmed and wriggled with delight licking the man's face. He held her close and crooned back at her.

"So that's the lever is it," I said. "I was wondering what they used for blackmail."

"You shut your face and bugger off back where you came from," he snarled and carried the dog into the house and banged the kitchen door. Unfortunately, he banged it too hard and as he disappeared into the sitting room, the kitchen door swung open again.

I walked purposefully down the passageway, letting my boots echo against the concrete. Then I waited. Everything was silent. I slipped off my boots and bare-footed my way gingerly back to the kitchen door. There was no sign of Felton. Without making a sound, I entered the dingy kitchen and tip toed over the cracked lino to the sitting room door. I placed my ear close to the hinge and listened.

"I'm telling you," Felton's voice said quite plainly, "she's on to him. She knows he told you to set it up." There was a moments silence and then he said, "she knows it's him all right Mr Snodgrass, she said so."

I held my breath, so there was a 'desperate client' behind it after all. The bluff was paying off although I'd meant Snodgrass had been the person giving the orders.

"What d'you want me to do then, warn him?" Felton's voice sounded hoarse and scared. "No, no she didn't say his name, but I'll do anything you say. If you want me to ring Mr . . ." His next words were drowned by my scream.

Four red-hot spikes had been driven into my left calf. Or that's what it felt like. Millie, the Jack Russell, had come up soundlessly behind me and sunk her jaws into my leg. She kept them sunk, whilst managing to make horrible growling noises. I swung my leg wide with pain trying to dislodge her. I heard the rattle of the 'phone as Felton dropped it on his way back to the kitchen. The dog still held on, front paws off the ground now. Blood flowed down coating my stocking, covering her muzzle and spattering onto the floor. I dropped to my knees, grabbed a handful of loose skin at the back of her head and thrust it forward between her ears. She yelped and let go simultaneously and I lurched out the back door. Hopping and running alternatively, I cleared the passageway, snatched up my boots and reached the car before Felton reached me. Slamming the door shut, narrowly missing the Jack Russell's nose, I agitatedly twisted the ignition key. True to its beautiful reliable self, the Triumph fired immediately and I stamped the clutch into first. Biting hard on my lip to counteract the stabs of agony, I burned petrol and banged the gears up to fourth. A glance in the rear view mirror was reassuring. Felton was a small figure way behind under the light of a street lamp. He was waving both arms in the air. Even as I watched he reached the tiny white blob in the middle of the tarmac where it had come to a barking halt and grabbed it up. I had the distinct impression that it hadn't been a case of Felton chasing me but simply chasing his beloved Millie. I kept in top gear and let the car race on.

To stem the blood flow I pressed my left leg hard against the edge of the driving seat and tried to ignore the burning throb. To get as many miles as possible between me and Bishop's Cleeve was the first priority. When all sensation seemed to be disappearing from my leg and a curious numbness started taking over, I swung off the main route and with a dexterity born of desperation, operated the clutch with my right foot. Following several jolts the car finally came to a stop. The light from the tiny overhead bulb showed up the bloody mess that was my calf. I stripped off my stocking and wiped up as much of the undried blood as possible with a box of tissues from the dashboard. Like all jockeys I was more hardened to the sight of blood than normal and appreciated that it always looked a lot worse than it actually was.

I sloshed some 70% proof whisky against the four puncture marks. It was like a burning firebrand going in. When the pain subsided I unclenched my hands from the steering wheel and wiped the sickly cold sweat from where it stood out from my forehead. Making a pad of tissues I placed them directly on the wound and bound it firmly in place with my stocking. Winding down the window I sat there taking a few deep breaths and steadying my shattered nerves. Felton wasn't tracking me that was pretty certain. For one thing he hadn't a vehicle of his own. The thought plagued me however that on returning he might have told Snodgrass which direction I'd taken. With spending time on repairs to my leg valuable mileage had been lost.

I started up the Triumph and turned her red nose towards home. It was just as well there weren't any police about because I trod the accelerator and kept up the pressure. Passing the half-way mark the lights of a cafe winked enticingly up ahead but the looks which would accompany my entrance caked in dried blood wearing only one stocking could be strongly visualized. I allowed myself one swig from the whisky flask and savoured the glorious warmth. Despite the heater going full bore I felt very cold and shivery. I cursed myself for not being more observant when the dog came at me. I'd been so engrossed in listening to the conversation through the crack in the door that no thought of watching the rear had occurred to me. It was a sobering thought that Felton's van driver friend, the gorilla in flat cap might have returned instead. It was a salutory lesson that I intended to heed. However, the dog's timing had been perfect. Another second and Felton would have spilled out the name behind it all. But did Felton know I hadn't heard? The last audible word had been 'Mr' but he could have said the surname at precisely the same moment that I'd screamed as the dog's jaws anchored themselves in my flesh. It was impossible to know. Felton thought I knew who the man was but if I'd heard the name from his own lips it would have clinched it. The bars on Snodgrass's cage had, however, been rattled and I could expect anything to happen from now on.

I drove past the cafe's welcoming light and on again into the darkness of the winter evening. It seemed an interminable time until I reached the familiar Nottinghamshire boundaries and finally the lane leading to Hunters. Kenneth Graham's mole couldn't have found the sight of his own front door more welcoming than I as the car's headlights picked out the big gates standing open waiting to greet me. Both David and Freda would have gone home hours ago so there wouldn't be an inquest on the bloody state of my person. I acknowledged even to myself that I'd had enough and that waves of weariness had been sweeping over me for the last hour which threatened to send me off to sleep at the wheel. A stiff whisky and a bowl of warm water to soak off the stiff, blood-caked tissues from my calf were all my thoughts were dwelling on. I turned in and drove over the gravel.

A moment later, injury forgotten, I slammed both feet out and clawed the wheel round frantically. The dark figure of a man had just stepped out of a car parked inside the gates. My side wing caught him and he went sprawling amongst the stones. The Triumph stopped and flaring agony in my leg started. I gritted my teeth. Fear, anger and pain roared through me. What now? Did I get out and see who the man was I'd knocked over or did I get the hell out of it and drive furiously on to the house and safety?

I got out.

Chapter Eleven

I STOOD on one foot and leaned against the car. The
man was just picking himself up. It certainly wasn't the
flat capped gorilla. He was only of small build. He
started towards me, obviously unhurt. I took a step
forward onto the dicky leg, a pebble twisted under my
unbalanced weight and I fell flat on my face.

"What a novel way to greet a visitor." Strong arms
went round me and sat me up. "Don't think it will
catch on though."

The voice was familiar. I peered up at him in the
dark. "Paul?"

"On the button little lady."

Then I was laughing and crying in dizzy relief.
"Thank heavens it's only you."

His arms were still round me and although they
tightened appreciably I didn't care. "There's no-one I'd
rather be knocked over by than you Tal." His face was
very close to me.

"I haven't hurt you have I."

"No," he laughed, "it only brushed me. How about
you? Can you stand?"

"Don't know to be honest."

"Which bit of you is in question?"

"My left leg."

He turned and looked at it. "What I can see looks a
mess." There was concern in his voice. "Come on Tal,
up you get. Try putting your weight on it."

I tried and managed to hobble a step or two.

"I see." Paul said. Before I could complain he swept
me up and my arms went round his neck automatically.
"Easier to carry you to the house than stuff you in and

out of a car. I'll sort those out later." He took charge matter of factly and the way I was feeling I was glad to let him. It was comforting to lean against the firmness of his body for although lightly built he was as strong as steel. For a few moments on the walk back I closed my eyes and enjoyed being weak and womanly. "This is a far better way to travel than by car." Paul said in a whisper and let his lips brush my cheek. I opened my eyes. Our faces were very close.

"Definitely couldn't drive a car like this," I tried to quip but my voice had a small choke to it. All the strong magnetism of the man radiated from him and the pull was almost irresistible. In my weakened state any defences I had were definitely down. He kissed my cheek again, softly, tenderly.

Rookey greeted us uproariously outside the kitchen door. Paul unclipped the leash and he bounded round us pleased to see someone home.

"Have you the key Tal?"

"Left mine in the car," I said, "but we can use the other one."

The half-coconut hanging by the kitchen window provided the spare and Paul carried me in and sat me on a pine chair in the kitchen.

"You first request madam?" He gave a sweeping bow.

"Two large whiskys please."

"Two?" His eyebrows went up.

"One each, you fool," I laughed.

He returned a few moments later minus the drinks. "Up you come," he picked me up and carried me through to the lounge. Two drinks stood ready on the side table and he'd pulled the settee up close to the bright, burning fire. "More comfortable for you to put your leg up." He arranged me carefully, propping pillows behind my head and gently raising the level of my injured leg.

"Actually it happened quite a while back. I think it's stopped bleeding now."

"It will help to discourage losing any more."

I sipped my whisky appreciatively, the warmth running through me like liquid fire. "Blood group 'A' Rh.

D. Positive nurse," I murmured drowsily, "but I don't think a transfusion is required this time." There had been times in the past when the automatic trotting out of the correct blood group had been very useful. Most jockeys had the sense to learn their own.

"Same as mine then." Paul turned the point of the poker into a half-burnt log splitting it in two. Sparks showered up inside the grate: warmth radiated out. After the traumatic time I'd spent it was very cosy and peaceful.

Paul fetched towels, the first-aid box and a bowl of warm water and proceeded to bathe my leg himself. "Just lie back and think of the old country, isn't that what you Brits say?" He said, waving aside my protests to do it myself.

"Something like that," I laughed.

After a few minutes he said, "It looks better now its cleaned up, but the wound is nasty." He dabbed on antiseptic and I gave a squeak of pain.

"Baby," he teased and gently tugged my hair.

"Baby yourself, that hurts!" I protested.

"How did it happen Tal?"

"A dog bit me – hard!"

It was his turn to laugh. "Well you do have a very tasty leg."

"Thank heavens my tetanus jabs are all up to date. Saves a lot of bother troubling doctors."

Paul padded off on stockinged feet to the kitchen and returned with a tray of coffee and cheese crackers.

We sipped and munched and enjoyed the fire, just the two of us. There was a comfortable ease between us which was a far cry from the last time Paul had been here.

"By the way, what were you doing parked by the gates?"

"I'd been up to the house but no-one was home and as I got back to the gates I could feel the car pulling. Reckoned it might be a puncture. Of course, when a guy gets out to check, what happens? Along comes a female and knocks him flat."

"Yes, but what did you call for?" I said pulling a face at him.

"Oh yes," his voice sobered, "no can do next week Tal, sorry."

"What next week?"

"Racing. David somebody rang me."

"You're talking about riding Bright Boy?" He nodded. "And you can't manage it?"

"Sorry, I'm riding for Mr Brice in the same race."

I loosed a sigh. Of course he would be. "Hot Chocolate?"

"Right first time."

The horse was favourite at the moment with Bright Boy third or fourth in the betting. "That should make it odds-on then," I said, hoping the disappointment I felt wasn't detectable in my voice.

"Could well do. I expect to win on him." His confidence was certainly sky-high still.

A smoulder of resentment started up inside. A tiny demon I was well used to clamoured for me to rise up in challenge. And why not? If Paul was already booked that was that. To put up another replacement would be easier. There were a lot of good jockeys waiting for chances of rides. But that's all they were – good. Paul was in a class of his own. I didn't shirk from admitting it to myself. Paul and my father had the same kind of extra magic about their riding that put them ahead of the field. It wasn't going to give me any edge over Hot Chocolate to simply put up another man. So why not me? One simple answer, Lord Vardy. But all he was after was a win, wasn't it? If I rode and won he wouldn't care a toss. Supposing though, Bright Boy were to lose? I shivered slightly at what could result. We could lose his horses from our stables and, more important, lose the other owners confidence.

"You cold Tal?" Paul stood up and threw another log on.

"No I'm fine Paul. Just someone walking over my grave."

"Huh?"

"Another old saying we have over here."

"A great lot for your sayings aren't you? Still its what the States doesn't have. A history stretching back. I should think it's the one thing we covert from you. And the one thing we shall never have."

"It's nice to know we've got something to hang onto."

Paul dropped heavily in his seat, "So, what will you do about Bright Boy?"

"I shall ride him myself." The words were out before I'd even thought of them. They took both of us by surprise.

"But this David fella said you needed a guy to ride for you."

"Hmm. It was the original idea but I've changed my mind."

"A woman's privilege."

"I'm in charge of Hunters, until father returns and I have to take the decisions. If an idea proves unworkable I have to decide on another course. One that's best for Hunters."

"And you think if you ride Bright Boy, you'd win?" There was a mocking quality in his voice.

"Yes, I think it's possible."

He blew deprecatingly down his nose. "Come on Tal, where's your objectivity?"

"I take it you think I have no chance?"

"Aw, no. I'm not saying it. You work it out."

I smouldered a bit more. The tiny demon clamoured harder. "Could it be you might be worried I'll win?" I hadn't meant to say the words but he'd provoked me. He rose abruptly, mouth drawn in a tight line.

"Me? Am I worried you'll take the race?"

"Yes," I said softly, "are you?"

"No I'm bloody well not!"

"You're shouting Paul. Me thinks you doth protest too much."

"What's that, another of your quotations?"

"Slightly mis-quoted but it says what I think."

He bent down to put his face close to mine. "Look Tal, nobody, but nobody will be taking that race from me! It's as good as mine now. The others might as well pull out to start with and we'll call it a walk-over." His annoyance dropped away and he smiled suddenly as if the race were already over and he'd won. "What are we

118

fighting for? After such a pleasant evening it's a shame. We sound like an old married couple."

"I wouldn't know. Not having mother here there's no-one for father to fight with."

"I'm sorry Tal." His manner softened. "I didn't mean anything by it."

"It's O.K. Paul. I know you didn't."

"What happened? Did she pass away when you were a kid?"

I stared at him. "Don't you know?"

He shook his head. "Guess not."

"I should have thought playing cards with father and Turton, you would have known."

"Do you want to tell me? Say if you don't." He took my hand and stroked it, not looking at me. "It obviously hurts."

"It's so long ago, I can't even remember her really. She went off with another man."

"That's too bad! How old were you?"

"Not very old. About three."

He shook his head in bewildered disgust. "How could she do it?"

"She fell in love with another man."

"It must have been a pretty powerful love for her to leave you behind."

"I guess it was. But I was always father's girl. If you know what I mean. It would have devastated him if she'd taken me with her. Maybe she did care for him a little and that's why she went on her own."

We sat for a few minutes in silence. Paul still held my hand.

"Have you ever thought of getting married Tal?" He said suddenly.

His words took me completely off-guard and I said automatically, "Yes, once, but I've changed my mind."

"He must have been pretty cut up about it, this guy. You're a lovely woman Albertine."

I floundered, awash with guilt because David didn't know yet I'd decided against marrying him. It was the first time too that Paul had used my proper name and it disturbed me very much. I think I knew what he was going to say next but it still came as a thunderbolt. "Would you consider marrying me?" His grip on my hand tightened.

Whatever else I'd anticipated happening tonight, to receive a proposal of marriage had been odds of a million to one.

"Paul . . . I . . . think what you're saying . . ." I know it was a great surprise to me and I felt that his words were also something of a shock to him. Something that he'd blurted out, just as I had said I'd ride Bright Boy, without due consideration.

"I know what I'm saying. Believe me, Tal, it's something I've thought about a great deal. When I came here to play poker, I always went home thinking about marrying you."

I gaped at him. "I'd no idea! You've taken me completely by surprise."

"Think about it eh? I'm dead serious, I want to marry you."

I shook my head slowly. "No Paul. I'm not in the marrying stakes."

"Give yourself time. I guess I've sprung it on you." He raised my hand to his lips and kissed it victorian fashion.

"I'm sorry Paul. I'm not letting you go on thinking I might change my mind, I won't."

"But you've changed your mind before. What about this other guy?"

"That's exactly why. He's been hoping, expecting for a long time. I should have told him ages ago. Marriage just isn't for me."

"A woman saying that, it's incredible! I don't believe it."

"You'll have to believe it Paul, there's something more important to me at this stage in my life."

"This other guy," his voice hardened, "he's prepared to wait possibly years?"

I nodded slowly thinking about it. "Yes, I honestly believe he is."

"Well more fool him. I'm not! Life's for having now whilst you've still got it." There was such harshness now in his voice that it frightened me a little. I tried to calm him.

"Don't you think at your age you've plenty of time?"

He stood up and strode across to the window. The curtains were not yet pulled and he stood, legs apart a little, hands on both hips aggressively staring out at the moonlit trees.

"How does any of us know what time is left?"

"Are you all right Paul?" I struggled to my feet.

"Sure I am." He still had his back to me.

"You sound very strange. You're not ill are you?" I tried walking towards him and was relieved to find I could put a little weight on the toes of my left foot now which I hadn't been able to earlier.

"Oh no," he said, "I'm not ill."

There seemed to me to be a slight emphasis on the word 'I'm'.

"But someone else is?" I probed gently.

"What's with you?" he grated, swinging round. "Leave it! I've said I'm all right."

I raised a placating palm towards him. "O.K., O.K. Don't get so tense."

His shoulders dropped a little. "I'm not tense," he said quietly, a weariness now replacing the harshness, "just disappointed."

I didn't know how to reply to him. It was something he had to adjust to himself but it would take time. What he needed was diverting at the moment. I put a hand on his arm. "Since you seem to have made such a good job of my leg could I ask a favour?"

"Ask away."

"I need to go to the stables and check one of the horses. How's your supporting arm?"

"At your service m'am." He obligingly stuck out an elbow.

I drew in a deep breath very glad that the atmosphere had lightened, but the quietness between us as we made our way slowly to the horses was a heavy one, not a companionable one as before. It probably never would be again now he'd spoken those words. Not for him a waiting game but a snatch life now attitude. I could understand it. I'd had years of practice living with father and his similar impatience. It stemmed in father's case from my grandmother who had indulged him.

I wondered if Paul's mother pandered to his every whim. His reaction had seemed to me rather like a petulant child wanting a chocolate bar and being forbidden to eat it. "Does your mother live with you in America?"

He stopped suddenly. "Why ask that?"

"I was thinking about her, wondering what she was like."

He didn't reply straight away but started walking again towards the first of the boxes. "Yes." he said. I felt he was about to say more and kept quiet. He opened the Tack room door and sat me on the same hay bale Turton and I had used. He stood looking down at me, hands once more on hips. "She has cancer," he said in a cold voice. "A slow one but a killer nevertheless."

I drew in my breath sharply. The horror in that one word was sufficient to chill apart from the ice in his voice. "How awful . . . for her . . . and for you."

"They don't know how long," Paul continued. "It could be two years. A lot depends on the individual's fighting spirit." He dropped his hands and I watched him aimlessly wander slowly round the Tack room absently fingering the hanging bridles. "There's nothing wrong with her spirit." His voice had a warmer quality about it now. "No sir! That lady has enough spirit in her to move a mountain."

I watched him, saw the agony buried beneath his words and bled for him.

He swung round to me, caught my face between his two hands. "Don't cry," he demanded urgently, "don't cry – she doesn't!"

"Paul . . . I didn't know I was." But as I said it, I could feel the hot betraying trickle down the shape of my cheeks. He put a forefinger against my face and caught the tear before it dropped. His eyes held mine with that strange magnetism. I watched, hypnotised, as he put his fingertip to his lips and delicately kissed the tear.

"Salt," he murmured caressing my face gently. "Salt, it fires the wound, yet cleanses and heals too."

Down the yard one of the horses stamped and whinnied. The sound ripped through the silence following Paul's words breaking the spell between us. He took his hands from my face and said, "Thank you for your compassion, I won't forget it." He proffered an arm. "Shall we have a look at that horse?" I nodded, deliberately holding back tears that would flow in the darkness and privacy of my room later.

We went slowly down the line of boxes. "Second from the end," I said and he reached for the door and slid the bolts back. Calypso had snorted and swung round to see who was invading his peace at this late hour.

"O.K. my lad, you're O.K." I murmured sliding a hand over his intelligent face. I undid both buckles around his chest and flipped the two triangles of rug over his back. The surcingle held them firmly from going further but it was sufficient for me to inspect the wound in his side. Turton had obviously bathed it during the tea-time session for the hair around was still a little damp. I gently pressed the lips of the flesh apart and puss began to bubble up again. It looked very inflamed.

"Looks nasty," Paul was peering over my shoulder. "Has he had an injection?"

"Oh yes. We had the vet this morning. It's a matter of keep bathing and let nature take over really."

Paul rubbed the horse's nose. "How did he manage it?"

"He's the horse father was riding when he came off."

Paul stiffened, he was standing so close to me I could feel him.

"Is he?" He didn't say it as a question but more as a statement.

"We think it was done deliberately."

"Deliberately? By whom?"

"That we don't know."

"But why? What would be gained by harming the horse?"

"Father's accident – it wasn't an accident. Someone

intended him to get injured, maybe they hoped it would kill him."

"No! No, Tal, surely you can't think that?"

I turned to look at him. His face was shocked.

"I'm sorry Paul but it looks very much like it."

He shook his head gently. "I think you're wrong."

"Maybe,' I said, "but I shall find out, what it was done for and, more importantly, who did it."

We rugged up the horse and walked slowly back to the house.

"Sit down Tal. I'll go and unscramble the cars off the drive."

I was glad to let him and be on my own for a few minutes. It had been more of a shock than I realised to hear of Paul's mother dying. I had been and still was, concerned over father, yet he wasn't going to die. We were not to be parted permanently. But it was an unescapable fact that Paul was going to lose his mother. Once she had died he would never see her again this side of the grave. There was a terrible finality about it. And to lose her to cancer was dreadful to contemplate. Two years Paul had said. Two years of agony faced that unknown woman overseas. Yet he was right. She might be unknown to me but I still felt a compassion towards her. If she had been a horse or a dog there would have been a quick, clean death in front, a cessation of suffering. For humans there was no such merciful release. We paid the price in full until God released us. I heard a car reversing outside. Hobbling through to the drinks cabinet in the lounge I poured two small whiskys. Paul came in rubbing hands together.

"To warm you," I said and passed him a drink. His fingers closed over mine round the chunkily cut glass.

"It was never on the cards Tal. Falling for you. I didn't intend to you know. It makes life more complicated than ever."

"Drink your whisky," I said softly.

"Reconsider Tal," his fingers tightened. "If it's the thought of moving away from here, forget it. That would be the last thing I'd do. We would live here, together. You'd never have to move."

"But won't you be returning home, to America?" I nearly added, to be with your mother, but stopped just in time. He could have read my thoughts for he said, "Yes, when I've finished over here, I shall return to her. For the time she has left."

"And then?"

"I shall decide. Either to live on in America, or to come back over here." He tossed off the whisky. "I'm not the sort of person who can live in hope. I'm impatient. Either I go all out and get what I want or I cut loose. I have to make decisions, that's the sort of person I am. Not a glowing character reference but an honest one. So," he took a deep breath, "it's up to you. What do you say Tal? Which way would you have it?"

Chapter Twelve

I SET DOWN my glass because my hand was shaking. Paul had been honest with me. He wasn't David, content to tag on and hope, playing a slow waiting game. It was now or not at all. He had been the one person I'd looked for in my anguish after father's accident. His the one face in the crowd to run to. I knew what I felt for Paul was a kind of love. But there are many kinds of love. And this one wasn't right for marriage. "No Paul. Let me be honest, neither of us really want marriage. It's hard to say it but easier than yes."

He didn't answer, his face was inscrutable as he stared at me.

"Don't make it difficult Paul," I thrust a nervous hand through my hair and pushed it back, "say something."

For an answer he moved to the window, slipped the catch and let the cold night air spill into the room. Deliberately aiming the whisky glass he flung it with maximum force at the trunk of a holly tree growing close to the house. The glass hit its target and splintered with a loud tinkling. He swung the window to and fastened it. "Like my hopes," he said, "shattered on cold thorns. Two women – one I've just lost and one I will lose very soon."

I didn't know what to do or say but he didn't wait for a reply. Turning on his heel he crossed to the door. With a small lift of a hand he said, "Goodbye Tal. Our private lives won't cross again and on the race course, you'll just be one more to beat." The coldness in his voice held me where I was. He closed the door behind him.

I remained motionless like a fly in amber, listening to

the sound of his car starting up and swiftly driving away.

Released from his spell, I went upstairs and flung myself on the bed fully dressed. But strangely no tears flowed, indeed, if they had, I wouldn't have known whether they were for Paul, his mother, or myself.

Despite a long, hot shower next morning, my leg was pretty stiff and painful as I limped my way round the stable yard. It was still very early as I opened the top halves of the box doors. Most of the horses swung inquisitive heads over. "You're all going to have to shape up," I addressed several heads collectively. "What we need are a few winners." Swishing the mucking out fork in an easy rhythm toned up my circulation and despite the cold rawness of the morning, as I humped the muck sack to the heap, a muscle-loosening warmth had spread from top to toe.

"What happened to your leg?" Turton rode precariously into the yard on his rattle trap of a bike. "You're hopping about like a sparrow with gout."

"You can keep your cheeky remarks to yourself my man. Tug your forelock and all that when you speak to the master's daughter."

He guffawed loudly and dipped into the drying room emerging straight away again with another fork. He flung a thin sinewy arm around my shoulders. "I'm right glad to see you in one piece gel. Did you get to see Felton?"

"Yes," I said, "and his bloody dog."

"I knew you'd go." His laughter peeled round the yard but I could tell it was tension being released. He had genuinely been anxious about my safety. He sobered up. "What d'you make out?"

"Snodgrass isn't the brains behind it. But he pulls Felton's strings."

"Huh, so whose working Snodgrass?"

"Big question." I filled him in on what had happened. "And Felton was adamant that no-one else was near at the fence when father came off." I finished.

"There was Reynolds, he won the race; he must have been fairly near."

"Yes, the rest of the field were lengths behind."

"Well, reckon we'd better ask him then."

"Forget it." I said. "After last night, I don't think he'll be approachable."

Turton looked speculatively at me. "Do I get to know about 'last night'?" He emphasised the last two words as though they had a nasty taste.

"You're as bad as a parent," I smiled and rubbed my knuckles across his jaw. "Don't worry, my honour is still intact I assure you."

"But you reckon we won't get anything out of him?"

"Sure of it. Oh and by the way, he's not riding Bright Boy for us."

Turton sniffed. "Not eh? In a way I'm not sorry but you've got to admit he's probably the best jockey putting up." Then he added hastily, "Now your dad's out of action o' course."

"Which is the reason I asked David to approach him in the first place. Anyway, he's riding Hot Chocolate for Brice."

"It leaves us in a spot don't it?"

"I hope not."

"You've someone else in mind?"

"Hmm," I nodded, "yours truly."

"Gawd help us!" Turton's mouth dropped open. "You're not serious?"

"Absolutely."

"But what about his Lordship?" His orders were for a chap to ride."

"Yes, I know, but all Lord Vardy is interested in is a win. As long as he gets that he won't be worrying whose drawing the ten percent."

Turton whistled through his teeth. "Phew, you're taking a mighty big risk gel. Supposing you don't win. I mean . . . think of Reynolds riding against you for a start."

"Let's not suppose Turton. I'm going to use that extra bit of help that Paul uses."

"Eh? What's that then?"

"Confidence Turton. He's got it – 101% of it. And he wins."

"Yes but . . ."

"No buts. I'm not even going to let the thought of losing cross my mind. I'm just visualizing myself and Bright Boy flashing past the post – in front."

He stared at me for a few seconds with pursed lips. "You know something gel?"

"What?"

"If you've got confidence to gamble the stables on this ride, you've already got confidence to win."

"Thanks Turton." I squeezed his hand. "We'll pull it off, both of us, for father's sake. Just think what a marvellous boost it will be for him."

"How d'you find him yesterday Tal?"

"Better, a good deal better. I'd forgotten I've not seen you since I came back. There's some good news."

"He's coming home?" Turton asked eagerly.

"Well not quite that good. He's being moved to the Queens Hospital in Nottingham in the next day or so."

"Aw good, champion. Next best thing. I can have a run over and see him meself." Turton was obviously delighted and I hesitated before telling him about the forthcoming operation.

He brushed aside the possibility of failure. "He'll make it gel, don't you fret yourself. Tough as they come is Jack. Nothing wrong with his fighting spirit."

"That's the second time in twelve hours I've been told of the power of having a fighting spirit," I said.

"Oh yeah?"

"Referring to Paul's mother. It was quite a shock when he told me about her."

"What about her?"

"She's dying Turton, of cancer."

"No!"

"Wish it wasn't true but it is. Paul told me last night, down here in the Tack Room. He said she had enough spirit to move a mountain."

"The poor woman," he said sadly, "she'll need every bit she's got."

"He's terribly cut up about it," I went on. "He does a first class job of hiding it but underneath he's red raw."

129

"Poor sod!" exclaimed Turton. "I don't care for the chap but I'm right sorry for him all the same."

"Yes, I feel the same. And I've kicked him again whilst he's down. Come to think about it, he probably wouldn't have asked if he hadn't been emotionally churned up."

"Asked what?"

I looked squarely at Turton. "Last night, Paul asked me to marry him."

"Gawd blimey!" Turton nearly choked. "He did what!" It wasn't really a question so I didn't bother to repeat myself. He clutched my arm. "Tell me you turned him down gel. You did, didn't you?"

"It's O.K." I was startled by the man's anxiety. "Calm down, yes, I turned him down."

Turton expelled pent up breath in a huge sigh of relief. "Phew, you really had me worried there." He rubbed a gaudily checked handkerchief across his upper lip and moustache.

"Would it have been such a disaster if I'd accepted?"

"It would," he said with feeling. "He'd have been boss here then."

"Well I said no. He won't ask again. I doubt very much if he will even come again either."

"That'll suit me."

"But you and father used to play cards with him. You know him probably better than I do."

"Jack likes his cards," said Turton stubbornly. "I just go along with him. Don't mean I have to like the other fella."

"Still it's a pity I didn't ask him about the accident before all this blew up. Now it's too late."

"Don't suppose he'd have been able to tell us anything if you had."

I was forced to agree. "Looks like a dead-end."

"P'raps Jack will be able to remember, when he gets up and about. Maybe when he sees Calypso Lad it might jog his memory y'never know. He'd have won that race for sure."

I nodded. "Yes, as near a certainty as you can get in racing. Oh . . ." a thought struck me. "Did you know about the old photograph?"

Turton parried the question warily. "What photograph's that?"

"It's one father kept hidden away – except when he won a race. It was a sort of ritual I suppose. He kept it inside his racing mascot and took it out after a win. I didn't know about it myself until today. Strange to think you can live with someone for years and find out that they still have secrets."

"I didn't know either." Turton said in a flat tone. "It's your mother I suppose."

"No, no it's not. I should have thought the same if I'd not seen it. Actually, he didn't mean me to see it. I took the mascot to the hospital for him, a little bit of home making him feel closer and all that. Anyway, whilst he was fingering it he caught the mechanism and a portion of the front slid sideways. The photograph was tucked inside."

Turton looked at me incredulously. "And who is it of?"

"My mother's father."

"Aah!" Turton stepped back as though I'd struck him.

"What on earth's the matter? You look as if you've seen a ghost."

"That's just about what I have," he said hoarsely. "And he's had it all these years?"

"Yes, it's pretty battered."

He turned his head from me and thumped the prongs of the mucking out fork into the ground in agitation, "Aw, Jack, aw Jack . . ."

His words were only just audible but the anguish in them was strong.

I put out a hand and grasped the fork. "Turton. What's troubling you man?"

"I thought he was over it, put it behind him. Now . . . now . . . It's still with him . . . all this long time, he's not forgotten."

"For goodness sake, what are you talking about?"

But Turton just kept on shaking his head and walked drunkenly off into Calypso's box. I stood perplexed looking after him. "I've brought the photograph home with me if you'd like to see it."

Turton stopped before closing the door, swung round slowly and looked at me. "No thanks gel. I knew the man for a good while. Can't remember exactly what he looks like but I don't want to be reminded." He turned to close the door muttering to himself, "Can't understand why Jack's rubbing in salt."

I followed him and leaned against the door jamb. "I brought it home to compare it with the other."

Turton stiffened, one hand on the horse's withers. "What other?"

"The photograph of mother."

There was no response from him, he could have been turned to stone.

"There's only one feature that seems the same to me."

He turned a white face to me. "You told me you never saw her, so how could you have a 'photo?"

"Father destroyed all the others but gave me the last one of her."

"I couldn't . . ." he stopped and clamped his lips firmly together.

"Yes?"

He stood rigidly shaking his head.

"You're infuriating at times Turton," I said in exasperation.

"Likely I am." He grunted and turned back to the horse unbuckling the rug straps.

"I checked him last night," I said. "There was still a lot of infection when Paul and I had a look."

"He was down here as well then?" Turton gave a loud sniff of disgust.

"I used his supporting arm in lieu of my leg." I felt annoyed at having to justify myself.

The situation was eased by the sound of approaching footsteps down the yard. "Mornin' Miss." The stable lad touched his cap.

"Morning Jimmy," I said. "I'm glad you've arrived. Grab a fork. You're riding out first lot on Court Jester."

"Yes Miss."

"Just a minute, hang on!" I caught his wrist. The remains of a lighted cigarette was held between his fingers. "You know it's against stable rules to smoke."

"It's only a stub Miss. I lit up before I got here."

"Well you can just put it out again."

"Yes Miss." He gave it a hard squeeze and put it inside his jacket pocket. As he brought his hand out again, he held a new cigarette lighter with the initial 'J' inscribed on the front. "Me dad gave me this for my birthday last Sunday. Nice 'en it?" he said proudly.

"Belated birthday wishes, Jimmy," I said. "I'm sorry I didn't remember the day. But leave the lighter and cigarettes at home, O.K.? I don't want to see them here again."

"Sure," he grinned and thrust the lighter back in his pocket.

I was hard put not to grin back but just managed to keep up the firm disciplinarian front until Jimmy trotted off for a fork. What a relief it was to fall back into the familiar business of running the yard and let the long ago intrigues fade into the background, for the moment at least.

If I'd expected fireworks following my visit to Felton, I was disappointed – if that was the right word. Nothing threatening arrived by mail and no undesirable visitors put in an appearance. For several days everything ran on quiet, well-oiled wheels. None of the horses went lame, a trainer's nightmare, no irate owner rang up to withdraw any from the yard and Calypso Lad made a swift recovery.

Turton and I worked on Bright Boy to bring him to a peak for Wednesday's race. He was a sure jumper and my heart lifted with excitement and expectation as I schooled him over jumps. I knew he was improving and ready to take on rivals like Hot Chocolate. I believed he could beat the horse given a small amount of luck on the day. That element should be written into Contracts. Very often its presence makes the hair's-breadth difference needed.

On the Monday afternoon I took a 'phone call from the Hospital. Father had been transferred to the Queens in Nottingham and would undergo surgery on Tuesday. They were quietly confident of the outcome. I replaced the receiver with a mixture of feelings. It would be marvellous to have him so close yet that was linked with his gamble on the operation. Although I had told father I was right behind him, which I was, to eradicate every tiny twinge of fear and doubt was not humanly possible.

Turton was mixing feed down the yard. He straightened up, tugged off his cap, wiping his forehead on his jacket sleeve as I hurried to tell him. My leg had healed well over the week-end and gave only a minimum of discomfort which I ignored. The news of father's transfer to Nottingham delighted him. "Strictly no visitors Tuesday though." I said. "We'll ring up later in the day and make sure he's O.K. after the operation."

"Shouldn't think he'll be able to see straight away. I reckon it'll be a day or two after his bandages come off."

"I don't really know. It's bound to be the hardest part for him, having to wait and not knowing."

"He'll make it Tal. Y'know deep down in your heart he'll be all right. A tough 'un is Jack." Turton turned back to his work, whistling happily through his teeth. The sound brought horses heads up over doors, ears pricked towards the sound. A lump rose in my throat as I stood and looked round the dear, familiar, old yard. It was all so precious to me. And if I felt so strongly about it, what must father feel?

I hadn't planned on visiting him today, but now the news had come through there was no reason at all why I shouldn't slip over to the hospital tonight to rejoice with him on being one step nearer home. It was only a matter of a few minutes by car. I swallowed the lump in my throat determinedly. I was behaving as though it were all being taken away which was a stupid and dangerous way of thinking. I would hang on to Hunters with the edge of my nails if need be.

I caught up a bucket and pushed it under the hose. The metal handle was cold in the early evening air and water splashed on my hand stung and turned my fingers blue.

"Could be a frost tonight Turton," I called.

"Feels that way," he agreed.

"Did you hear the weather forecast at lunch?"

"Naw, fell asleep."

"Lazy beggar!"

"We don't want a frost yet gel, not afore Wednesday's race."

"Exactly what I was thinking." I carried on with the watering. The contrast between the cold yard and the warmth inside the boxes was appreciable. The big animals, well rugged up, seemed to generate their own central heating. If frost did come and turned the ground to rock hardness, there was no way I'd run any of them. The risk of damage to their legs was too high. But I desperately wanted to race. Mentally I'd been preparing myself ever since I'd told Paul that I would ride. My confidence was rising nicely. By Wednesday it should be sky-high and that was the way I wanted it. Sky-high and dead certain. I returned to the hose humming gently under my breath. Things were certainly beginning to run right. Snodgrass hadn't made a move for days and probably realised the futility of trying to buy Hunters. Whoever his eager client was, faced with a situation where no matter what price, the Hunter establishment wasn't for sale, he was probably astute enough to know when to give in. When evening stables finished I walked back to the house. I entered the kitchen and savoured both warmth and smell that enfolded me.

"Succotash, Freda?"

"Yes, there was a lot of chicken left and I know you like it."

"Lovely, smells superb. By the way, father's back in Nottingham, at the Queens."

"Oh that is good news!"

"His operation's tomorrow and then, then we pray he'll be back at Hunters in a few more days."

"I'm so pleased for you. It's been a terrible time since the accident."

"Yes, still, it's nearly over now, thank heavens."

Whilst we talked I washed stable hands off at the kitchen sink. Freda flipped across the hand towel.

"I cleared up some broken glass earlier. All around

135

the big holly tree it was. You know, opposite the lounge window?"

"Hmm." I nodded, "Sorry Freda, I should have remembered to do it myself."

"I didn't want Rookey to cut his paws on it."

"It was remiss of me to leave it. It took me by surprise when he did it."

Freda's eyebrows lifted enquiringly.

"Paul, Paul Reynolds. He upped and threw a whisky glass out of the window. It smashed on the holly tree."

She sniffed primly. "What a shocking waste of a good glass."

"Yes it was rather," I smiled, "but it did emphasise a point. I don't think Mr Reynolds will be calling round any more Freda."

"A good job, too," she sniffed again, "can't afford to keep on having glasses broken."

She served up the meal, steaming and appetising. After a long, cold day outside it was spot on.

"You know Freda," I said, between forkfuls, "as a cook you get better and better."

Her ears turned a warm shade of pink. "Thanks very much."

"Wait 'til father gets home and tastes your food again, it will speed his recovery."

"Nice of you to say so. Do give him my best when you see him."

"Tell you what, why not leave the pan to soak in the sink and slip off early tonight. There's nothing spoiling."

"That'd be lovely if you're sure. I'm going to see a film tonight."

"Settled then, you slip off and I'll see you to-morrow."

Freda took off her apron and departed happily leaving me to finish off my meal with just Rookey for company. I tossed him a piece of chicken. "And that's all," I said as he stood, stumpy tail wagging, eyes fixed on my plate. "You've had a bowl of dinner." I put the plate into the sink. "Come on, let's give you a quick run 'cos I'm going out."

We strolled to the end of the drive and back. Well, I strolled, Rookey gambolled madly. Back at the house, I fastened his lead and left him on guard outside.

I did a quick change into a warm trousersuit, made sure I had the 'photo to put back inside the Buddha and headed for the garage. It was a delight to know, as I turned West out the main gate, that at most there was only fifteen miles drive ahead.

Most of the approach to Nottingham was down dual-carriageway and the Triumph sailed along. A pity it was such raw weather or I could have had the top down. I noted with a certain satisfaction as I parked up outside the Queens that it had only taken thirteen minutes. But it took me nearly as long inside to locate father's room. It was a veritable mole heap with corridors running off corridors and yet more corridors connecting and branching off. I found it very disconcerting that many of them were without natural light, being so far inside the building that no windows were possible. The whole effect was claustrophobic, smothering. Emerging from the corridors it was a relief to discover the wards had large windows showing wide expanses of sky. I felt like a diver coming up for air.

Father's room was on the right. I turned the handle and went in. My words of welcome died before they were said. Standing by the bed was a tall, fat man. He was pressing a pen into father's hand. Lying on the bedcover was a sheet of paper. What the paper was I didn't know, but I knew the man. It was Snodgrass.

Chapter Thirteen

I WAS ACROSS the room and snatching the paper from the bed before he realised who I was. "What the hell do you think you're doing Snodgrass? Get out of here. Leave father alone."

Recognition dawned on his ugly, pocked face. "I might have known you'd show-up," he spat the words at me.

"How dare you come in here bothering him."

"Tal? Tal, what's going on?" Father rubbed a frustrated hand across his bandaged eyes in agitation.

"You're O.K. father. I'm here now."

"He says you want me to sign a Contract for sale, that you've had a marvellous offer for Hunters."

I whirled round on Snodgrass. "See this?" I gritted and jammed the paper under his nose. "This is what you can do with it." I ripped it viciously into shreds.

His eyes blazed in rage. "If you hadn't shown up, he'd have signed." He thrust out his chin so his face was only a couple of inches away from me. His breath was heavy with stale tobacco as he hissed, "And then where would you be my pretty madam?"

I stepped back with revulsion at the closeness of him. "Get out you creep. Hunters will never be for sale. It will always be ours."

He laughed nastily as he marched to the door. "There's more than one way to skin a cat my dear, so, watch out for your fur!" He slammed the door behind him.

"What's going on?" Father was tugging furiously at the bandages.

"Steady on," I caught his hands, "You mustn't take the bandages off. it's O.K., he's gone now."

"What's it all about. Have you agreed a sale?"

"Of course not, how could I. Hunters belongs to you."

He dropped his hands in weariness. "He said you'd never manage Hunters on your own. If I thought anything about you I'd sign."

"Rubbish," I said firmly, settling him back against the pillows. "I shan't be on my own anyway. After your operation you'll be there to take over most of it again."

He shook his head. "Not according to him. He said why didn't I wake up. I'm going to be blind for the rest of my life. This operation is a Beecher's Brook and I'm on a horse with three legs."

"He's about the lowest form of life going," I said trying desperately to contain the anger roaring through me. "He wants you to think negatively. Well you're not going to. This operation is going to restore your sight and give you back your old life at Hunters. A piece of wreckage like Snodgrass isn't going to take away your fighting spirit. It's part of you father, the biggest part."

He was still shaking his head.

In desperation I said. "If we lose Hunters, my life won't be worth having. You know that don't you?

After a second or two he began to nod. "Yes girl, I know it's your whole life. But you need some support and right now I can't give it."

"But you will! Three legs or not, you're going to clear Beecher's." I held my breath. Slowly a faint smile began to break through.

"By God Tal," he said at last, "You've got enough spirit and guts for the pair of us."

I dropped to my knees and hugged him tightly hoping the wetness from my tears wasn't sufficient to penetrate his pyjamas and give me away.

I drove back from the hospital at a sober pace. My mind was busy with Snodgrass's implications. As I saw it, the best way of beating him was by winning races. Whilst ever the owners had sufficient faith in Hunters we were all right. Lose that faith and it would play into his hands. All of which added up to Bright Boy being first past the post on Wednesday. For a second I allowed myself to think of putting up one of the other jockeys. There was no doubt I was sticking my neck out under the guillotine putting up in the race. But it was only for a second. On a good horse I could match any man and Bright Boy was one very good horse. During his concentrated training we had come to know each other well. Besides, I had to admit being selfish, there was a hunger driving through me. A hunger for wins. The desire to win was a fire within me which I had deliberately fed with fuel until it burned so strongly nothing else mattered but the race. I swung into the drive at Hunters, the headlights beaming over the edge of the grass verge. A silver icing shone on the edge of the blades and I swore gently under my breath. Frost was another enemy just now. Too much and the race would be off. Rookey barked furiously when he saw the car and bounded around my legs when I released him. He led the way to the back door and clouted it with a huge, furry paw.

"A bit cold for you out here, Rookey boy?" I said and let him in.

Instead of exploring for morsels left in his dinner bowl as he usually did, he slipped through the door to the hall. I heard him bark and pound up the staircase. With misgivings I followed him.

The hall light wasn't on and in the dusk along the landing I saw the outline of a dark figure. For a moment I thought it might be Freda and then remembered I'd sent her home early. My heart began to beat overtime and I extended my fingers and grasped hold of the only possible weapon nearest to me, the oak–handled warming pan.

"I can see you up there, come on down!" It was supposed to have been said as a strong command and I was mortified when it came out a strangled squeak. My anger at myself negated the fear. "Come down here you!" I bellowed. The figure turned and came towards me. I jerked the copper pan from the wall and advanced to meet it. All the anger I'd controlled in the hospital welled up. "Snodgrass sent you did he? Come here, I'll show you what he's up against!"

The figure held up a pacifying hand. "Hold on Tal."

The use of my name stopped me short. It crossed my mind it could be a trick. Of course Snodgrass knew my name so it followed that his underlings probably did to. Then Rookey surprised me. He stopped dancing round the figure and trotted back sedately downstairs. He would never have done that unless he knew who the figure was.

"O.K." I said, "so I know you do I? Well don't be shy, tell me your name."

"Tal, it's me." The dark figure cleared the landing and started down the stairs.

Now I could see who it was. "Turton!" I exploded. "What the hell do you think you're doing? You frightened me half to death."

"I'm sorry gel." He negotiated the last stair and stood beside me in the hall. "I wouldn't have given you that scare for the world. I thought you were out, visiting Jack."

"And the coast was clear?" The hurt and disgust in my voice made him wince.

"Please, Tal, don't be like that."

"What do you expect me to be like." I turned away from him and with trembling fingers re-hung the warming pan. "You'd better come through to the kitchen and explain. I'm going to make a drink." He followed me and dropped into a pine chair.

"What's it all about Turton? Forget something from your last try at breaking and entering?" I hated myself for the sarcasm in my voice but the blow to my faith in the man hurt like the devil. He was the last person I'd expected to walk down those stairs. I'd come to lean on him almost like a second father and this seeming betrayal made me feel physically sick.

"You've every right to be hopping mad. I guess I shouldn't have done it."

I'm not mad – I'm hurt, I wanted to scream at him but the words stayed in my head.

"I didn't want you to know. I thought by the time you were back from the hospital I'd have been out of the house."

The sickness inside me increased and my head swam giddily. "You're admitting you're a thief?"

"No!" his head jerked up. "You don't understand Tal, you don't understand at all. I didn't want you to know because of what it might do to you."

I stared in baffled bewilderment. He fumbled in an inside pocket and produced a battered old lighter and lit one of his distinctive menthol cigarettes. I drew out another chair and sat down facing him.

"Turton, for pity's sake just give me a reason for being upstairs, in the dark, when you thought I was out." I had to stop myself from adding, any reason just as long as my trust is restored.

"Last time," he began hesitatingly, "last time, I was looking for something. O.K.?"

I nodded.

"Well I didn't find it. In fact afterwards I was convinced it had been destroyed, no longer existed. Until you told me you'd actually still got it."

"I told you?"

"Yes Tal. In a roundabout way you told me. Oh you didn't realise at the time but as soon as you'd spoken I just knew I had to have another go at finding it." He took a deep drag on the cigarette.

"Go on," I encouraged. "How did you get into the house with Rookey on guard?"

He smiled wryly. "It was easy. I'd been waiting for a chance ever since. I saw Freda go cycling off early and then you took woofter for a run."

"You actually slipped in before I went to the hospital?"

"Yeah, that's about the size of it."

"And I locked you in and went to visit father." I concluded.

He inclined his head in agreement.

"So just what is this 'thing' you're so desperate to get hold of?"

He didn't answer immediately and I was impatient. "Did you find it this time?"

Without replying he slipped a hand in his jacket pocket and drew out something covered with a hand- kerchief. I watched in disbelief as he unfolded the material and exposed a photograph. It was the one from my jewellery box - the photograph of my mother. We sat looking at each other, the photograph on the table between us.

I managed one word. "Why?"

He gave the tiniest of shrugs and just stared down at it, his face haunted.

"Turton, were you in love with my mother?" It was a question I hardly dared ask and yet it would explain his desire to find the photograph.

"You give me your word of honour not to breathe a word of this to Jack?"

Impulsively, I put my hand over his. "There's two of us and four walls here, that's how far it goes."

"You're a good girl, Tal. Jack's a lucky man to have you for a daughter."

"Is she the reason why you never married Turton?"

"You could say that." He raised his eyes from the 'photo. "She burned me up inside. She was Jack's wife and God help me, I wanted her."

The words seemed incongruous coming from the little, dried-up old chap. I tried to picture him in his youth all those years back.

"She was the sort of woman who put a spell on men. Made them do things against their better judgement. They couldn't help themselves. I . . . I couldn't help myself. Like just now, when I found the 'photo, I knew I should go straight away, before you came home but I couldn't. So I just sat . . . sat and looked at her. That's why you found me."

My heart went out to him. "If she can still have that effect after all these years, I can guess what you must have gone through at the time."

"I had one night with her." His voice was so low I could scarcely catch the words. "Just the one night. It made the fire inside me roar like a furnace yet at the same time, it burned it out. The next day, I couldn't look Jack in the face. I've never felt so low. no self-respect left y'see, just a burned out shell. My God, it's a terrible thing for a man to lose his self-respect. When that's gone, everything's gone."

A devastating thought came into my mind: I had to nerve myself to ask him. "Turton, was that before or after I was born?"

He saw in an instant what I was getting at. "You see!" He said almost angrily. "You see what it's putting you through? No, no Tal, my ducky, you're Jack's girl all right." His voice lost the anger and dropped reflectively. "You were all black curls and rompers then . . . pulling yourself up by the table leg, tiny toes curling . . ." He drew hard on his cigarette for the last time and searched around for something to stub it in. I fetched an ash-tray from the study.

"Need something stronger than coffee Turton?"

"Naw, I'm O.K. gel," He pushed the 'photo towards me. "I've seen all I need to. Here, put it away safe. it's the only one of her."

"I'm not sure I should. Maybe it would be better to do what father did and destroy it. She's caused so much heartbreak."

"And then what would you tell your own young 'uns? There was one photograph of your grandma and I threw it away? No, Tal, you keep it somewhere safe."

I smiled at him. "By the time I get married, I'll be too old for young 'uns, as you put it."

He wagged a finger at me, "Don't be so sure. Love could come knocking at the door tomorrow."

"Possibly, but unlikely." I said and poured him a drink. "I'm glad you're here tonight anyway Turton. I could do with a shoulder. Father already had a visitor when I went to visit him."

"Who might that have been?" Turton lifted up his cup.

"Snodgrass."

He spluttered and choked, clapping a handkerchief to his dripping moustache. "You're joking!".

I shook my head. "Afraid not. The old devil was spinning a con yarn and trying to persuade father to sign a sale contract."

"For Gawd's sake! He didn't sign it Tal?"

"No, fortunately he didn't. It must have been a good line Snodgrass was telling though because father was wavering when I got there."

"By, I wish I'd been there. I'd have given him what for!" Turton's eyes blazed. "Poor old Jack, stuck in bed with the operation tomorrow and that sod pushing him. . .. I'd like to do him up proper."

"I felt the same. I tore his contract up and told him what to do with it."

"And did he threaten you again?" Turton asked perceptively.

"Hmm. But I'll watch my step."

"And so shall I. There's no harm going to come to you Tal, not if I can help it." His tone was fiercely protective and I loved him for it.

"You're a good chap to have on our side."

"I'm glad you still think so gel, after what I've admitted to."

"Forget it. I'm going to. People do things they regret bitterly afterwards. You can't change the past, it is past. Now is the important bit."

"Thanks gel, you're quite right." He nodded sagely, "and tomorrow's even more important."

"Yes."

We locked hands hard almost without being aware of reaching out for each other.

"He'll make it—he's got to make it." Insisted Turton and it could have been myself speaking.

I opened the bedroom curtains next morning to lashing rain. All trace of frost gone. "And the going will be good to soft," I murmured as I slipped downstairs to let Rookey out. He was reluctant to go and I gave him a push. He was out and back in two minutes – a quick trot to the nearest tree, a balance on three legs whilst he assisted the flow of rainwater and a mad scamper back. "Not keen on rain are you my sunshine?" He leaned hard against my leg, stumpy tail a blur of happy wagging. He was good company in the big, empty house. "Guess you wonder where your master is don't you?" I patted him firmly on the shoulder. The dog squirmed with pleasure. "He'll be back in a few days, Rookey, good as new." And as I filled the kettle, I added, "God willing." I determinedly put all thoughts of father from me and geared myself to concentrate on the horses. And one horse in particular – Bright Boy.

The stable yard gleamed wetly as I switched on the lights a few minutes later. Two or three horses whickered a greeting as they heard my footsteps. I went along the line, bolting back the top halves. Despite the dark miserable morning, my spirits started to rise. It was all up to me and the bay now. Tomorrow's win would secure Hunters an all important breathing space.

"Don't you ever sleep," Turton grunted, trundling his decrepit bike into a disused stable and parking it.

"Don't know why you bother putting that old thing under cover. It couldn't get much more rusty." I countered.

He pitched a horse nut at me which I fielded and returned. It bounced off the peak of his cap. "Watch it gel. You're still not too big for a spanking."

"No." I agreed. "'course, you've got to catch me first."

He lunged towards me and I laughingly skipped out of his reach.

Bright Boy whinnied and kicked hard in his box.

"Full of it, ain't he?" Turton said happily.

"Right on top form," I agreed, "He's going to show the rest of them the way home."

"And then it's Calypso Lad."

"One thing at a time Turton. Let's get tomorrow's race won."

"A walk over." He said and stumped off whistling loudly through his teeth.

Bright Boy seemed to think so too as I led him fully tacked from his box. He avoided me adroitly and swirled around getting in a few bucks.

"Save it for tomorrow my lovely," I said and a squirm of excitement started low in my stomach. I was going to win that race and no other horse and jockey was going to take it from me.

"Want a leg-up?" Turton tossed down a muck sack he was carrying.

"Might help." I grinned.

"You look like a cat that's been at the cream," he commented.

"It's the thought of going in the winners enclosure tomorrow. it always puts a silly smirk on my face."

"Get away with you. Go and exercise the horse." Turton slapped Bright Boy's neck.

"Yessir, right away sir." I tugged a mock forelock submissively.

Bright Boy sensed the removal of a hand and reared suddenly.

"Git down!" Turton bellowed.

I stopped fooling about, bridged my reins and took the horse out the stable yard. We trotted as far as the gallops. "Let's pop over a few fences shall we boy?" The horse's ears flicked back and forward, catching my voice yet eager to be away down the turf. He danced and sidewalked and I let him run. We swept down the field to the first hefty fence, all planks and brushwood and above that padded uprights. He jumped fluidly with inches to spare. He was a brilliant jumper, never running in the bottom or misjudging and putting in extra strides. It was a joy to be riding him. We cleared a second fence cleanly and I urged him to a flat gallop. He needed little urging. We went down the straight at a tremendous pace. I pulled him up with some difficulty, he seemed to have a deep reservoir of energy that would have kept him going forever had I let him. The winners enclosure seemed to swim before me with clarity in all it's vivid detail. Bright Boy and I were being led in, straight to the number one place and I was wearing Lord Vardy's colours. It was no wishful dream–tomorrow I would make it fact. The horse and I hacked back to the stables.

"How did he go?" Turton peered over the half-door as I untacked.

"In a word–beautifully." There was little sweat on him and I slapped his shoulder. It was firm solid muscle. "He's going to go like a bomb tomorrow. He's jumping out of his shoes now."

"Good," said Turton and gave a loud sniff of satisfaction.

By unspoken agreement neither of us mentioned father's operation and the yard work kept us busy the entire morning. But as we were finishing straightening up the Tack room he turned to me. "Jack'll have had the operation by now. When were you thinking of ringing up?"

"As soon as I get back up the house."

"I'll come with you then gel. I'll enjoy me dinner better when I know he's O.K."

"Might as well call it a day now," I said adjusting the last bridle on its peg.

"Right y'are. Just get me transport." He trundled the ancient bicycle across the yard and we fell into step back to the house. David's car was parked outside and at the sight of it I felt a stab of guilt. I should have to tell him my mind was made up on the question of marriage. It was unfair to keep him hanging on, hoping that the waiting would be worthwhile in the end when I married him. There wasn't going to be any marriage. Life suddenly became complicated. Whilst I was down with the horses I could forget everything but away from the yard, life came back at me with a bang. I took a deep breath and went in at the kitchen door with Turton.

"Come through to the study, we'll probably find David there."

He was. Surrounded by office accounts and with a brand new pair of glasses perched self-consciously on his nose. "Ha, hello you two. Come to use the 'phone?"

I nodded. "The operation should be well over by now." I pulled the 'phone towards me. "How come the 'specs.?" He jabbed a forefinger at the bridge of his nose and they retreated to the right position.

"The Optician said I needed them. Getting old I suppose."

"Aren't we all."

"Some of us more than others my girl."

"All right, grandad."

"She was never respectful to her elders y'know," said Turton and tweaked my ear.

"You'll all be singing a different tune tomorrow. It will be tenpence to speak to me then." I dialled the hospital number.

"Hark at it!" chortled Turton.

David put the back of his hand to the side of his

mouth and said in a loud whisper. "It's called getting swelled-headed."

The operator answered and I asked for father's ward. The banter stopped and the three of us waited. There was a tension now in the room. I felt I could put out my hand and grasp it. Just about everything depended on this operation and we all knew it. The Ward Sister answered the 'phone.

I spoke for the three of us. "Mr. Hunter. He was to have an eye operation this morning. Could you tell me how he is please? And is it too soon to say if the operation has . . . restored his sight?"

Time stopped whilst we waited for the answer.

Chapter Fourteen

THE THREE of us huddled round the receiver to hear her reply.

"Mr. Hunter is fine. He's had his operation and the doctor considers it a success. We can't obviously say one hundred per cent if Mr. Hunter can see because of course he is bandaged at the moment, but the doctor is confident everything will be all right."

"Thank you very much," I said shakily, "give him all our love. We shall be in tomorrow evening to see him." I replaced the receiver.

"Well," I said in the silence that followed, "what are you both waiting for? Let's have a drink to celebrate."

Turton gave a whoop of delight and tossed his scruffy, old cap into the air. "He's made it, by Gawd, he's made it!"

"Yes, thank God he's O.K." said David with feeling and hurried to fetch a bottle. The champagne popped and gurgled into glasses.

"You'll have to stop Tal," said Turton. "Can't have you watering down a good drink."

I put a hand to my cheek. It came away wet with the tears that were streaming down my face, unnoticed until his words.

"You've shown more emotion in the last week or so than I've ever seen before," said David handing me a glass. "Chin up Tally Ho, it's almost over. Jack will be home shortly, they're desperate for beds. The old rogue is too healthy to take someone else's right to a place in hospital."

"Let me give you a toast," Turton clinked his glass against David's and mine. "To Jack. May he make a complete recovery and a speedy return to Hunters."

"To Jack." We said.

It was not the right moment, even after Turton departed for lunch, to tell David my decision. We were all riding on the wave of exultation at the success of the operation and it woud be too cruel to dash him from such heights. It would have to wait. I'd much rather have it over and said but that was a selfish way of looking at it.

"Will you stay for lunch?" I asked him.

"Not today Tally Ho. I promised Mary I would be back at twelve-thirty sharp for a meal. Tim likes to come home for lunch now. Mind you, Mary's cooking is a vast improvement on school dinners."

"It's still working out O.K.?"

"Couldn't be better," enthused David. "The change in the child is enormous since she took over the running of the house. No more nightmares, packs away tremendous meals, he's great. Much happier altogether. In fact we all went to the zoo on Saturday. I've shot a complete roll of film. Should turn out well. I'll let you have a look when they're back from being developed."

"I'd like to see them. The last time I saw Tim he was such a solemn, little boy."

"Well he's not anymore," David drained his glass. "Must go. I'll be in tomorrow morning before you leave."

"Fair enough. See you then."

"This morning's good news will give you an even greater zip to win I expect." He shovelled papers into his briefcase.

"Mentally, I'm there already."

He smiled briefly at me and snapped the catch. "Yes, I can see you are. It means such a lot to you Tally doesn't it, winning?"

"Racing is what I live for, what I was born for."

He cupped my face between his hands and kissed me gently. "Go to it then girl. Show them how it's done."

"Do my best." I caught hold of his hand and pressed it against my lips. I felt too choked inside to say more.

When he'd left I went upstairs and stretched out on the bed. Perhaps David was right, too much emotion packed into a short time had resulted in a feeling of exhaustion. And as I sleepily drifted off to oblivion, I realised he hadn't known half that had gone on either.

It was after four when I woke from a dream tossed sleep and peered in the dressing-table mirror. I recoiled at the sight and stumbled to the bathroom and sloshed my face with warm water. It didn't wash away the dark rings around my eyes but it did wake me up. A drink of honeyed coffee downstairs completed my return to life and I realised that having a sleep instead of lunch was fine except it left you feeling pretty hungry when you woke up. I knocked together a quick sandwich and munched it on my way down to the stables. Jimmy and Turton were already half-way through the afternoon feeding.

"Hello part-timer," said Turton clattering a scoop into the feed bucket.

"Perks of being the boss."

"Huh. What makes you think you're boss?"

I grabbed the peak of his cap as he bent over the bucket and pulled it down hard over his eyes.

"Geroff!"

Jimmy sniggered, was treated to a hard look from Turton and hastily took himself off to the hay barn.

"Lord Vardy done any checking up yet?" enquired Turton adjusting his old cap lovingly.

"No, you think he will?"

"I'd 'ave thought so. With Jack not being here, he's like a hen sitting on a hot egg."

"How do you mean?"

"Unsettled. Likely to jump in any direction. If he knows there ain't a chap riding t'hoss tomorrow, he'll be up in the air."

"True. But as yet he doesn't know. I think he's still out of the country."

"Let's hope he stays out."

"After two-thirty tomorrow it won't matter anyway."

"What time are we off in the morning?"

"As late as possible I think. Whilst Bright Boy is here nobody will be getting at him. Once we make a move, he's open to risk."

"And yourself, Tal, don't forget."

"I won't forget."

Turton looked so anxious I leaned forward and patted his cheek.

"Don't worry! I'll double check the bolts on the big front door tonight. A girl can't say fairer than that." It was meant as a joke but he took it seriously.

"Yes, do that. And I should leave Rookey the run of the house, don't shut him in the kitchen."

"You're a whittling old fool," I said, "but I love you."

"I'll feel a lot happier when Jack's back home. Say," he grabbed my arm, "you could stay the night with me and mother. What do you think?"

I gently put his arm away from me. "I think the stables need me around tonight–and I need them. No disrespects intended, Turton and thanks for the offer, but I need to be near the horses right up until the time of the race. I don't want a break in concentration. You do understand?"

He pursed his lips briefly, "Yes, yes, I guess you're right. Well, I'm only on the other end of the 'phone if you need me."

I couldn't resist it. "And you'll come charging to my assistance on your trusty steed–that ancient rattletrap of a bike."

"Why, you ungrateful little . . ." he growled and I ran. Straight into the safety of the Tack room. I leaned my back against the door laughing as Turton pounded his fists on it. "One of these days, my girl . . . I'll get hold of you . . . You've got more sauce than a bottle of ketchup."

"But you've got to admit, I'm twice as sweet."

He stumped off chuntering to himself. I gave him a couple of seconds then slipped out the door. From half-way down the yard he shook a fist at me. I gave him a cute little wave.

When we finished at six o'clock I returned to the house for a meal. It would be the last main meal before the race. I usually ate very little on race-days, not so much because of weight problems but because I felt more alert and active without a full stomach.

Tonight Freda had one of my favourite vegetarian meals waiting, Red Dragon Pie. I took a tray through to the fireside and watched the news as I ate. There were some repairs needed on one of the rugs where the binding around the edge had come loose and it was all I intended during this evening. A gentle unwinding couple of hours stitching, a sloshy, warm bath and an early night. Tomorrow should see me relaxed and refreshed. I returned my tray to the kitchen. Freda had already cleared up and had coffee bubbling ready for me.

"Delicious Freda, thanks. Will you have a coffee too?"

She shook her head. "I've a friend coming round tonight for a bite to eat."

"The way you cook Freda, it's a wonder he's not round every night."

She blushed, "He does keep coming, it's true."

"You'll have the neighbours talking," I pulled her leg.

She laughed. "Let them, if they want to. I'll see you tomorrow, it that's all right?"

"Of course, good night Freda, take care cycling back."

"I will." She disappeared into the darkness of the winter evening.

I finished my drink and sat content with my own company, thimble on finger, stitching the stiff cloth of the horse rug. Whilst my fingers were busy so too were my thoughts. I ran through all the jumps I would meet tomorrow, mentally judging where the best position would be at specific parts of the course. The preparation before racing was an important part as far as I was concerned. It left me free whilst riding the actual race to put into practice all the advance planning. I worked on the race until there was a clear blue-print in my mind of how it should be run. Finally, satisfied, I dropped the heavy rug to the floor and stretched back in the armchair, yawning widely. It was surprising that I felt so tired when this afternoon had been lost to sleep. I bent and tossed another log on the fire. Rookey stirred by my feet.

"Did I wake you?" I rubbed a stockinged foot up and down his black back.

He sat up and growled. His sleepiness dropped away and he was all attentive listening, head cocked on one side.

Something other than myself had disturbed and awakened him. The growls rumbled low in his throat and he stood up stiff-legged.

"What is it boy, what've you heard?"

We both listened together: I could hear nothing, Rookey continued to growl.

"I can't hear anything, you've got an over-active imagination," I ribbed him. "Probably you were dreaming. Come on," I patted the rug, "lie down."

The dog refused. His growls grew nastier and along his spine the hair rose. I stopped cajoling him and strained my human ear to catch what came so clearly to his canine one. I could hear only the silence of the empty house around me broken by the crackles of the log in the fire and the dog's growls. Then into that silence pealed a single, long ring from the front door. It was so loud I jumped and Rookey shot from the room barking wildly. My heart started pumping faster and I sat quite still in the chair. No-one was expected and if there had been they would have used the back door. So – who? Obviously it was someone unfamiliar with Hunters. It was not a friend, which left . . . The bell rang again.

I rose and went into the hall. Rookey was snuffling loudly against the crack of the door trying to decide if he knew who it was. He barked once, stumpy tail stiff and straight. Definitely a stranger. Walking closer to the door, I said, fatuously, to the inert oak panels. "What do you want?"

A muffled reply came back. "I would like to speak with Miss Albertine Hunter."

It was a man's voice but definitely not one of the Snodgrass brigade. The tone was far more cultured. Not without trepidation, I began to draw back the heavy bolts. Turton need not have worried, the bolts were in place all the time and were stiff with disuse.

I opened the door all of four inches and peeped round into the dark night. "Who are you?"

In anticipation of being asked, the man slipped me a business card. "Sorry if I startled you," he said.

I looked at the card and one word stood out from all the others. Vardy. With a gasp I swung wide the oak door and faced him. But as the hall light spilled out in an illuminating glow, I could see it certainly wasn't Lord Vardy on the doorstep. I looked at him. "You're not Lord Vardy."

"No," he agreed staring back at me. And suddenly it didn't matter who he was. This was the man I had subconsciously waited for. He knew it, so did I, but neither spoke. We just stood on the threshold whilst Rookey sniffed around his shoes and our eyes said everything that on first meeting couldn't possibly be said in words. It was a fugue in time. Whatever romantic novels said of love at first sight, they hadn't described it by a syllable. they had not, could not, begin to capture this . . . essence. And it was simply just that – essence.

"Knock, and the door will open," he murmured.

There was only one response, I made it. "Seek and ye shall find."

But the words were superfluous. We didn't need them. There was a fourth dimension quality about it, we had evolved down the centuries for this moment, a moment that I knew with utter conviction would never happen again in my lifetime. I put out my hand, took his and drew him over the doorstep into the house.

"Now I know what I was born for." He said softly.

We walked slowly to the lounge and sat down beside the fire.

"I cannot describe what is happening to me," he said still holding on tightly to my hand, "you feel it too, don't you?"

I nodded without a word.

"So, this is what they call, falling in love. I feel I'm falling down a well and there's no bottom to it. How is it for you?"

"I don't know," I said, "I feel as if my soul has stepped out from my body and merged with yours."

We sat silently together for several minutes, each of us waiting for our feet to touch ground again yet somehow wishing they never would and we could experience this exquisiteness forever–created solely for each other. No other person existed on this earth.

The curse of mankind chose the unique moment to come to life. The telephone rang.

The magical bubble surrounding us splintered and was lost to reality.

I went to answer the infernal invention.

"You all right Tal?" Turton was on the other end.

"Fine, yes . . . I'm fine."

"Just thought I'd make sure you haven't had an unwelcome visitor."

"No, no, I haven't."

"Your voice sounds a bit strange. You sure you're O.K.?"

"Perfectly. I've never felt more completely well and alive in my life."

"Take care then gel, and if you want me, you know where I am."

"Thanks Turton." A thought occurred. "What you said to me a little while back, it's actually happened."

'What was that?" the puzzlement in his voice came down the wires.

"Love knocked on the door." I put down the 'phone.

In the lounge, he was standing with his hands on the mantlepiece staring down into the flames. He looked up as I came in.

"My head lad . . . just checking if everything is . . . O.K."

"Everything O.K.?" he rolled the words round in his mouth, "not normal, but yes . . . everything very much O.K." We smiled at each other. "Never moreso is how I'd describe it." He hesitated. "Not that it matters in any way but, you are Albertine Hunter?"

"Oh absolutely." We both laughed. "And yourself? You're far too young to be Lord Vardy. You had me worried for a moment, I must admit when I thought you were."

"Why, would it have troubled you?"

"He's the last person I want to see. There's something I'm keeping very squat about."

"Pardon?"

"Quiet about."

"And is it important, this 'something'?"

'Definitely. If it wasn't important it wouldn't matter."

"Can I ask what?"

"You promise not to breathe a word to his Lordship?"

The man hesitated a second. "You're not planning his assassination or anything?"

"Good grief! Of course not. What do you take me for?"

He smiled. "Better or worse . . . and . . . I promise I won't say a word to Lord Vardy."

"I'm not sure whether I've just been proposed to or not." I said, taken aback by his words.

"The formal one comes later." He put in swiftly. "Now, tell me what is this secret that cannot be revealed?"

I gathered myself with an effort. "His horse, Bright Boy. We have him in our yard. Tomorrow we'll be running him and Lord Vardy has stated he wishes him to be ridden by a man."

"Well he would, wouldn't he." The man threw back his head and roared with laughter, a resounding happy sound that sprang back from the wooden beams and seemed to kindle a special warmth in the room not attributable to the fire. "He could hardly be ridden by anything else could he?" He struggled to control his laughter. "What a girl! Tell me, who is riding him?"

"I am."

His laughter dissolved like a snowflake on one of the hot logs.

"What, a girl?" His incredulity was obvious.

I looked at him levelly. "If you visit the race course tomorrow, you'll see me win."

"I've not given it much thought, I suppose, of course there are ladies races. But this is a man's race, a big one."

"Sorry," I shook my head, "the rules do not say 'girls prohibited'."

"Even so, the top jockeys are riding. Your father should have been riding. By the way, I'm sorry to hear of his accident."

"Thanks, yes, he should have been in the saddle but since he can't be . . ."

"In effect then, what you're saying is, you're taking his place?"

"Not entirely. Nobody can take his place. He was a brilliant jockey."

"But you are riding Bright Boy?"

"Yes."

"Well I'm damned!"

"You needn't look so sand-bagged. I'm quite a capable jockey."

He raised both eyebrows. "I'm sure you are, the point is, does Lord Vardy think so?"

I grinned. "He'll run me out the county if he knows."

"Ooooh." He said it gustily, blowing the vowels between his lips. There was a depth of meaning wrapped up in the word.

"O.K. say whatever it is you're thinking. Something's obviously on your mind."

He stared at me. "I'm just wondering . . . did I ought to tell him?"

"What!"

"Is it fair not to tell him?"

"Is it fair to break a promise? You did promise!"

"Hmm . . . yes, I forgot that, I did promise didn't I."

"You certainly did. I wouldn't have told you otherwise."

We stood and stared at each other. "So?" I challenged.

He smiled wryly, "My word . . . and all that. Of course I can't tell him."

I gave a great sigh of relief. "Boy! You had me worried. Hey, wait though, just why should you be interested in letting him know? You're not his fully paid up spy or something are you?"

He looked embarrassed and turned away from me, pushing a log further into the flames with the toe of his expensive tan shoe. He said in a muffled voice. "Or something."

I reached out and caught his arm, turning him to face

159

me. "Give." It came out in a tone that I used with Rookey when he'd picked up something harmful. He looked me squarely in the eye and I felt a tremor of apprehension.

"We've had our few minutes 'beyond the pale'. Nothing can alter that. It's stamped in the history books of our mind. Irreversibly. What I say to you now might change how you feel. And I don't want it to. You're the girl I've been searching for to share my life. To find you and lose you almost in the space of a heartbeat would be devastating."

I began to tremble. "Tell me who you are."

"I feel like the hangman releasing the trapdoor but I'm also the man with the noose around his neck."

"Please . . . I'd rather know." My mouth was so dry the words came out a whisper.

"Until this moment, I've always been proud of who I am. Right now, to be someone else . . ." the words tailed off. He hesitated, then added flatly, " . . . but I'm not. You're asking who I am, I'll tell you . . . I am Adrian Vardy, Lord Vardy's son.

Chapter Fifteen

I SLEPT very little that night and rose early next morning heavy-headed and emotionally drained. It took me ages to get beyond first gear and then only after three cups of coffee. Food I didn't want to know. The previous evening could have happened in another world so far away did it seem and when I thought back it appeared dream-like.

Turton was waiting for me down in the stables. He scanned my face anxiously. "You don't look too hot gel."

"Maybe that's because I don't feel it."

"I thought you were bedding down early last night so's to be fresh this morning."

"Life seldom does what you plan."

"Yeah, but it's a big one today. I should have thought . . ." he shrugged his shoulders and huffed away to himself, obviously disappointed in me.

"Please Turton, no recriminations. Last night was . . . was a crossroads in my life. When I decide which road I'm on, well, I'll forge along."

He wasn't impressed. "Just forge along the race course this afternoon and it'll do me. Everything's balancing on it y'know."

"I haven't forgotten. Stop sweating up about it Turton. I'll be right on the button when the tape goes up. I just need this morning to put the pieces together."

"If you hadn't had a bloke round last night, you wouldn't be in pieces now," he growled, very put out.

"I didn't invite him. He just turned up on my doorstep."

Turton went red. "You could have told him goodbye. Didn't think you were like that . . ."

"And I'm not. As you very well know. As to telling him goodbye . . . you can't say a thing like that to Lord Vardy's son."

"What!" The pitchfork Turton was holding clattered to the concrete and he went rapidly from red to white as the blood drained from his face. "Who did you say?"

"Adrian Vardy, Lord Vardy's son."

"Oh my Gawd! We're for it now all right. He'll have those horses out of here so fast all you'll see is the dust from the horse box." He leaned against the nearest stable wall and yanked off his old cap and scratched his head furiously. "What's to do now?"

"He's not telling Lord Vardy. I made him promise he wouldn't."

Hope flickered on Turton's face. "D'you think he'll keep to it?"

"I know he will. He's a man of honour. Mind you, if he hadn't given his word first, it might have been a different tale."

"But what about afterwards?"

"Won't matter will it, not after I've won."

"You're playing poker all right gel, is all I can say." Turton broke the stable rule and fished into his pocket and lit up a menthol cigarette. I didn't say anything but watched as he drew in a large lungful. "I'm getting a bit long in the tooth for all these shocks," he said, by way of apology. I was concerned to see that his hand did have a slight shake to it.

"Father will be home soon then he'll take back the responsibility." I reassured him.

'Aye," he brightened up, "he'll not be long afore he's home." The thought seemed to strengthen him and he flung the cigarette to the floor and ground it under his Derri boot. "Better make a start gel, don't want to be running late."

The morning routine slipped past and I rode out Calypso Lad. He was coming along marvellously. His injury now completely healed, he galloped as strongly and fluidly as ever. I pulled up feeling a trickle of sweat run down between my shoulder blades despite the rawness of the morning. "You'll do," I said patting his neck firmly. "Next race–Nottingham." The big animal flexed his neck several times, making spittle fly. Obviously he'd enjoyed the gallop. So had I. Last night was last night but now it was back to business. My pieces were rapidly putting themselves back together. We hacked back sedately and I jumped down in the yard. "He's terrific, Turton. Going like a rocket."

"Aye. Reckon the race at Nottingham is a fair gamble for him."

"You bet it is. We'll be there old chap won't we?" I pulled his left ear and he blew out his nostrils and shook his head jangling the bit.

"Best get the show on the road then." Turton took Calypso's bridle. "You slip off and get showered if you want. I'll see to him."

"Thanks, I'll only be a half-hour."

I jog-trotted back to the house and bumped into David who was making himself a coffee in the kitchen. "Fancy one Tal?" he waved a mug in front of me.

"Not just now David thanks. I'm going up to change."

He reached out a hand and plucked a wisp of hay from my hair. "You'll have a great day Tally. I'm sure of it. He bent and kissed my cheek affectionately. "You'll come home covered in glory."

"Covered in mud more like," I laughed. "Not so sure about the glory."

I took the stairs two at a time and splashed and paddled happily under the shower for ten minutes. When I came back downstairs, David had a piping hot drink all fixed for me. "You're an angel, thanks very much," I said taking it from him. "Will you be here when I get back?"

"No afraid not. We're going to see a film tonight. Early sitting."

"Something interesting?"

"A Walt Disney. The 101. Timothy missed it last time it was on. I promised I'd take him if it came round again. In fact he's putting on the squeeze for me to buy him a dog of his own."

"Every boy should have one."

"Yes, I think the responsibility would be good for him. Not to mention the pleasure."

"Well, I'll see you tomorrow then." I said slipping on my racing ring and grabbing my coat. "Visiting father tonight by the way, I'll give him your love."

A rather strained look came over David's face but he said quickly enough. "Do that. I'll be over to see him myself first chance."

"Right, bye now."

"All the luck in the world, Tally Ho."

There was a fair turn out of boxes already parked when we reached Warwick race course. Many of them I recognised but the distinctive blue and red of Brice's was missing from the scene. For a glorious few moments I allowed myself to wonder if they might have scratched Hot Chocolate. Unhappily it was only a few moments. Checking my parking in the rear mirror revealed the unmistakeable horse box turning in at the entrance. Hot Chocolate was going to be the biggest danger and I wasn't going to make the mistake of underestimating him. With arguably the best pilot on board in Paul Reynolds, he commanded fullest respect. Paul hadn't travelled with the horse box but I didn't need to see him to know his confidence would be oozing out of his ears. The mental blue-print of how I'd planned out the race came into my mind and immediately raised the slight sag of spirits seeing the box had engendered. Nothing was going to go wrong. Bright Boy was well able to take on the others and whilst not under-estimating Hot Chocolate I didn't intend to be over-awed by him either. It was going to be a close run race whichever way you looked at it.

By the time I made the weighing room, Paul was already there chatting to the other jockeys. A couple of young ones treated him with unmistakeable deference but to give Paul his due, he appeared unaware of it.

In a break in conversation I moved up to him. "Hello Paul."

He looked at me in a cold, detached manner and gave the briefest of nods.

Stupidly I said, "How's your mother?" It was meant as a genuine inquiry but wasn't received as such. Pure hatred flashed across Paul's handsome face. I realised he thought I'd asked about her on purpose to take his mind from the race.

"She can do without you asking – and so can I." He said in a low, steely voice so that only I could hear him. "I'm taking this race so you might as well withdraw."

"No chance." I replied stung by his words. "If you want it – tough! All you'll be seeing is Bright Boy's plates."

He sniffed contemptuously. "Go home and play with your dollies. Leave the racing to men." His voice had risen a few octaves and one or two other jockeys, hearing the animosity, looked questioningly at us. A full scale shouting match was not my idea of a pre-race starter and I abruptly left him. Getting angry was not worth what it would do to my chances of winning. All the energy dissipated in having a row would be better used in urging Bright Boy home. I was annoyed at myself for being so tactless. It was undoubtedly my asking about his mother that had upset him, but the damage was done. It was going to add an even keener edge to the race now with no quarter being given. I weighed out and waited for the bell. On cue when it rang, I streamed out with the other jockeys to the parade ring. Bright Boy looked great. His ears were forward and questioning and his whole manner alert and ready. He stamped a white-marked hind leg and swished his tail forcibly. I could tell he wanted to get out on the turf and go. A corresponding thrill of excitement ran through me.

"You ready gel?" Turton legged me up and the

horse, feeling my weight, pranced with impatience to be off. "Do your best for Jack eh?" Turton looked anxiously up at me. I bent forward.

"This one's for him."

It was all I had time to say for the other horses were being paraded. We fell into stride behind them and I was looking down onto a wide border of heads and hats. I stared straight between the horse's ears and saw the race course as I'd planned it. All I required now was that certain little bit of luck, the unknown factor, which could clinch it or send the whole thing out of the window. I raised my hand to my mouth and passed my lips over the black ring. "This one for father," I whispered and then added entreatingly, "please!"

Bright Boy quickened, we were moving through onto the course. Dropping my hands we cantered away down the turf. I used the rails as a guide and turned his head as I felt the power leap up in him. To be run away with at the start was not part of the blue-print.

We circled around behind the tape and I picked out my place. Third in, front line. Bright Boy was a front runner who took a breather and then came back on the bridle over the last four furlongs. I just needed to keep that little bit in the tank for the last half furlong.

The starter was bawling for us to cut the noise and get into line.

I reached up and pulled down the goggles, squeezing the horse's responsive body as near the line as possible. I didn't intend to lose even an inch at the start if I could help it. That inch would make or break in a 'photo-finish. The tape flew high and we were away, pounding down to the first with the field sorting itself out as jockeys carried out trainers' instructions.

I let Bright Boy have a run right to the first, steadied him for take-off and let him run again. We were in front as I'd planned we would be. We raced on over two, three and four. He was practically swimming over the jumps without a break in his rhythm. Although we were out in front of the rest of the field, it was the horse in front at the winning post that mattered. Eight out, I could feel the check in him and knew this was the time to ease him up. We bowled along steadily and five more horses came from behind and went on. One of them was Hot Chocolate and Paul. He was giving all his concentration to his riding and didn't give us a glance. But I knew he was aware of us from a sudden, wolfish grin that split his face as Hot Chocolate's hooves thundered by, stretching leg muscles eating turf and thrusting them a length in front. Bright Boy cruised on. Seven horses were now in front of us. There was a faller at the next who interfered with two others. Right then I asked for more from the horse and got it. He nipped over the jump, pulling right to avoid the tangle of flailing hooves and rolling jockeys and moved up to fourth place. Three and a half furlongs to go now and the crowd on the stands roared encouragement and a weak sun caught and winked on binocular lenses. Bright Boy was making ground now as I knew he would. Being work jockey as well as racing him, I was accustomed to his pace and style of racing. We jumped the last and made up ground on the third horse. Less than two furlongs to go, I pressed the button and Bright Boy responded magnificently. We were gaining on the second horse with every stride and I could see it's tongue lolling tiredly from the side of it's mouth. I urged Bright Boy on using hands and heels only still. We came upsides of the tiring animal and for a second were racing neck and neck. But with some petrol still left in the tank, we went into second place-behind Hot Chocolate. Half a furlong left now. Paul's head swivelled sideways to see where the danger was. I could tell by the way he snatched it back again and worked on the horse he hadn't expected to see me. Doubtless having passed me way back down the course, he'd mentally written me off at that point. Well he was about due for another shock. All I needed from my horse was just one more effort.

I pulled the whip out and gave him a back hander then carried on waving it alongside to urge him to the maximum. He came on like a rocket disliking to see another horse in front of him, just as he did on the gallops at home.

We levelled with Paul. The wolfish grin had turned into a fiendish grimace that drew his lips back showing white teeth tightly clenched. He was using the whip excessively now, desperately trying to hold off Bright Boy's challenge. but with the crowd screaming hysterically and only a few yards to go, I knew I was going to take the race and so did he. He whipped Hot Chocolate unmercifully now, savagely determined to keep trying but Bright Boy was a short head in front, half a length in front and the post came up fast and flashed by. We'd made it!.

I raised a clenched fist in the air and punched towards the sky. Exhilaration ripped through me and I screamed inside, "All for you father!" Bending forwards, I patted the hot, damp neck under me. "Well done lad, you're a cracker." His ear twitched backwards as he slowed to a canter. He knew he'd won and was well pleased with himself.

As we cantered back, I shot a look at Hot Chocolate. He was streaked dark with sweat. Paul would be in trouble. The stewards would be down on him immediately for excessive use of the whip. Uncharitably I thought, serve him right. But then I thought of the animal and decided it wasn't uncharitable but merely justice. To abuse a horse in that way deserved the recriminations.

I dismissed Paul from my thoughts as Turton appeared at my side and took hold of Bright Boy. "You show'd 'em gel!" he said with great glee. "What a race. Your dad would have been that proud to have seen you."

"It's surely going to please him," I said and ruffled the hair on top of his head affectionately. "Hey, where's your old cap then?"

He chuckled. "Guess I got a bit carried away and threw it in the air. It's somewhere on the lads' stand. I'll get it later."

He walked us proudly to the winners' enclosure and I

dropped the reins over Bright Boy's head. Just as I was about to dismount a man strode up.

"Very well done Albertine. A superb race." He slapped the horse's neck. "The first time I've seen one of our horses actually win on a course."

Turton's face was screwed up with puzzlement. With legs suddenly weak which wasn't anything to do with riding reaction, I jumped down. "Thank you Adrian." I introduced them. "Turton, this is Adrian, Lord Vardy's son. You know, I mentioned him this morning.?"

"Oh, ah," Turton chewed the inside of his lip and looked embarrassed. He shot out a hand, "Very pleased to meet you, sir."

Adrian shook his hand. "No need for the sirs, Turton. I don't like ceremony."

"Very good sir, er, Mr. Vardy."

Adrian turned to me as I unsaddled. "Need any assistance?"

"No thanks. Must go and weigh-in."

He nodded. "I'll still be here."

"Were you here all afternoon, keeping squat?"

"You could say that," he chuckled, "just didn't want to throw you before the race."

"Thanks. It would have done if I'd known you were watching."

"Am I that much of an ogre?" He raised his eyebrows.

"You're a . . ."

"Yes?"

"A Vardy." I pulled the girth over the saddle and walked to the weighing room. I didn't have to consider what would have happened if I'd lost the race. Without doubt Adrian would have to report back to his father. I sat on the scales and was passed as correct, the race officially mine. Up and down the country now blue "Weighed-in" stickers would be smacked on Betting Shop lists.

Paul was slumped dejectedly on a bench moodily

tapping his whip against his boot. I passed him but he didn't look up.

The picture of him stayed in my mind as I changed out of Lord Vardy's colours. Something in my brain niggled away like a maggot in an over-ripe apple. The sight of him today reminded me of the time I'd seen him dressed in the same lemon coloured silks on the day of father's accident. In my mind I could still picture him in detail as he rode back to the winners' enclosure on Black Monarch. I'd run up to catch him before the owner. Paul had told me father had fallen at the third last. What else? I let the maggot niggle a little more. There had been something. At the time, I'd felt I'd unconsciously registered some fact that refused to be recalled. Absently I buttoned on my jacket, fingers working automatically. My brain, put into reverse gear, suddenly clicked and tossed me a golden nugget of information. My fingers froze on the buttons. No! It couldn't be! It was too late now, there was no evidence to back it up. But my brain stubbornly refused to withdraw it. I had had the blinkers pulled away and my narrow field of vision was abruptly widened.

As I carried on getting dressed, my fingers felt like a bunch of carrots.

Chapter Sixteen

ADRIAN'S Mercedes followed the horse box all the way back to Hunters. It was a long drive but strangely I didn't feel tired. The elation of winning had increased my flow of energy and I was still surfing along on the wave of it. What I had remembered in the weighing-room was a piece of jig-saw. It was a significant piece which linked with others and made sense of at least part of the picture. There was a sense of the inevitability of the entire picture revealing itself to me and I was content to push it from my mind right now and enjoy the present. I felt a delightful sense of anticipation at the thought of Adrian's company. He'd wanted to come home with us so that he could have the chance of meeting father later.

Turton stirred in his seat beside me. "You could do a lot worse."

I shot a glance at him. He was nodding slowly, "Yep, a lot worse."

"What are you on about?"

He jerked his head backward. "Young Vardy. Reckon he's all right."

I smothered a bubble of laughter that threatened to escape. "Glad you approve."

"Aye and I bet Jack will an' all."

I concentrated on the road but his words kept repeating themselves in my brain. Father had to like him. I realised just how important it was to me that he did like Adrian. Up until last night father had been the most important man in my life and now, quite suddenly, he wasn't. It was a sobering thought. Would he feel jealous? Fathers were supposed to. After all, he'd had me to rear on his own. He was bound to feel displaced from the central point of my life. He'd never shown any signs of jealousy over David's attentions. But father was shrewd, knowing me better than I did myself, he'd realised David was no threat.

"Got champagne in the cupboard Tal?"

"Hmmm . . .?"

"Well I know I haven't and a bit of a celebration's called for."

"Yes, we should have some."

"Reckon Mr. Vardy's probably used to it. 'Course a drop of beer's more to my taste."

"You can have exactly what you want Turton. We're not just celebrating my win, after all, what we're celebrating is a reprieve for Hunters."

We exchanged wide grins.

"You reckon we could slip a drop into Hospital? Jack must be getting a mite dry after all this time."

"You're a terrible man Turton. You make father sound like an alcoholic."

"One thing's sure, he ain't got to watch his weight anymore. Betcha your drinks bill will go up a bit now."

"How do you like to walk home?"

He guffawed.

The champagne waited: the fire didn't.

We could see it from the main road. It lit up the dark evening sky like a red sun. My strangled shriek of "Look!" died in my throat.

"Bloody hell!" Turton exploded, pounding clenched fists up and down on his knees in a frenzy.

I couldn't make a sound. Fear steel banded my throat and I prayed desperately inside. The horses, dear God, the horses, if we can only be in time to save them.

The mercedes gave a loud blast of horn and leapt past in a flash. The box lurched wildly as I stamped the accelerator and took off after him. By the time we'd made Hunters drive, our swathing headlights showed the silver and red barrier of a fire engine parked in front of the house itself. We left the box in safety where it was and raced to the stables on foot. An efficient team of helmetted fire-men were winning the battle to save the end stable from igniting the rest. The fire was spreading in the other direction through the crackling branches of an old overhanging tree.

"The horses, what about the horses," I bawled to the nearest figure.

"Don't worry Miss, they're all O.K." he reassured revealing white teeth in a blackened face. "The lad kept his head. He'd got the nearest three out before we arrived."

Jimmy came up. "It'd started Miss when I got here."

"What time was that Jimmy?"

"'Bout half-past four Miss."

"Carry on."

"I didn't ring for the fire-engine," he said licking his lips nervously and rubbing his palms down his jacket. "I just thought, get the horses out . . ."

"Don't sweat Jimmy, you've done well. Just tell me."

"They were spooky but I shoved a saddle rug over their heads and took them into the paddock."

"Well done, lad." Turton clappd a hand on Jimmy's shoulder.

"I was just leading out Larioka when the firemen came racing down."

"So you didn't actually get to ring up?"

"No Miss."

"I wonder who did? Still, doesn't matter, they're here now. It doesn't look too bad."

The end stable was a write-off, the roof had caved in as flames had engulfed the joists but it was separate from the continuous run of stables and the firemen had soaked the nearest box, which whilst considerably smoke blackened was unharmd and no flames had spread. Fortunately, the stiff breeze was blowing away and towards the tree lined drive. The fire fighters were aware of this and had now turned a hose on the burning tree. Unchecked it could conceivably have run riot down the line of trees as many of them had interlocking

173

bare branches, black skeletons in the approaching winter. The house itself was in no danger at all.

Turton, who had hared off to the paddock, came dashing back to report. "All O.K. Tal. Jumpy as salmon but otherwise fine."

"Thank heavens for that," I said with heartfelt relief.

"What I'd like to know," Turton bristled, "is how the bugger started?"

The head fire officer came up. "Not too bad Miss, just the one building gone. The rest is perfectly safe and no danger to persons or lifestock."

"Thank God for that!"

"Dead right!" Turton agreed looking shocked.

"Yes, indeed," the fire officer said. "Could have been a lot nastier, if the wind had been in the other direction . . ." He didn't need to finish, it was all too clear what the outcome would have been.

"You've done a great job. I'll get some trays of tea set up."

"That'd be much appreciated by the chaps thank you."

"Any ideas how it started officer?" I queried.

"A difficult one that. I'm not happy about how the tree took hold so fast."

"Well, it is bare, no juicy leaves to make it smoulder."

"Yes, Miss, but just 'cos it looks dry and ideal for catching fire doesn't mean the branches aren't still holding sap. No, it went to fast straight away for my liking."

"What are you getting at?"

Before he could reply, Adrian came up. "Ha, Albertine, there you are." He still looked surprisingly immaculate apart from his wet brogues and dirtied hands. As he spoke he brushed his palms together." Just beeen shifting saddles down to the end stable in case this next one caught fire but it seems to have escaped, thank heavens."

"Thanks a lot Adrian."

He smiled briefly, "Nasty business fire, especially if it

174

had took hold of this run of buildings. Thankfully, the wind is blowing towards the trees."

"Exactly what I was thinking sir." The fireman was standing very four square with lips pursed.

"What do you mean officer?" Adrian cocked an eyebrow at him.

"Too soon to say sir what caused it but it looks very much as if someone started it deliberately, knowing the way it would go – away from the main line and out to the trees."

"Arson?" I said incredulously.

"Could be Miss. I'm not saying it was, I'm not saying it wasn't."

"Look here," Adrian chipped in, "if it was arson surely they would have started it off in the fodder store. That's attached to the main run."

"Exactly sir, but it wasn't started there. That is why it is perplexing. But I'd stake a quid or two that the tree which is burning was sloshed along the nearest branches with petrol. From the way it burned, it looks like it to me."

I felt my jaw drop. A deliberate attempt to trigger off a fire. One that wasn't meant to gut the place but solely act as a frightener.

Adrian looked grim faced. "Could it be Albertine?" There was a depth of hidden question contained in the four words. He hadn't said, are you being threatened, is someone out to scare you, is somebody putting a squeeze on, but they were all there in the one question. The fireman was watching me closely.

I lied through my teeth. "Of course not, what a strange thing to suggest. I'm sure it must have started accidentally. Possibly the tree had been dead at the end of those branches. It would have burned swiftly then."

"Ye..es," the fireman grudgingly admitted it was a possibility. Still the insurance assessors will doubtless tell you what they think caused it."

"Who called you out officer?" Adrian asked.

"Couldn't rightly say sir. Message timed at 4.18p.m. but no name given."

175

"I see. The fact is, I telephoned from my car as soon as I saw the fire from the main road but of course you chaps had already arrived and it was under control."

"Quick thinking Adrian." I was impressed.

"We'd sooner get several calls reporting the same fire than everybody leaving it to someone else. I've attended fires that have completely destroyed property and found that people round about assumed someone else had already reported it so they didn't."

"Did you have more than one call? Apart from my own of course." Adrian quizzed.

"Just the one, sir."

At that moment a very scared Freda came dashing into the yard. "Oooh Tal! What's happened. Is anybody hurt?"

"Everything's under control Freda," I soothed her down. "Fortunately nobody's hurt. The horses are O.K. Just one stable damaged and that can be repaired."

"What a relief! Couldn't believe my eyes when I came up on my bike and saw the fire-engine stuck outside the house."

"You didn't 'phone the Fire Brigade then obviously," I said.

"Me? No."

"It's a mystery who called them out."

"More a mystery who started it I'd say." Freda narrowed her eyes. "You're sure it wasn't Jimmy?"

"Gracious no. Jimmy's quick acting may well have saved the horses. Why do you say that?"

"He smokes as shouldn't in the stables." she said darkly. "I'm not telling tales but it's not safe. Proves it doesn't it?" She flung an arm out towards the damage.

"But it wasn't Jimmy, it couldn't have been. He didn't get here until 4.30p.m. and the fire was reported at 4.18p.m." I said.

The last flames had flickered and gone out leaving a black sky above.

"I'll just check everything's safe then Miss." The firemen lifted his right index finger in semi-salute and strode off.

"Perhaps you could rustle up mugs of tea for the men Freda please."

"Oh yes, sure. I'll put the kettle on straight away." She scampered off.

"The whole thing's extremely odd." Adrian cupped a palm round his chin and tapped his cheek thoughtfully. "If I had to give an opinion, I'd say this fire was started deliberately."

"If it had been surely it would have been the house."

"Not necessarily. Not if it was done simply to frighten you instead of cause too much damage. And there again, that seems to indicate an interest in the property." He swung round to face me. "Have you had an offer to buy Hunter's Stables?"

Put like that, there was no option but to admit it. "I suppose you could say I had, through an agent though. I don't know who the interested party is."

"I see, so it could be anybody – it could even be me."

I gasped at his words.

"Don't fret yourself, of course it wasn't but I'm just illustrating that because you don't know who it was, it could virtually be anybody."

"There's no possibility of Hunters being sold."

"When is your father due back from hospital?"

"A few days at most now."

"Good. You'll be much safer with a man around than living here by yourself."

"Woman's lib. would just love you."

His face remained hard and worried. "I'd move in myself, just until Mr. Hunter gets back but there's your reputation to be considered. Freda doesn't live in does she?"

"No."

"Thought not. Could she be persuaded to?"

"Dear Adrian, stop fussing. I shall be perfectly safe. You can be of use at the moment though."

"I can?"

"The horses need catching up if the fire's out. They certainly can't stay in the paddock all night."

His face was a picture. "I've never caught a horse before in my life."

"Well now's your chance."

An hour later, firemen gone and lifestock settled in, we sat down to welcome hot soup and salad.

"It's a lovely place you've got here Albertine."

"Do call me Tal. Everyone does. Yes, it's a super place. I can't imagine living anywhere else."

"Oh." He was silent whilst dipping his spoon in the minestrone. As he sipped, he said thoughtfully, "What about if you were to marry. You'd have to leave then."

"Since I'd only marry someone in the racing world, they could probably live here. I need to race you see."

"It means that much does it?"

"That much."

"What race are you in next?"

"A local one. Nottingham race course, in a few days time."

"What horse is it?"

"Your father's."

"Really!"

"Hmm . . .Calypso Lad."

"The one Mr. Hunter had his accident with. I see. Just how safe is the horse?"

"As safe as the next. Look Adrian, racing's a tough life. It's not a game and it's not all glamour. It's hard work and accepting falls and injuries. You can't escape them and if you can't accept them, will you find something else to do with your life."

"And you've never considered anything else?"

"No."

There was something of a constrained atmosphere between us. I broke into it. "Am I reading you right Adrian?"

"How do you mean?"

"I get the impression you're sounding me out as a prospective bride."

"Not just a bride, Tal. I wonder if it's fair on you for me to want you for my wife – because I do."

I dared not look at him. "One thing you can bet on with certainty, life is never fair."

"Would your answer be yes . . . or no?" He persisted.

I parried his question desperately. "It's hardly the time for a proposal, supping soup."

"Name the time, I'll do it properly, bended knee and all that."

"You're serious aren't you?"

"Of course."

I didn't know my hand was shaking until the soup spoon rattled in the bowl. "All my thoughts at the moment have to be with my father, until he comes home. I couldn't possibly see him in hospital and tell him I'd accepted a marriage proposal during the short time he's been away. It wouldn't be right."

Adrian's eyes twinkled. "That means you're going to say yes."

"No it doesn't," I floundered, "it means you can ask me when father comes home and I'll think about it."

"Sounds hopeful to me." Adrian helped himself to the salad. "Are we seeing Mr. Hunter tonight? It's later than we intended."

"Of course we're visiting tonight. Turton's coming round in . . ." I checked my watch, "about three-quarters of an hour. We're all going together to celebrate the success of his operation."

"But he'll still be bandaged."

"Doubter! He's going to be fine. The doctor said the operation went very smoothly and there was every reason to think it would be a success."

Adrian stopped twinkling, "Believe me, my love, I seriously wish the chap well and I'm sure he'll be fine. If he's like his daughter, he'll refuse to be anything he doesn't want to be."

We finished the meal in silence but this time it was a comfortable, old slipper silence that enclosed us both and fitted perfectly.

I was washed and changed before Turton showed up and the three of us climbed into Adrian's car.

"Hang on!" Turton scrambled out again. "The house keys, Tal."

I passed them over to him. "What have you forgotten?"

"Be back in a minute." He disappeared.

Adrian slipped an arm round my shoulders and drew me to him. I rested my head against the thick tweed of his car coat. It seemed very right. "He can take all night if he likes." Adrian whispered and tilted my head and kissed me very gently, little more than brushing my lips with his own but my heart responded joyously.

Turton reappeared. "Here we are. Damn nearly forgot." He pushed a bottle of whisky and a bottle of champagne into my hands.

"What about glasses, bet you didn't remember those?"

"Ha, you're wrong there Tal me duck. Here we go," He produced four whisky tumblers from the capacious pocket of his mac like a conjurer producing white rabbits.

"We all set now then?" Adrian started the engine.

"We surely are," I said hugging the bottles tightly whilst a surge of happiness flooded through me. "I can't wait to see father and tell him we won this afternoon's race. He'll be over the moon."

What I didn't say was I couldn't wait to introduce Adrian to father.

Chapter Seventeen

WHEN ADRIAN finally drove away from Hunters around midnight, it wasn't just father who was over the moon, I was as well. The visit to the hospital had been a great success. No-one had mentioned the fire. It was a unanimous verdict that nothing would be gained and the less father knew the less he would worry.

Father hit it off from the start with Adrian saying, "I like your handshake, firm, dependable. Nothing weak about it. What our Tal needs is a firm man, she's a bit headstrong you know. Could do with taming a bit."

I had blushed crimson but Adrian had quipped back that fillies needed to be spirited. The news of Bright Boy's win was like a tonic to father.

"Pity we can't celebrate properly. You didn't bring a bottle by any chance did you Turton?" he'd asked.

Turton had produced the bottle and poured the drinks with a wide grin. The quick, if sneaky, toast was to the future success of Hunters. I treasured father's last words as we were all leaving.

"I shan't be racing again. I accept that. Hunters has dropped into Tal's lap but there's not another jockey alive I'd rather have in charge. God bless you my sweetheart."

There had been a lump still in my throat as the car sped homewards.

I sat now in the kitchen with a hot drink and Rookey leaning companionably against my legs. Soon, very soon, now, father would be home for good. Once he was back I could give my full consideration to Adrian's proposal. I knew without any deliberation that I was in love with him but there was another love in my life that, in a different way, was equally as strong. The question I had to ask myself was could the two work successfully together or would one have to be sacrificed? There had been no sign of hostility whatever in father's manner and he seemed genuinely pleased at the possibility Adrian might end up in the role of son-in-law. I sighed contentedly. The biggest hurdle jumped successfully, the rest should surely fall into place. I went off in a delicious self-indulgent day-dream in which Adrian and I were married and living happily at Hunters with myself still following my career and riding winner after winner. I'd even got as far as one or two little Adrians running around the stable yard when there was a smack of the front door letter box falling smartly into place, Rookey shot to his feet and took off down the hall barking frenziedly. I froze in the chair, my day-dream light years away already. I looked at the clock, 12.30 a.m. Not a time for a postman to call. Rookey trotted back to the kitchen with a letter in his mouth. He stood expectantly in front of me, tail wagging.

"Good boy." I said automatically, "Give."

He let go reluctantly. Slitting the envelope I took out the single sheet of paper inside. It didn't take much reading. "Name your price – you have no choice. We could have started the fire from the other end. What price then for Hunters or the burning horseflesh?" I screwed the envelope up into a tight ball and flung it far from me.

Rookey was already tearing it to shreds as I lurched for the cloakroom to rid myself of the vomit rising in my throat.

I didn't bother going to bed. There was no point. Beds were primarily for sleeping in and it was more than odds-on, it was a walk-over that sleep and I wouldn't meet that night. I wasn't in a hurry to come face to face with the deliverer of the letter either and double checked all the windows and doors and closed all undrawn curtains. With the lounge fire stoked to fullest capacity and a brandy within easy reach I sat curled on the settee and wished Adrian's concern for my reputation wasn't so high and he could have spent the night with me. I longed to feel the comfort of his arms around me taking some of the burden of responsibility away. As it stood now, the lives of all our horses were in my hands. If I didn't comply they stood a fair chance of falling innocent victims to another mad arson attack. Without the protection of a 24 hour surveillance there was no way I could prevent another fire breaking out.

I shivered violently as in my frightened, distorted thoughts, I could actually hear the shrill screams of pain from tortured animals. At this point I grasped the brandy glass and downed the whole lot, spluttering and gasping as the amber fluid hit my throat. How long had I got? That was the question. A point of contact had to be arranged before any further fiendish vendetta was carried out. For all they knew, I was now a quivering jelly ready to give in. And I very nearly was. Fortunately, the brandy had a steadying effect and logic, commonsense, or desperation, whatever, started working. It seemed whoever was trying to get Hunters was doing so whilst father was still away. Would they give up trying when he came back? I just didn't know. One thing was sure. Once he was back, invalid or not, Jack Hunter wouldn't part with the stables. As long as the owners had confidence, nothing else mattered especially after one or two wins in succession. That line of reasoning brought me squarely to Nottingham races.

Father had hinted tonight he might be home on the 26th – the day of the races. The doctors wouldn't commit themselves but it was a distinct possibility if he continued his present speedy recovery. So now I had three days to sweat it out. And I was sweating. It wasn't just the heat from the fire it was the next thought that occurred to me. Whoever had delivered the missive must have been waiting close to the house. Waiting and watching for Adrian to leave so that I was alone when I read it and therefore the impact would be magnified. Possibly they had been hanging around since the fire, waiting until everybody had left. The more I thought about it the more certain I became that that is what had happened.

The next races to attend was the Nottingham fixture which meant during daylight hours at least the stables would be constantly manned. Which left the after dark hours. Short of employing a security firm, it meant Turton and Jimmy policing in alternative shifts, if of course they were willing, and one man on duty couldn't be expected to cover the house and grounds as well. He would have his hands full coping with just the stables. If he had also worked all day, as well, he wasn't going to be at his best.

Thoughts churned around in my brain burning up valuable mental energy until I heard the hall clock strike four. I stretched out on the settee, totally exhausted. Rookey had never had it so good. He'd been asleep for hours laid out with belly to the fire snoring blissfully. I closed my eyes briefly. It seemed like two seconds later he was whining to be let out. Wearily, I swung my legs off the settee and glanced at my watch. It was gone seven. The morning routine pointed an accusing finger at me. I should have been up an hour since.

Down in the yard Turton informed me Bright Boy had a strain in his nearside front fetlock.

"I've bandaged it up. There's a bit of heat and tenderness but it's not too bad. How's your hang-over?"

"Haven't got one."

"Give over," he chortled, "You walk in about in time for afternoon feeding, looking as though you haven't slept. Don't give me that." He carried on mixing feed still chortling. The elation of Bright Boy's win was obviously still in his system.

It hurt me to take away his happy mood but it had to be done. I pushed the sheet of paper under his nose.

"Eh? What's this?"

"Just read it."

His face paled. "It was for real then, yesterday." He looked up the other end of the yard where the ugly blackened stable stood silent testimony that we hadn't dreamed it. He tapped a forefinger against the paper. "Police. It's the first solid evidence we've had. They must be getting desperate to take chances writing a clear threat."

"If we go to the Police we shall have to tell them everything right back to father's accident. And what will they do? They can't manage to post a guard on us until father comes home."

"No . . . but they can give us a visit now and again."

"It won't do Turton." I told him how the man must have waited in hiding last night until Adrian left before putting the letter through the box.

"By Gawd, Tal. You're in serious danger. You can't stay up the house on your own. It isn't safe!"

"Not very," I admitted, "that's why I'm going to ask if you and Jimmy could split night watching for the next few nights until father gets home. I can't take chances with the horses."

"Bugger the horses! What about you?"

"Look, I'm O.K."

He did a big sniff of disagreement.

"Please Turton. What do you say to doing night patrolling? You can have time off in the morning for catching up on some sleep."

"If it's what you want Tal, o'course I'll do it. Jimmy will an' all. At his age, he'll think it's a lark. He'll be fancying himself as a T.V. cop."

I had to smile. "I guess he will. It's settled then. Starting tonight. Just the stables, mind. No slipping off to see if I'm all right. Is that clear?"

"Yes, yes," Turton said tetchily. "What you want to do gel, is get that bloke to stay with you."

"What bloke?" I deliberately put on an innocent look.

"Vardy. Who the devil else do you think I mean."

"Really Turton, my reputation will be ruined."

"Be buggered to your reputation. I'd sooner see you with a reputation in ruins than not see you at all. What good's an unblemished reputation if you're not alive to enjoy it?"

"They're not going to knock me off if there's any chance of my agreeing to sell are they?"

He grudgingly acknowledged the logic of it.

"Anyway, Adrian's gone abroad on business today. He told me last night before he left. Should be back sometime around the beginning of next week, most likely on Tuesday."

"Pity."

"Do give over. I'll be perfectly safe. It was the horses that were threatened, not me."

"All right then, I'll just concentrate on the horses safety. Reckon a four hours on, four off, should do it and I'll bed down in the hay bales on tap like."

"Good man, I knew I could rely on you."

For the next two days it worked like a charm. In the evenings I drove over to visit father and stable routine during the day with no race course visits meant that there was always someone around. The gap between morning and evening work didn't make a great deal of difference as Jimmy and Turton took turns cat-napping and keeping surveillance. During the afternoons when I returned to the house, David was usually around. He always parked his white Rover outside the back door which very nicely and conspicuously advertised his presence to the world.

The day after Bright Boy's win, David drew up at lunch time and emerged from the car almost invisible behind a gorgeous bouquet of autumn toned chrysanthemums.

"For me?" I said with delight.

"But of course. Congratulations on yesterday's win."

"Thanks David, what a lovely thought. Come along, you can give me a hand displaying them to their best advantage."

He helped by filling a big, stoneware jug and carrying it through to the hall table. All the while I arranged the magnificent blooms my conscience pricked harder and sharper than a needle. I had still not come clean with him about my decision not to marry. Not only had I intended to say marriage was out with him but with any other man. Now, to complicate matters, Adrian had arrived on the scene and it was a pretty good bet that when he asked me to marry him I'd say yes. I groaned inwardly. It would have been one thing to level with David on the subject of not marrying at all but to say there was another man . . . ouch! I tossed words around in my head whilst my hands manipulated the blooms in the jug. It didn't get me any nearer to saying the right thing but at least the arrangement was spot on. The big hall mirror on the wall behind the table picked up the image of the flowers and threw them back like a visual echo.

"They really do look grand." David stepped back admiringly.

"David . . . there's something you have to know . . ." I began screwing up courage.

"If you don't mind Tally ho, I'd rather say something to you first. Shall we go through to Jack's study and talk?"

I nodded reluctantly, feeling thwarted. He led me through and sat down in father's swivel chair and fiddled with a stray biro on the desk top.

"Spit it out David. You look like an employer whose about to tell me I'm fired."

"In a way, that's exactly what I am doing." he said it soberly.

"Say again?"

"Tally, for a long time now we've had an 'understanding'."

"David, I must . . . "

"Be quiet a moment. Just listen to me first. I've always known your first love was, is, racing. I accepted that even should we marry, racing would still claim the biggest part of you. I didn't let it worry me. For myself that small part was infinitely preferable to not having you at all."

I stared miserably at the floor. To hear him humbling himself like this and knowing how shallowly I'd valued his love was a chastening experience.

"But I'm not a free man who can indulge himself." David continued. "By marrying you I'd have a part-time wife but I'd also be giving Timothy a part-time mum. I'd thought by employing Mary as housekeeper, and Timothy really does think she's the cats whiskers, that it would solve my problem. It won't. If I have a small part of you and I'd like to think you care about

187

me a little, how much smaller would be the part left for another woman's son?"

I didn't say anything. There was nothing to say. It was all true and I couldn't defend myself against the truth.

"He's had one bad experience with his first mother. It would be incredibly selfish of me to offer him a part-time second mother. You do see Tally, don't you what I'm leading up to?"

"Our 'understanding' is off."

"Not only that," he wriggled self-consciously in the chair. "It's very hard to tell you but . . . I'm sorry, Tally . . . I'm going to marry Mary." He dropped his bombshell and it's only effect upon me was one of relief. Even as I felt the liberation of relief, self-dislike topped it. David must have agonised over his unselfish decision. I wasn't worth his love, never had been. The gentle love, almost adoration, he had shown me, I'd tossed back in his face.

"Say something to me Tally." He dropped the biro back on the desk top and clenched both hands together.

"Right now, I hate myself. It's all absolutely true what you've said. I can't deny a word of it."

He started up in his chair. "That's not what I want! I don't want you to feel guilty."

"I'm sorry, I'm sorry, you see, there I go again, being selfish, thinking how I feel." I grasped his hands. "David, truly I'm pleased for you. For you and Timothy. If you've chosen Mary, she must be the right one, for both of you. I do wish you all the best. Don't look back, go all out and marry her, have a happy life together."

He drew a shuddering breath and for a dreadful moment, I thought he was going to break down. He contained himself with great effort. "And that's it?"

"What else can I say? I give you both my blessing."

His shoulders dropped and he sank back in the chair. "You were going to say something to me in the hall. What was it?" His voice was stiff, businesslike.

I was nonplussed by his swift change of mood. "I, it's difficult . . . I don't know how to tell you."

"Unless you try I shan't find out what it is shall I?"

"A few days ago, I was sure of what to say."

"Tell me."

"Marriage was out, with you or anybody else. I wasn't ready for it: other things mattered more."

"Like racing." There was an edge to his voice.

"Yes. And a secret dream. A dream that one day I might actually ride in the Cheltenham Gold Cup or the National at Aintree and win."

"The moon's too high for you to catch hold of Tally, but that's what you're trying to do."

"Maybe. Who knows. A woman's got to win one day, it's the law of averages. It might as well be me as anyone else."

He shook his head in disbelief. "It will never happen."

"We'll see."

"So what else do you want to tell me?"

I cursed inwardly, it was harder trying to tell him than I'd imagined, much harder. Before I could begin he beat me to it.

"There's someone else, is that it? Someone you might even consider giving racing up for?"

"It's a blunt way of putting it."

"But true?"

"Ye . . . es."

"So. I'd already lost you." He passed a hand across his eyes.

"I'm very sorry David, it should have been said days ago."

He stood up. "Well, if you'll excuse me Tally, there are papers to fetch from the car. Work has to be done."

"Aren't you going to ask who the other man is, wish us well?"

He was round the desk so fast it took me by complete surprise.

"No." He said harshly, grabbing my shoulders and crushing me against him. "Does it matter? It's some other man, that's all, that's all!" He kissed me hard, possessively with a passion I would never have believed him capable of. It seemed to go on and on. "There!" he panted, releasing me at last. "I'll have one last kiss before he takes over."

"Please David, don't. Let me go. I've released you. Give me your blessing." I was so choked by unshed tears the words barely came out.

"I can't!" he shouted it at me.

"But why? I've no quarrel with Mary. I hope you'll both be happy," I could feel the tears now running down my face and was powerless to stop them.

"Because my darling," his voice dropped to a whisper and this time he drew me to him gently, and stroked my hair lovingly, "because you don't love me, there's no open wound to pour the iodine of jealousy into. It's easy for you to say it, so easy. But it's like a razor cutting through me. Oh yes, I'll be a good husband to Mary, she's a fine girl but you will always have me Tally, until the day I die. That's why it's so hard for me."

"Oh David," I could see the deep sadness in his face.

He put a hand under my chin, lifting my face to his and looking deeply into my eyes. "You see Tally," the words were said so softly, tenderly, "I love you. I shall *always* love you."

Chapter Eighteen

THE WEST WIND cut icily across the gallops sending the dark, cumulous clouds racing towards the east where a weak sun tried its best to give what warmth it had to the earth. It was persistent, I'll say that for it, disappearing behind clouds to re-emerge again as the shadows chased across its face, alternatively dappling the grass in greys and lemon, never giving up.

David had given up. I put a gloved hand to my face, brushed away a strand of hair and pushed it under my crash cap with one finger. Mustn't think about David, it was too painful. Must concentrate on controlling the firecracker under me. Calypso Lad was at peak condition and let me know it by doing several wicked bucks. I grabbed the neck strap. "No you don't Lad! You don't get rid of me that easy." Jimmy was having problems too and circling his horse. "Better let me go first," I called. "Follow Calypso down but don't get too close. We're not riding upsides this morning."

"Gotcha." He did another circle.

I released the brakes and Calypso took off, scorching down towards the thicket of trees at the far end. Familiar excitement thrilled through me at the speed he was producing. He had every chance at Nottingham on Saturday. It would be just what Hunters needed – two wins from two starts.

A cloud scudded past and the lemon sun shone through. Something in the trees caught it and flashed brightly. I registered what it was a second before a flying divott struck me stingingly in the eye. After that it was a case of riding part blind as the affected eye watered magnificently and vision was obliterated. But the divott didn't stop my brain from working. What I'd just glimpsed was sunlight catching binoculars. Someone was holed up in the trees watching. I pulled on the nearside rein, feet thrust forward to slow the horse down and cut the corner before we reached the thicket heading back the way we had come. I let Calypso have his head and he ate up distance. The glasses could belong to a snoop checking the horse's speed or they could belong to someone with a more sinister motive, maybe even possessing a shotgun. Somehow I didn't go for the snoop theory.

I pulled Calypso to a snorting, prancing halt at the far end. Despite being worried, part of me was elated to note he still had plenty left in the tank. Clawing off my glove, I dabbed the streaming eye.

Jimmy came pounding up. "Thought we were stopping at the trees."

"No brakes." It satisfied him. He probably hadn't noticed the flash from the binoculars.

It was the last ride out of the morning and I was smugly confident that nothing would be tried on until they could catch me on my own. Rain started spotting as we walked the horses back and before we reached the yard it was a deluge. I chuckled inwardly at the thought of the unknown lurker in the trees. He was more than likely still there waiting for the next non-existent ride out in case I was stupid enough to go alone. He'd be absolutely saturated.

Thursday and Friday passed uneventfully. I was humbly grateful for David's magnanimous attitude. He emphatically declared that although painful to him he would still be working for us until Jack could manage without him. I intended to level with father at the earliest opportunity to save him from further hurt. But in the meantime, I was very glad of the protection his presence afforded.

On Friday tea-time David was packing his brief-case into the car.

"Do come," I urged him, leaning on the door handle. "It's just a little celebration to welcome father home. Just a drink and a few nibbles."

"You're sure he's coming out tomorrow?"

"He's seeing the doctor later in the morning and he'll know for sure then."

"What I think would be best is if I give you a ring about 7.00–7.30 to find out."

"Fair enough. I'm keeping my fingers crossed. I'll be fetching him from the hospital in my car after the race."

"O.K." David started the engine. "Oh, and good luck to you as well Tally Ho. I hope you win on Calypso."

"You've a heart as big as a house."

He smiled ruefully and drove away. I watched the tail lights until the insistent ringing of the 'phone drew me indoors.

"Your meal's ready in twenty minutes," said Freda studying profoundly some delicacy she was stirring on the cooker. "If I leave this to answer the 'phone it will spoil so . . ."

"Don't worry. I'll get it." I dashed to the study. "Hello, Hunters."

There was a long moment of silence and then a voice that reminded me of a snake slithering along a rock said in a silky low whisper, "You did read the midnight message, didn't you?"

I did an involuntary intake of breath and dropped into the swivel chair which revolved half a turn and left me facing the window.

"Name the price. We don't wish to be unfair."

I clenched my hand hard round the white plastic. "What if I say, no sale?"

There was a dry little laugh on the other end. "Come now Miss Hunter. It is ours already; we're being generous paying you, but let's keep it strictly legal. Couldn't have you just giving it away could we?"

"I don't know what you're talking about." My hand felt slippery with cold sweat.

"Perhaps you don't, but Jack Hunter knows. Now, the price!"

"I can't give one . . . not instantly, just like that . . ."
I played for time trying to think of a way out.

"One more day. That's all the time you have."

"No! No, I can't. I'm racing tomorrow. You, you

won't be able to contact me. Sunday, make it Sunday."
I crossed my fingers in desperation. If I could stall them until then father should be back home.

A nerve-jangling silence stretched out for almost a minute before the voice said very softly, "Agreed. Sunday."

My heart jumped with premature relief.

"Just one more thing," again the dry laugh, totally mirthless, "the race tomorrow. You will lose it."

"I don't intend to . . . "

"Miss Hunter, you misunderstand," the voice chopped me off. "We're telling you. Lose it!"

"Not bad news about Mr. Hunter surely?" Freda looked at me with concern across the pan handle she was holding. "You're as white as chalk."

"I'm O.K." I struggled to stop my wobbly legs betraying me. "It wasn't about father. Just stable business."

"Hmm. You look a bit dicky to me."

"It's called hunger."

"Ha . . . " She perked up. "Won't be long now. Give you a bit of go this will."

"I'm saving all my go for tomorrow."

"Pooh! You'll do it easy. It'll be just what Mr. Hunter needs to hear. Another win for the yard."

"If I win," I murmured it half to myself, thinking about the last two words on the 'phone.

Freda pounced on me. "Thought you were always a positive thinker. What's happened? You go on at everybody else for their negative thinking and now you're doing it yourself. Shame on you!"

Despite myself, I grinned at her. "Quite right Freda. Next time I do it I give you full permission to bawl me out."

"Right, you're on!" She returned to her stirring on the stove with renewed vigour.

I left her to it and went upstairs for a quick shower. By the time the icy water had glugged it's way down the plug-hole and I'd scrubbed myself vigorously with the twisted towel, positivity had taken over again. Who the hell did snake-voice think he was? No-one told me to pull a race. A slow burning anger replaced the fear and suddenly I couldn't wait for 2.30 p.m. tomorrow to arrive. If I never won another race it wouldn't matter just as long as Calypso and I won this one. I smiled grimly into the bathroom mirror. If Freda was happily awaiting the chance of bawling me out, she'd have to wait a devil of a while.

Saturday morning was cold and foggy; not sufficient to stop racing but enough to be unpleasant and wetting. Visibility was not great but by the time I took Calypso for a short loosener, it had started to lift a little. There was no problem with the hidden lurker in the trees this time. I didn't expect to see anyone. They would 'phone tomorrow so why bother wasting man-power today?

After I'd seen Calypso fed and rugged up, Felton and I checked over the racing equipment needed and, accompanied by Jimmy, went in for breakfast.

"What time you ringing the hospital gel?"

"They said later in the morning."

"It is later."

"Perhaps by our time but I reckon they meant around ten or eleven."

Turton grunted in disgust. "I call that more like afternoon."

"You're an old grump, do you know," I laughed at him, "like a child wanting to unwrap a Christmas present. Talking of which, Christmas is only about two weeks now."

"Having Jack back is all the Christmas present I want," Turton retaliated.

"It's all any of us want."

"I'm hoping for a new radio," said Jimmy.

"You can always hope lad."

"Take no notice Jimmy."

I slid a piece of toast off my plate onto Turton's. "Can you manage this, I'm full."

"Reckon I could just about ram it down."

"Do that. I'll 'phone the hospital just in case."

It's not easy crossing the fingers on both hands when trying to hold a telephone but I tried.

"Mr. Hunter is being discharged today. He can be picked up later when you're ready."

If I'd been there, I'd have given Sister Mason a rapturous hug. As it was all I could do was transmit my joy to the lady.

"Thank you very much, thank you all. You've worked a miracle. We're greatly endebted to you. I'll pick him up after my race this afternoon, before 3.30 p.m."

I headed back to the kitchen. "Santa's arrived two weeks early!"

"Get away! D'you mean he's really out?"

"Will be when I pick him up."

"Great," mumbled Jimmy through a mouthful of toast.

"When you fetching him?" said Turton

"I'll take my car to the race course. I can drive up the hospital after the race. You'll have to drive the box back home with Calypso."

"Righto gel," he rubbed his hands together gleefully. "I've missed the old skunk y'know."

I grinned. "Father would be delighted to hear what you think of him."

"A lot gel, a bloody lot." He scraped his chair back. "C'mon young Jim lad, let's be having you."

Jimmy crammed another half slice of toast into his mouth and followed Turton out.

I brought myself down from an emotional high and checked over my personal items to take to the course. Finally I put the black cat ring in my bag. It might be an inanimate object but it had power psychologically. I didn't intend to race without it.

I'd mentally gone round the Nottingham course last night, seeing myself in the right spots during the race. Hot Chocolate was the only real danger and he was a predictable front runner. He would try and lead the field for the first two-thirds of the race, dying only to get a second wind. I had to make up ground at the time he fell back, if it was sufficient, Hot Chocolate would have too much to do to head the race in the home straight.

With three of the four parts working in union, physical, emotional and mental, I went to the study and prayed. Dropping on my knees on the carpet, I thanked God gratefully for father's recovery and hospital discharge. When I stood up a beautiful calm swept over me. A calm against which butterflies in the stomach couldn't compete.

The number one priority today was not the race, nor the winning, but father being restored to me and to Hunters.

The foggy weather hadn't dampened the enthusiasm of punters. Already there was a fair turn out of cars as I drove the Triumph along Colwick Road and swung into the race course car park. I picked a spot right at the top where I could drive away quickly after the race. It meant a longer walk from the weighing room afterwards but at least there was no chance of being boxed in by other vehicles. Father would be waiting to be collected and the sooner the better.

I checked with Turton and saw Calypso Lad safely boxed before heading for the weighing room. It was almost time for the earlier race and most of the jockeys were already there including Paul. I carried my gear across towards the girls' changing room as they were called to get ready. Unfortunately, just as the bell rang, Paul dashed past in a great hurry and collided with me on his way out.

"Watch out!" He spat the words at me.

I didn't bother to speak. The look on his face was sufficient. It hardly seemed credible he could be the same man who had so lovingly wiped a tear from my face in the tack room at Hunters. As all the jockeys streamed past me, I noticed a piece of paper lying open on the floor. Instinctively I picked it up. I didn't mean to read the contents but simply who it belonged to. However, it was impossible not to read the one sentence written in large spidery handwriting. 'Hurry up,' it said, 'finish the job. Your mother has slipped suddenly and is very much worse.' The letter belonged to Paul. I hastily slipped it across to the Clerk of the Scales.

"Found this on the floor, I think it's Reynold's."

Leaving my gear in the changing room on the same peg as the one I'd used last time I'd won and, no doubt, upholding the belief that jockeys are a pretty superstitious lot, I went into the toilet as the jockeys returned from the race. No wonder Paul's temper was so foul, he must be worried sick. The more I could keep out of his way the better. There was little time to spare between races and I was first out the weighing room door for the 2.30.

Calypso Lad was looking pretty good in the parade ring. He was all attention, dancing on his toes and Turton was soothing him with gentle strokes from poll to withers. He hoisted me up sharply and Calypso did a quick buck.

"The lad's full of it ain't he?" Turton said proudly.

"Just as well if you look at the opposition."

We both looked. Hot Chocolate was giving his lad a hard time. A coiled spring waiting to be released could best describe him. An unpleasant flutter of nerves in my stomach made me feel a bit sick. The horse was going to take some beating. Turton was looking up at my face and reading the apprehension which was surely written upon it in big letters.

"He'll burn out before the two furlong mark," said Turton.

I gave him a quick nod of appreciation. "Sure."

We went round twice but after the first circuit of the parade ring, the apprehension had disappeared. Calypso went superbly for my father, but the horse and I got on very well. I could tune in to his feelings and today he was full of confidence. My heart rose to be riding him.

The fog of early morning was coming down again in wraith like swirls and I was glad to be riding in one of the earlier races. It was quite possible later races might have to be abandoned.

The horses pulled off from the ring and out onto the course; Calypso and I were right with them. Predictably as the tape flew high, Hot Chocolate was first away from the pack. I let him go. Turton's words flashed through my thoughts. Whoever took the lead in the early part of the race, the horse going strongest in the last two furlongs would be the one. Calypso was a stayer and this race was two and a half miles. Plenty of time to wear the others down. I kept a steady pace and did just that. Two thirds round the course three horses were in front with another jockey and I joint fourth. It was still Hot Chocolate in the lead but I could see he was beginning to tire. At this point I needed to give Calypso the advantage of putting more ground between us to counteract his one pace at the end. He was a horse that didn't finish fast but with enough ground in hand, could hold off Hot Chocolate.

We approached the next fence in a bunch. Paul took it slightly ahead. I was now close enough to see the horse had misjudged his take-off. His nose went down fast as he scrambled over and Paul had no chance. He went out the side door. The four of us immediately behind cleared the fence and in the blur of hooves I could see the lemon and white colours balled-up and rolling. Saliva flooded from my mouth. It needed a miracle if none of those wickedly cutting hooves were to connect with him. But in a race it's the concentration of getting to the post ahead which counts. My job was to get Calypso's head past first. Already I knew first-aid officials would be running to assist Paul.

I cleared the picture of the balled silks from my mind and gave everything I'd got to winning.

The cheer that went up from the crowd was nothing to the cheer that rose up inside me as Calypso stretched for the line and we flashed over a good length and a half in front of the nearest horse. As we slowed to a canter, I flung an arm down and gave him a hard congratulatory pat. His ears twitched backwards. He knew he'd won and it gave him a kick too. I headed for the gate.

Turton gleefully reached for the reins. "Good 'un gel! Jack'll be sky-high. What a home-coming!" He led the way in triumph to the number one spot in the winners enclosure.

The crowd closed round us with a roar of sound. I grinned and raised a hand in salute. It raised another cheer and I slid from the horse feeling about nine feet tall. What a great present for father to return home to. Two wins from two starts. Marvellous. Turton was chirping away like a canary with a nest. I reached under the flaps and let down the girth.

"Leave Calypso with you. Get him boxed and back to Hunters and I'll see you later."

"You bet. All right if I pop up the house after feeding, 'bout 6.30 tonight. Can't wait to see Jack."

"Need you ask? He'll be dying to see you as well."

I left him and went to get weighed in. What made me glance to my right just before I went through the door I don't know, sixth sense maybe. A man was standing on the edge of the crowd at the corner of the first-aid room and looking straight at me. At that very moment I saw him, he looked to his left and gave an affirmative inclination of his head. I followed the direction and saw with a sickening jolt a big man with cap pulled low over his eyes. Snodgrass and the gorilla.

I scurried through the weighing room door as if it were the devil himself following. All exhilaration had drained and as I was O.K.'ed from the chair, I remembered the last two words over the 'phone. "Lose it." Snodgrass was the last person I'd expected to see at Nottingham. Complacently, I'd put him from my mind expecting a Sunday call when father had already come back home and I would no longer be on my vulnerable own. Stupid woman. My anger began to rise at my own naivety. My win today had been like putting a foot straight into a wasps nest. I leaned on my peg and thought desperately how to get out of the situation.

I knew they would be waiting for me leaving through the door of the weighing room. It could be there were more than just the two I'd seen: they'd simply be unknown faces in the crowd. For all I knew there might be a third waiting and watching Hunters horse box. Obviously no quick escape route in that direction. If I could leave the weighing room unnoticed there was a chance of picking up my car. It was parked at the entrance to the car park with luck I might do it. But not if I walked brazenly out through the usual door under the bell. So it had to be a window. One that I could leave by with no-one the wiser. One of the other jockeys called to the valet and enquired how Reynolds was. Despite my predicament, I listened to his reply. Taken to hospital, suspected concussion and a broken collar bone. Not crippling thank heavens but nasty enough. He was going to be feeling like nothing on earth when he came round. Could have told them his blood group if a transfusion had been needed. He didn't need this added burden just now on top of his mother's relapse. It would probably cost him the championship too.

I went through to the toilet, locked the door, sat down on the unopened toilet seat cover and buried my face in both hands. The black cat ring pressed against my cheek-bone. It had at least brought me the luck of a winner. My mind skipped irrationally to father's Buddha. Perhaps I should have worn that as well. Had it have been father, no doubt by now he'd have slipped the safety catch and taken out the old sepia photograph to acknowledge his win.

I leapt up as though I'd been shot. What a bloody stupid fool I'd been! Of course, that was why the 'photo seemed familiar. It explained everything!

Chapter Nineteen

THE JIG-SAW pieces crowded in thick and fast, dropping into place and the picture formed with shattering clarity. When I thought of what had so nearly occurred my stomach heaved with revulsion. Whipping up the toilet seat, I retched violently as the ghastly truth sank in, the shock making me shake like a nervous dog.

I flushed the toilet, turned the handbasin hot tap full on and splashed purifying water over my face. It couldn't wash away what had already happened but I thanked God it had gone no further. The revelation I'd just experienced could explain my reluctance to approach the police. Subconsciously, I believed I had known the truth since the day at Warwick races but some safety valve in the nervous system had refused to allow it to surface.

The first priority now was to get out of here fast and fetch father. What the truth would do to him I couldn't begin to comprehend. I checked my watch. It was approaching time for the three o'clock race. Cautiously I took the catch off the small window; with care I could wriggle through and be away without Snodgrass being any the wiser.

Outside the punters had already sighed, cried and cheered according to their luck in the 2.30 and with hope springing anew, were now surging forward to the rails to watch the 3.00. Nobody saw me slide out. I edged my way round the wall, slipped through the jockeys entrance and out into the car park. Slipping between parked vehicles, I made ground towards my car.

A little weasel of a man was standing with his back to me by the driver's side of the Triumph. He had tow coloured hair sticking out above his ears. I cursed silently, of course, Felton, over a barrel, would be swelling the ranks whether he wanted to or not. He turned, I ducked, but not quickly enough. The glaringly obvious purple racing silks must have stuck out a mile. He raised a yell and I turned and ran. It wasn't easy. The cars were parked tightly and I had to weave in and out. A quick glance back showed Felton had abandoned the hard way of following and was sprinting down the Colwick Road side of the car park.

A big red car was driving slowly down Colwick Road, it honked several times and a hand waved in my direction. Felton, obedient to his master's voice, left the easy way and wormed his body like lightening through the parked vehicles. I'd seen enough to know that if I headed for the road Snodgrass, who presumably was driving the red peril, would have no difficulty in picking me off. The best chance, which would also lessen the odds on the pursuers, would be to cut across country.

I headed south-east into Colwick Park away from the road, running like a hare, I left the race course behind. Trees and shrubs grew in profusion here and I dodged from cover to cover putting as much distance between me and Felton as possible. Finally, blowing like a whale, I flung myself down onto the wet grass behind a semi-circle of bushes. Lying with my chin just skimming the grass tussocks, I was much less visible and had a wide sweep of view to the north. This was partly obscured by the wreathing fog, but the fog cut both ways. It would give me cover just the same as it did Felton. I also knew the fog would be far denser the nearer one was to the river Trent. Even as the thought came I saw Felton searching for me, doubling back on his tracks checking thickly wooded spots that might offer concealment and looking for all the world like a terrier dog. People were supposed to grow like their animals and right now all he lacked was a wagging tail. What disturbed me more however was the sight of a bulky man bringing up the rear. Even from here I could see the inevitable cap pulled low. I shivered with fear. If the gorilla were to get his hands on me I wouldn't stand a chance. I forced myself to wait for the right moment when they were looking away and then scurried over the ground, keeping low and praying they wouldn't see me. A distant roar, which wouldn't have disgraced a caged lion, blew any hopes.

It had to be the river then, it was my only chance. At this point it was probably only a mile or thereabouts away and Roger Bannister would doubtless have applauded from the side lines. I had the advantage of local knowledge on my side which the two pursuers did not and I found the stretch of river with no problem. Different types of boats were moored along the banks at this point and I urgently scanned the bobbing crafts.

A motor cruiser was just being cast off. I hailed the owner. "It's very important. Could you take me across?"

He pushed a fancy red and white cap back and scratched his head in amazement. "Looks like you've lost your horse."

From the periphery of my vision I could see the two men catching up fast.

"Please, I'm desperate to get over!"

"Yeah, why not?" He extended a brawny arm and gave me a pull up.

"Thank a million, you're a life-saver!"

"What happened to you then?"

"A long story and very boring."

"In other words, mind my own business. Fair enough." he said good humouredly, sending the boat throbbing out away from the bank. "Will it do you if I drop you off at the lock? Take a few minutes after that getting through d'you see."

"Great. The Holme Pierrepont Water Sports Centre's on the other side isn't it?"

"Yeah, complete with Slalom."

I risked a quick look over my shoulder. Through the thick fog which hung low over the water, the two men were just discernible hurrying back in the direction of the race course. I had a sneaking feeling they might be thinking of motoring over Trent Bridge and cutting me off on the A.52 which ran the other side of the Water Sports Complex. Happily, the man beside me seemed oblivious to the pursuers existance. I kept him talking.

"I've never actually seen the Slalom."

"Have you not? It's impressive. Like a miniature rapids."

"Does it run fast?"

"You bet your sweet life it does. Takes a deal of nerve I dare say to have a bash at that."

"Must do with the sound of it."

"You're headed for the complex then?"

Obviously the opposite bank was a safer place at the moment.

"Yes."

"Some sort of fancy dress is it?" The man asked curiously, eyeing my racing gear.

"It's a game," I said crossing my fingers.

He appeared satisfied.

We travelled across the water at an angle and I could see the lock coming up. Before we reached it I could see iron rungs set in concrete reaching to the top of the bank.

"If you climb up yon rungs, it will bring you right up to the Slalom." said the man and manouvered his boat expertly alongside.

"You've done me a big favour. I'm very grateful." I said and shook his hand.

"Well, if you can't give anybody a bit of help it's a bad job." he replied.

We parted company, he headed into the lock and I climbed the iron rungs. At the top I paused for breath. It was good job I did for my first sight of the Slalom was sufficient to make me gasp in wonder. Impressive the boatman had said and it was all of that. Water foaming and bubbling down the man-made waterway raced at speed over ledges and steps below the surface causing an extremely fast flow. It reminded me of a continuous low weir complete with noise and flying specks of spray. But the swift current churning along wasn't a natural one, this was driven by electrical power.

I must have gaped at it for several minutes so

arresting a sight was it. Mentally I gave myself a shake. What to do now was the pressing thing. I looked back across the Trent. The far bank was obscured by fog but I knew the two men had high-tailed in the opposite direction. They expected me to continue on over the river and try to reach the nearest road. I made up my mind quickly. They wouldn't expect to see me back at the race course. In fact, it would probably be the safest place right now. And my clothes and car were still there. I looked down at the lock. The water level had risen high and the motor cruiser would soon be leaving through the far end gates. The boatman was a good sort. If I could reach him before the boat gained speed after leaving the lock, perhaps he could be persuaded to tack back across the water and drop me off on the other side. It would be the most unexpected thing to do. Snodgrass and company certainly wouldn't anticipate me doing it. I began to run along the concrete banks of the Slalom towards the far end gates.

All I was thinking about was getting there before the boat and I didn't allow for the sharp slope of the concrete which was wet and slippery with the spray. I skidded and my paper-thin racing boots gave no grip whatsoever. I teetered wildly, waving my arms to try to gain balance but I'd passed the angle of no return. With an almighty splash I hit the water of the Slalom. For a second it bounced me up before snatching me away down the course in the teeth of the current. I fought to keep my face above the water. There was no prospect of swimming – continuing to breathe took all my strength.

I vaguely heard the cries from people along the bank but they were powerless to do anything. The only hope was to give in to the pull of the water and let it take me down the course to the end. And it did with a vengeance, buffeting me before it like a tiny plastic doll.

Sky and water merged together, a crashing icy grey nightmare which seemed to last forever but in reality was over very quickly. A great yellow shape threw itself up out of the water and I frantically grabbed at it and clung on. Arms reached to me from the bank and I was pulled from the grip of the water and laid on firm ground.

An enthusiastic life-saver leapt upon me and began practising his resuscitation technique. I struggled up choking and gasping and pushed him away.

"Are you all right?" clamoured several anxious voices together but speech was beyond me at that moment. I nodded, coughing up river water.

"Good job you caught hold of the buoy," said someone else and a chorus of others affirmed it. I fervently concurred.

"Anything broken?" asked another practical soul.

I checked my limbs, although bruised and considerably battered, they worked.

"You'll be O.K." said one little ray of sunshine. "Canoeists fall in regularly."

"Thanks a lot," I said between coughs "It really brightens up my day knowing that."

I struggled to my feet, squeezing handfuls of water from my clinging, saturated silks.

"Anything we can do?" asked the practical soul.

I looked towards the lock. The motor cruiser was just nosing out.

"Could you flag down that boat. I need to get back across the Trent."

She looked at me in surprise, shrugged her shoulders then in a powerful voice, hailed the skipper.

I could have hugged him. Without a whinge, he hauled me aboard once more.

"Some game!" Was his only comment.

"I can't thank you enough. I'm so grateful."

He waved aside my thanks. "If you look in the locker under the bunk you'll find a clean towel to rub your hair with."

"I bet you think I'm nuts." I sat beside him, the towel turbanned around my head.

He turned from the wheel and grinned at me. "No, you're just a woman. I've got five daughters. Nothing surprises me anymore. They change their minds all the time."

He dropped me back on the far bank and pulled away.

Laboriously, I made my way back across country through Colwick Park. My legs felt like lead weights and I was shivering too much to make any pace to get warm. It seemed an eternity before I reached the race course. I was in no condition to take evasive action should Snodgrass appear but I was in luck, there was no sign of any of them.

Slipping through the jockeys entrance, I made the weighing room without attracting attention. The last race had finished and most of the jockeys had gone.

One of the few remaining spotted me. "Thought you'd fell down the bogs." he said rudely, peered closer and added, "Looks as if you did."

"Sorry to disappoint you," I drawled, "I've just been testing how cold the Trent is."

I left him gawping after me and went into the showers. The hot water cascading down over my shoulders was sheer bliss. I stood enveloped in steam and thawed out, my toes gave up being blue and transformed themselves into reasonable imitations of ripe radishes. The heat took a lot of the pain from my bruises, although no doubt tomorrow I'd be as stiff as a piece of tongued and grooved. With the greatest reluctance I stepped out and towelled gingerly. No vigorous rubbing, just gentle pats which even so had me ooohing and aaahing. I dressed and sat next to the hot radiator pulling on my outdoor boots.

All the jockeys had left now and the race course would be closing very shortly. I needed to ring the hospital first. The weighing room 'phone was the handiest. The sister on father's ward informed me that Mr. Hunter had waited until four o'clock before ringing for a taxi and returning home. Before she put down the receiver, I asked to be transferred to reception. The girl behind the desk kept me waiting for an age before she traced Paul's admittance.

"He's being kept in hospital is he?" I inquired.

She affirmed it. So that was that.

If father had left at four, he'd be home long since. No

urgency now to get back, thank heavens, with legs still on the wobble, I was in no shape to drive.

The prospect of some food and a whisky tempted beyond endurance. But not here. The nearest pub would be the Starting Gate on Colwick Road. I left the building and walked back across the almost deserted car park. My watch said 5.30 p.m. a bit early yet, the pub didn't open until around 6.00 p.m.

One or two car park attendants were scurrying about clearing litter. I kept a watchful eye on them but none appeared in the slightest suspicious. My car stuck out like an assassin's target surrounded by an expanse of green, very vulnerable and easy prey. I walked slowly towards it with thumping heart, expecting trouble to break at every step. Nothing happened.

With great relief I slipped into the driver's seat and let the tension drain away. The flask was still lying in the dashboard, an experimental shake confirmed it was empty. I tossed it back with disgust and turned on the ignition. The Triumph engine purred into life and together we bumped gently over the grass onto tarmac. Two minutes later I nosed into the forecourt of the Starting Gate and parked. The lights in the pub were already on and I walked stiffly across and pushed open the main door.

The brightness and warmth engulfed me immediately. I ordered a salad filled bun and a small whisky and sat as close to a radiator as possible. A delightful sense of safety and protection seemed to exude from the very bricks and I let it wash over me like a whale who had been stranded. The food and drink had a wonderfully reviving effect and my legs began to feel normal again instead of belonging to a jelly-baby. I sipped the last of the whisky and pictured father back in his usual chair by the fire. How lovely it would be, I'd missed him more than I realised. The weight of sole responsibility lifted from my shoulders and euphoric lightness filled me. All I wanted now was to get back, to be there with him, beside the fire, Hunters once more restored to normal. If I left now I could be home in ten minutes.

I left. Even the Triumph seemed to rejoice as it

gobbled up the miles. We swept through the gates of Hunters with a flourish and a spray of pea-gravel. A few seconds more and we would be re-united.

Up ahead, a car was parked by the front door. Visitors? Someone else couldn't wait to see father either. And then I realised it was red. I stepped hard on the brake, fear churning my insides. It was the same car that had driven down Colwick Road: the red peril.

It could only mean Snodgrass was inside.

Chapter Twenty

I LEAPT from the car leaving the door wide open and ran for the kitchen door, hit my foot against a yielding black heap on the ground and went sprawling. It was Rookey. I ran my hands over his head feeling the stickiness of congealing blood behind his ear. But, thank God, he was breathing steadily. I dropped my jacket over him to help the shock. It was all I could do. Father was inside with Snodgrass, he needed me.

I crashed open the door and ploughed through the kitchen upsetting the chairs in my haste. The noise I made was irrelevant, I had no weapon, no means of defence. There was only one possible ace up my sleeve and it didn't require quietness.

Felton's little weasel face was peeping round the study door. I smacked the door back wide, knocking him flying. Inside the study were Snodgrass and gorilla, guns sprouting from hands, one now trained on me and the other on Turton and father.

"Stay where you are Miss Hunter," Snodgrass lifted the tip of his gun slightly. "We were expecting you, in fact gentlemen, we were waiting for her weren't we?"

"You all right Tal, my love?" said father.

"Fine, has this creep harmed either of you?"

"No gel, we're both O.K." said Turton hoarsely.

"A little more respect, if you please," sneered Snodgrass, "or I might let Georgy off his lead."

The gorilla leered at me. "I could do her some damage."

Turton lunged towards him but weasel face, still half-down on the floor where I'd winded him, stuck out a foot and Turton ended up on the carpet as well.

"Come on!" snapped Snodgrass. "Now she's showed up let's get the bloody paper signed." He swung round to face father who was leaning with one hand on the desk and the other on his crutch for support. A foolscap sheet was laid out on the desk top in front of him.

"I'm not signing it," said father.

"You said you'd sign when she got here." ground out Snodgrass, "get on with it."

"Who is it that want's Hunters so bad? I want to know."

I held my breath. I could have told father, played my ace, but I might be wrong, very wrong, with all my heart I hoped so.

"You can want Hunter. I'm not paid to tell-tales. Now sign it." As he said it Snodgrass jammed the revolver hard against the side of father's temple.

I clenched my fist and started towards him but Felton was too quick and jammed my arms down at my sides.

Then father started to laugh. It started with a chuckle which swelling up into a loud, harsh bellow of laughter.

"What the hell . . . " Snodgrass slapped his face hard. "Cut the cackle . . . you off your soddin' rocker or what?"

Father sobered down. He shrugged his shoulders and still grinning said. "Hard luck, old buddy, but Hunters isn't mine to sell."

We all gaped at him.

"Don't give me that crap!" The revolver pushed harder against his head.

"It never was mine. It belongs to someone else."

"What bloody game do you think you're playing Hunter?"

"Morally and, I suppose legally, it belongs to Tal, or will do one day so she can do as she wishes with it. If the owner's already dead then it's Tally's right now. But they're most certainly not my stables."

"You don't expect us to believe that crap do you? Go on then, smart guy, who does Hunters belong to?"

Father looked round at everybody and then smiled gently at me.

"For more than a quarter of a century I've lived a lie. Like a poison wanting letting it worked inside me. My God, I'll be glad to let it out and tell you . . . "

"Jack!" Turton yelled out. "No Jack don't tell her . . . "

The gorilla silenced him with a fat smack from the barrel of his revolver.

"Carry on Hunter, we're all ears," sneered Snodgrass. "I haven't heard any good fairy stories lately."

"Believe me, this is on the level, every single word. Common knowledge anyway, some of it. I won Hunters in a card game."

"So what, it makes it yours."

"I rang my Solicitor yesterday from the hospital. Asked him to check the legal side of that. Gambling debts cannot be enforced in a Court of Law."

"Give over, it's still yours."

"Not when I cheated the cards to win."

A dead silence followed.

I felt my knees give as though a cricket bat had cracked them from behind. "Father, please, it's not true . . . surely it's not true."

"My darling. I'm only sorry I had to spill it in front of the hoodlums. I should have told you long since – just us, no outsiders listening."

"We're not bloody well listening, Hunter" snarled Snodgrass, "It's a load of cobblers."

"You see, when you tell the truth, people don't believe you," father tried a quip but it fell on stoney ground.

"O.K. Georgy, light one up." Snodgrass bared his teeth in what, for him, was probably a smile.

"Yes sir!"

The gorilla gleefully took a cigarette out, lit it and pulled hard to get it going.

A tense silence filled the room and I came out in a cold sweat. Dear God, surely they weren't going to try torture.

"Now, Hunter, we'll see if you're going to sign it or not."

Snodgrass lashed out with his foot and kicked the

crutch away from father's hand. It happened so fast it took us all by surprise. Father, off balance, flailed the air wildly but couldn't keep his balance. He fell backwards into the swivel chair which spun crazily from side to side with the sudden weight.

I back-kicked at Felton who still held my arms pinioned. The force behind it wouldn't have disgraced Calypso and the man let out a sob of pain.

A loud crack rang out as Snodgrass fired into the floor a few inches in front of me. "Don't bloody try it. The next one's got your name all over it." He spat at me. "Come on with that bloody fag, let's have it!"

Grinning like a maniac, the gorilla handed it across to him.

"Now, Mr. soddin' Hunter, we'll see who's the boss here. Sign it!" In a stride Snodgrass swung the chair round so father was facing away and encircled a left arm around him. Steadily he swung the chair back to face the desk and with his right hand, brought the lighted cigarette in an arc to where we could all see it.

"You bastards," screamed Turton but under the muzzle of the gorilla's gun was powerless to stop him.

We watched the glowing cigarette end like mesmerized rabbits watching a stoat. Snodgrass slowly brought the cigarette closer and closer to father's one remaining eye.

"Let me sign," I heard myself scream, "if the stables belong to me, let me sign. You can have them, just let father go. For God's sake, let him go!"

The study door slammed open. "Do as the lady says, scum. Let him go. No undue violence remember!"

We all spun round. Framed in the doorway was Paul Reynolds. His face the colour of a snow-sky in winter, grey and leaden. His jacket held in place by only one arm, his other strapped across his chest. But the deadly authority in his voice was enough.

Snodgrass threw the cigarette down into the ashtray.

"Reynolds, I was never more glad to see anyone in my whole life," said father thankfully snatching up his crutch.

"Amen to that!" I reiterated.

"Swines." Turton spat out, "Gawd, if you hadn't stopped 'em . . ."

"He won't sign the paper," shouted Snodgrass.

"They are not my stables," father bellowed in a mixture of rage and relief, "they belong to my wife."

"Your ex-wife," Turton bellowed back.

"Makes no odds, they're hers."

Paul took a roll of notes from his pocket. "Snodgrass, I don't want to see or hear from you or your backers-up again, ever. Understood? Now get out!"

Snodgrass snatched the notes. "You're paying, you're the boss . . ."

"Bloody hell . . ." Turton sat down suddenly in the nearest chair. The three men made a hurried exit.

"No!" Father was aghast. "You can't be the one after Hunters." He went as white as Paul was grey.

"He is." I said quietly. I took the ace from my sleeve with deep regret. "In fact, he's the one to blame for your accident. Aren't you Paul?"

"Tal, what are you saying girl?" Father dropped his crutch and took hold of my shoulders.

"Ask him father. He plugged the end of his riding whip with a hat pin, or similar, and when you were nearing the third last at Cheltenham he stuck it into Calypso."

"I never intended to hurt the animal." Paul said, clinging onto the door frame to stop himself swaying.

"And you paid Felton to keep his mouth shut at that fence whilst you brought father off, didn't you?"

"It went horribly wrong . . . I never intended Jack to get injured so badly."

"So that was why Felton was so shocked?"

"Yes, I admit everything. I was just trying to get him off the horse so I could win."

"The championship cannot be that important for God's sake," said father incredulously.

"No, no," Paul shook his head wearily.

"He was trying to put us out of business, weren't you?" I said.

"Yes," he looked at me, "how do you know?"

"Because you wanted Hunters back – for your mother – isn't that right?"

"Dead right."

"I don't believe this is happening," said Turton holding his head.

"Paul," I said screwing myself up for the words which had to be said, "did you know, you're my brother?"

His mouth dropped open. All the implications which had swamped me in Nottingham weighing room now hit him.

"Oh no," he slid slowly down the door frame and collapsed in a heap.

"Tal, are you off your head?" Father shook me.

"It's true father. Paul is your son. His mother is my mother."

"What have I done?" moaned Paul in agony. "Nearly blinding my own father, making love to my own sister, oh my God, I'm so desperately, desperately sorry . . . " He blacked out completely in a dead faint.

"The settee, Turton," ordered father, "get him onto it. Stupid sod should be in hospital with the look of him."

"He was until 5.30 p.m. this evening," I said, "He must have discharged himself. He came a crashing fall at Nottingham, in my race."

"Pour four whiskies out Tal. We all need a steadier," said father.

Paul came round slowly. I held a glass to his lips.

"When did you know I was your . . . brother?" he said brokenly. "Not from the first surely."

"Of course not," I said briskly, "don't be a silly fool. I was always intrigued by you, drawn to you in a strange way. I just interpreted it wrongly."

He sipped some of the whisky. "When did you know?"

"I suspected you'd caused the accident after the Warwick races. You were tapping your boot with the whip, of course there was no visible evidence then. After the accident at Cheltenham, when I rushed up to ask you about father, you told me he'd fallen at the third last and waved your whip backwards. I didn't register it at the time but there was something gleaming on the end of it, something that shouldn't have been there."

"I did it all for her," he said in a low voice. "She's

had a rough deal. Tom Reynolds went off with another woman years ago. After he'd gone she took me to live with her father, my grandfather. But she still thought of Britain as home. All she wanted since she knew about the cancer was to come back here to die. She said there was a stable run by a man called Hunter and she'd lived there before she was married. I tried to get the stables back in a card game, ironic isn't it," he choked a little. "But Jack's a better player than I'll ever be. So," he spread his hands, "I knew you would never sell the business, not unless it folded. I tried to make it fold."

"Only I kept getting winners," I said gently.

"Yes."

"The fire, it was only a warning?"

"I couldn't hurt horses like that. Not even for my mother. I might be a bastard but I'm not as big a one as that."

"And tonight? You must have instructed Snodgrass to come. The rotten beast knocked poor Rookey out. I must see to him in a minute but I don't think he's too bad."

"I'm very sorry but I was desperate."

"Because of your . . . our . . . mother's sudden relapse?"

His head jerked up. "You know?"

"Yes. You dropped a letter in the weighing room."

"But how did you really know I was your brother, Tal?"

"Jockeys always know their blood-group. Father's, yours and mine are all the same."

"It's not conclusive."

"Perhaps not, but your eyes are. They're exactly the same as mother's eyes in her photograph and the man in the Buddha's photograph, your grandfather. Isn't that what you were trying to check Turton, when you tried to find mother's photograph?" I turned to him.

He nodded, too overwhelmed to speak. I found myself wondering disconcertingly what Turton's blood group was, but his indiscretion with my mother was a secret between us and no way would I break his confidence.

"What's with this Buddha?" Paul looked blank.

I filled in the details. "It's father's racing mascot containing a 'photo of your grandfather."

"A self-imposed rack-torture," said father, still ashen-faced at the shock of it all. "After a win I'd take it out just to let him know this time I hadn't cheated. But all it did was scour the old wound and remind me I'd cheated him and your mother out of Hunters in the first place."

"It's over now father, you'll never have to do it again. You've spilt your last blood on the turf."

"True enough," father nodded. "I suppose to completely eliminate Tom Reynolds, we'd have to find out his blood-group." He came close to Paul and scrutinized him carefully. "Are you *really* my son?"

"There's only one person who could know that Jack."

Father nodded his head. "Yes, your mother."

"And mine," I said quietly.

We were all silent, thinking of her far away in America, dying of cancer.

Into the silence the telephone rang. "Bet it's David," I said and answered it. "Yes, he's home and everything's fine. Yes, Calypso Lad won. Of course I'll pass them on. All the best David." I replaced the receiver. "He's really pleased for you and sends all his good wishes."

Father nodded absently.

"So," I said as nobody else spoke. "That just about wraps up the mystery."

"A right relief it is too," said Turton with feeling.

Still nobody asked the question we were all thinking about.

I took hold of my courage and jumped in. "What do we all want to do about mother?"

"I know what I want," Paul said quickly, "but it's up to Jack."

We all looked at father. He hesitated only a moment. "She must be flown over if . . . if Tal's agreeable?" His face met mine and it was full of anguish.

"Of course," I put my arm through his. "Hunters is not just ours, as you said, it's hers too. And now, I think I'll get you three sick and injured boys ministered to and put to bed."

"Three?" said father.

"Hmmm. You, Paul . . . and Rookey."